MURDER CLUB

For the last decade and a half, Mark Pearson has worked as a full-time television scriptwriter on a variety of shows for the BBC and ITV, including *Doctors*, *Holby City* and *The Bill*. He lives in Norfolk. *Hard Evidence*, *Blood Work*, and *Death Row*, the first three novels in the Detective Inspector Jack Delaney series, are available in Arrow.

Praise for Mark Pearson

'A very good writer . . . Mark Pearson really brings to life the gritty underbelly of London'
James Patterson

'A cracking debut, matching gore with suspense. His TV scripting experience shows' *Bookseller*

'Jack Delaney is hard to forget' *Time Out*

'Pearson scores a hit first time out with Jack Delaney, ~~~~~~~~~~~~~~~~~~~~ John Rebus ~~~~~~~~~~~~~~~~~~~~ rd

'This is a ~~~~~~~~~~~~~~~~~~~~ flags, the di~~~~~~~~~~~~~~~~~~~~ r'

www.shotsmag.co.uk

Also available by Mark Pearson

Hard Evidence
Blood Work
Death Row

MURDER CLUB

MARK PEARSON

arrow books

Published by Arrow 2011

2 4 6 8 10 9 7 5 3 1

First published in Great Britain in 2011 by
Arrow Books
Random House, 20 Vauxhall Bridge Road,
London SW1V 2SA

www.randomhouse.co.uk

Addresses for companies within The Random House Group Limited can be
found at: www.randomhouse.co.uk/offices.htm

The Random House Group Limited Reg. No. 954009

A CIP catalogue record for this book
is available from the British Library

ISBN 9780099550884

The Random House Group Limited supports The Forest Stewardship Council
(FSC®), the leading international forest certification organisation. Our books
carrying the FSC label are printed on FSC® certified paper. FSC is the only
forest certification scheme endorsed by the leading environmental
organisations, including Greenpeace. Our paper procurement policy
can be found at www.randomhouse.co.uk/environment

Typeset by SX Composing DTP, Rayleigh, Essex
Printed and bound by CPI Group (UK) Ltd, Croydon, CR0 4YY

For Lynn and Shirley

The majority of women in society fear rape – no woman is allowed to ignore it. The majority of children are taught to be afraid of 'strange men' who offer us sweets, lifts, etc. We are taught as adults to keep our doors locked, not to be alone, not to look or act in any way that might 'bring rape upon ourselves'. Perhaps the most obvious situation in which we are taught to be afraid is when walking home alone at night. The threat of violence is a total intrusion into women's personal space and transforms a routine and/or potential pleasurable activity (for example, a walk in the park, a quiet evening at home, a long train journey) into a potentially upsetting, disturbing and often threatening experience.

40% of adults who are raped tell no one about it. 31% of children who are abused reach adulthood without having disclosed their abuse.

Only 15% of serious sexual offences against people 16 and over are reported to the police and of the rape offences that are reported, fewer than 6% result in an offender being convicted of this offence.

From the Rape Crisis (England and Wales) website, 2010

Prologue

Twelve Months ago . . . Christmas

'Fuck that!' said Jack Delaney.

The middle-aged woman dressed in a Salvation Army uniform looked horrified and would have backed away, but the pub was extremely busy, and she was jammed in tight amongst the revellers. Friday night at The Crooked Hat off the Goldhawk Road in Shepherd's Bush was always busy. But it was only a short while to the Christmas holidays and The Hat was packed with people, young and old alike, getting into the spirit of the season. Office parties mingled with the regulars and the pub was filled with laughter and shouting and the kind of unresolved sexual tension that usually leads to regret and red faces the morning after. The couple behind the Salvation Army woman were going some way to resolving that tension, however, if the way they seemed to be swallowing each other's tongues was anything to go by. Young women today, thought Delaney, you've got to love them.

But he wasn't smiling. Delaney wasn't getting into the spirit of the season, he was just getting into the spirit. Irish whiskey to be precise and drinking it without strict adherence to the guidelines about the number of units of alcohol it was safe to consume. Jack Delaney had already consumed more than a week's worth of them and tossed back another large Jameson's as he scowled at the woman holding a collecting box under his nose.

'Will you take a drink instead?' he said to the woman, who shook her head outraged.

'I don't drink alcohol,' she said. 'The Salvation Army is a temperate organisation. "It is not for kings, O Lemuel, it is not for kings to drink wine; nor for princes strong drink, lest they drink, and forget the law, and pervert the judgement of any of the afflicted. Give strong drink unto him that is ready to perish, and wine unto those that be of heavy hearts." Proverbs 31, 4 to 6!'

Delaney nodded at her and took a glug of his pint of Guinness. 'Psalm 104: 14–15 "He makes grass. grow for the cattle, and plants for man to cultivate – bringing forth food from the earth: wine that gladdens the heart of man, oil to make his face shine, and bread that sustains his heart." '

'You have studied the good book?' she asked surprised.

'I have studied man,' he replied. 'And was he not made in God's image?'

'So the Bible tells us.'

'Then I have no desire to meet the maker of such a despicable race. Troll your jolly bowl around somewhere else, lady!'

The woman's face flushed, whether with anger or embarrassment Delaney couldn't tell. He didn't care either way. 'Get us another whiskey here,' he shouted across at the barmaid, a young woman called Aysha, who winked and stuck her thumb up before fetching his drink.

'Oi, I was next.'

Delaney turned round to the man standing beside him. In his late twenties with a goatee beard, jeans and a loose, blue linen shirt. Probably working at the BBC, Delaney surmised, the place was filled with them nowadays. Creeping about from their numerous buildings around Shepherd's Bush and further up the road at White City and Television Centre. Turning a proper old boozer like The Hat into some kind of trendy, yuppie, yahoo nightmare. It had even started calling itself a gastropub, for Christ's sake. Delaney resisted the urge to smash his fist into the outraged prig's face. 'Fuck you!' he said instead and the man seeing the latent violence in Delaney's eyes backed away. Delaney wasn't a particularly big man, but he was six foot tall with broad enough shoulders, dark, curly Irish hair. And eyes that would have been blue in the spring sunshine of a May morning, had he been well rested and refrained from strong liquor. As it was, the blue was tinged with red, and his eyes were not peaceful, if they were, indeed, the windows to the soul the BBC script editor was gazing into a very dark place. Dark and dangerous. He held his hands up and backed away. As best as he could, that is, with his heehawing colleagues from Media Central clustered around him like so many braying donkeys.

'Cheers, darling,' he said as he took the drink from Aysha, an extremely pretty, young woman, with come-to-bed eyes and a full, womanly figure. 'Jeez,' he said, 'if I was ten years younger, I'd be having you in my bed faster than you can say "Christ on a bicycle".'

The Salvation Army officer took a deep intake of breath and made an involuntary sign of the cross on her chest.

'Come back tomorrow when you are sober enough to get it up, and I might let you, Jack,' said the barmaid with an earthy laugh.

The Salvation Army woman shook her head at Delaney with both contempt and sadness. 'I shall pray for you,' she said.

'Any woman gets down on her knees for me,' he replied, 'it's not her prayers I'll be wanting.'

'Blasphemy, drunkenness and sins of the flesh. You are an unhappy man. And you'll find no answers in that.'

She nodded at the whiskey glass in Delaney's hand.

'I'm not looking for answers, lectures or salvation, lady.'

'What are you looking for?'

'Oblivion,' he said and swallowed the rest of his whiskey.

A dark-haired woman, somewhere in her late thirties or early forties, threaded her way through the crowd towards him. A group of office workers in their best suits and dresses wearing novelty hats had struck up a chorus of 'Deck the halls with boughs of holly'. She was a curvaceous woman with thick, dark curly tresses, striking eyes and lipstick as red as a holly berry. She wore a short leather skirt, high-heeled boots and her ample chest was barely constrained by a tight bustier. She slipped her leather motorcycle jacket off as she approached the bar.

'Now I wouldn't mind putting something in her box,' said Jack Delaney to the Salvation Army woman, having to raise his voice to be heard. The woman pulled a face as if she had swallowed a pickled walnut and pushed her way through the crowd, heedless of the cries of protest as people spilled their drinks in her wake.

'Is that yourself, Jack?' said the dark-haired woman as she got to the bar.

'Who the fuck else would it be?' said Delaney. 'I'm sure as shit not the Pope.'

'No. You're not that. That's for sure.'

'Good to see you, Jackie,' he said, tilting his glass at her. 'What can I get ya?'

Jackie Malone leaned in and whispered in his ear, pushing her breasts into his chest as she did so. 'You wouldn't have something to perk a girl up, would you?' she said, with a deep, musical Irish accent.

Delaney smiled. 'Put your coat back on and let's repair to the beer garden,' he said.

'Repair?' replied Jackie Malone.

'I read a book once.' He grinned and steered her through the crowd to the back door.

Outside it was cold. Their breaths made mist-streams in the air as they leaned up against the back wall, away from the rear exit. The garden was enclosed but not overlooked, not at night, anyway, when the office block beyond was closed.

Delaney pushed her up against the rough surface of the brickwork and kissed her.

'You hungry tonight, Cowboy?' said Jackie Malone in a husky voice.

'Always hungry for you, Jackie.'

'Got a little something for me then?'

Delaney reached into his pocket, unscrewed a small cylinder and tapped some white powder onto his hand. Then held it up to her nose. She snorted it down, then Delaney poured some more onto his hand and did the same.

A drunken man stumbled out from the pub into the garden. Delaney reached into his pocket and pulled out his warrant card, which he held up to the man. 'The beer garden is closed,' he said. 'Fuck off.'

The man stumbled hurriedly back inside, as Jackie Malone undid Delaney's zip.

'Now where were we?' she said then gasped as Delaney entered her. 'Not such a little something after all,' she continued with a smile and gasped again as Delaney thrust hard, gripping her hips tight against the cold brickwork.

His eyes glazed over as he built a steady rhythm. Not oblivion but getting close to it. *La petite mort*, as the French called it, the little death.

And at that moment, a mile or so across London, a women was raped and mutilated.

'Happy fucking Christmas everyone!' shouted Delaney as he juddered to a climax.

2.

EARLIER

The woman pulled her coat around her and folded her arms.

She looked up at the monitor and again at her watch. It was ten o'clock. The sound of the train still rattled in the tunnel ahead. Normally she would have caught an earlier train. But the blind date she had met at Kettner's of Soho had ordered a bottle of Veuve Clicquot for them both after they had had a glass of unoaked Chardonnay, and it seemed rude to hurry it. It was Christmas after all. The season to be jolly and he had been easy company. She hadn't been on a date with a man since she had split up with her fiancé, some six months earlier.

She had returned from a business trip to Paris to discover her lover in bed with her best friend. It was hardly an original situation, but certainly never one she had had to deal with before. She was used to getting the man she chose, and, when things ended, she was the one ending it. True, she had done so with her fiancée but it wasn't quite the same thing. To come home and find him with her chief bridesmaid in her own bed was more than just a slap to her face; it was a complete blow to her self-esteem. She was a beautiful, confident, intelligent woman and she knew it. She attracted men as naturally as a magnet attracted iron filings, but all that had changed. At least her self-confidence had, or her tolerance for men. For sure they still approached her but they were met with a frosty reception. Worst of all she realised she hadn't really loved her fiancé in the first place. She had decided to marry him for all the wrong reasons, and realising that had made her doubt herself and her judgement even more.

But six months was long enough. Her female friends had been very supportive at first, but had now – almost as one – decided that it was time for her to get back in the dating game, as the Americans called it. She had looked at singles sites, even went on a speed-dating evening once, but that was a disaster and she had walked out on it after the second 'date'.

That was a month ago but, undaunted, her married and partnered friends had been relentless. For her own good, they called it, putting candidate after candidate before her. A brother, a husband's best friend, a really 'nice guy' from work, an ex-lover! In the end she had given in under the tsunami of pressure from them and agreed to meet the guy tonight. His name was John Smith. He was dressed in a dark two-piece suit with a white shirt and a blue tie. He might have been dressed for an interview. Maybe he had been. She smiled at the thought. John Smith looked like a salesman in the suit, but was in fact an opera singer. Only background character and chorus, he modestly pointed out. He was thirty-eight years old, had been divorced for four years (an amicable split apparently), was five foot eleven inches tall with sandy blond hair and really blue eyes. He reminded her of the younger Robert Redford maybe, or Heath Ledger. But if he was aware of his good looks, he certainly wasn't arrogant with it, as a lot of men were.

'You remind me of someone . . .' she had said.

'Do I?'

'Yes, can't put my finger on it. You probably get that a lot, do you?'

He had smiled. 'As long as it's not Brad Pitt.'

She had laughed, genuinely. The first time in a long while a man had made her do that.

'No. You're all right. It's not him.'

The conversation had flowed pretty smoothly after that. He was an entertainer, she knew, probably trained in breaking the ice. But there seemed nothing disingenuous in the way he held her gaze when talking, and his flirtatious comments were flattering and on the right side of fun. He didn't take himself too seriously and she liked that in a man. Her ex-fiancé, come to think of it, had been a bit of a stuffed shirt. In fact the more she did think about it, the more she realised how little there was that she really liked about the man.

So when her date had offered champagne, not only did it seem churlish to refuse, but it seemed somehow appropriate that a bottle of the Widow Ponsardin's finest drop, Veuve Clicquot La Grande Dame at £175 a pop, should signal the end of one chapter and the beginning of another. A baptism in wine: out with the old, in with the new. And the thing was, John wasn't being flash in ordering it, showing off. He had explained that he had just finished a good run with a show in the West End. Judging by his clothes, she reckoned it was not an uncommon occurrence. He explained that in truth he only did the singing part-time, couldn't afford to go full-time. When he was resting he did freelance sales work and that paid pretty well.

Stephanie had laughed, telling him that she had pegged him for it when she first saw him. She wasn't surprised he was good at his job: he had something about him – charisma, she supposed, or empathy; either way, he was certainly comfortable to talk with. To trust. She guessed that went with his job too, but suspected it was something innate rather than a learned skill. God knows she had been sold to (or they had attempted to) by enough salesmen and women to appreciate the difference. She reckoned John should be getting lead parts, and he had confessed that his telephone voice was better than his singing!

She looked up at the monitor again: four minutes to go. She had made a decision. John had said he would call her in a couple of days and, when he did, she would agree to see him again. She smiled to herself and felt the warmth of it spread through her body. And it wasn't just the champagne working.

Two minutes to go. Not only had she stayed later than she planned at Kettner's, but the automatic ticket gates hadn't been working at Piccadilly, wouldn't recognise her Oyster card, and she had had to wait for a guard to let her through.

She'd arrived on the platform just as the doors of her train closed and it had started to move away. She hated missing her train. Another eight minutes to the next one. She'd have to run to make the connection at Marylebone to catch the fast overland. If she missed it, it was another half-hour wait.

She shivered and turned around, suddenly getting the feeling she was being watched. There were a few other people on the platform: a group of young women in their twenties, giggling and dressed more for summer than winter! A girls' night out, by the look of it, and quite a drunken one. An office party or a hen-night. An older man further along the platform was pretending to read a poster on the wall, but she could see he kept flicking sideways glances at the group of laughing women. He caught her eye and looked away. More people piled onto the platform and a short while later the train arrived.

At Marylebone she ran as fast as she could; she wasn't exactly wearing high-heeled shoes, but she wasn't wearing flats either. People with the same idea flew past her, men mainly, who weren't hampered by their footwear.

She hurried up the stairs leading from the Underground, up and onto the concourse, and then ran up to the barrier connecting to the overland Chiltern Railways; she had to run up almost one entire platform and then sideways to another platform – the train was still there, and she made it inside with seconds to spare.

She smiled apologetically to the man sitting opposite her as she drew in deep breaths and ran her hand across her forehead. He nodded almost dismissively and returned to the crossword he was studying. She looked at the paper, the Saturday

Telegraph, and raised an eyebrow; he'd had long enough to complete it.

She looked at her reflection in the mirrored effect of the windows and smiled. She did look flushed, but happily flushed. She was pleased with what she saw. Today drew a line under everything. Today was going to change things. And so it would.

Just not in the way she imagined it.

Not in her worst nightmares.

3.

Easter week . . . Wednesday

Andrew Johnson was a pillar of his local community. And he was quite happy to tell that fact to anyone who would listen.

It wasn't entirely true.

He'd joined the Rotary Club at twenty-two years old and moved on to the Rotarians when he was past forty. He was a member of the local Masons' Lodge and had been invited to dine with the Lord Mayor of London on more than one occasion. He was maybe still a few years away from getting the pin-striped morning-suit trousers, but it was only a matter of time. Patience and perseverance. That was Andrew's mantra. All things come to he who waits. Even if you have to go out and get them sometimes.

He was the forty-five-year-old manager of a country pub called The Crawfish, in Lavenham, a pretty market town in Suffolk. He was married with no children. He had had a vasectomy at the age of thirty-eight, on his wife's urging. He hadn't baulked at the idea, having no particular desire himself to father children. The pub was medium-sized, with a lounge bar and a public bar. The lounge bar had a large open fire that was always lit on cold days, even in the summer, if it was wet enough out; and it was popular with the older local customers and the many thousands of tourists who flocked into the town. On one wall of the room hung an original Andrew Haslan – a local artist particularly renowned for his stunning wildlife paintings and etchings. It was of a hare in a wood under a full moon at winter, with snowflakes dancing in the air around him. It had the air of a 1930s Art Deco kind of illustration about it and Andrew Johnson particularly disliked it. But his wife had bought it at a charity auction, for a figure that still made his blood boil, and had insisted that it be proudly displayed so that the world would know what a charitable woman she was.

Charity should begin at home, Andrew would have told her, but he had learned in the many years of their marriage that it was simpler in the long run just to agree with what she wanted. One of these days he was going to toss the bloody painting in the open fire and see what she had to say when it went up in flames. For now, though, he gritted his teeth, sold pints of best or Broadside ale to the customers and listened to their inane CAMRA nonsense, contenting himself with the thought that fairly shortly he would be making one of his little trips. As far as his wife knew, he was going to London on Lodge business or to see his accountants. And sometimes that was true, but it wasn't the only reason he headed south

Every couple of months or so, when his patience had worn thin and his desires waxed large – desires that could not be satisfied by his wife, for all manner of reasons – he travelled on the railway down from the country to London. It was a six-mile drive to the nearby town of Sudbury, where he would park his car and catch the train to London's Liverpool Street. It was a pleasant journey with just one change at Marks Tey, and in an hour and twenty minutes he was in the capital.

Andrew liked travelling on the railway, for it gave him time to think of the pleasures that lay ahead. Anticipation was always nine-tenths of the pleasure after all, was it not, as he was wont to joke with his customers when they had to wait for him to change a barrel of the local ale from Adnams brewery. Most of the locals considered Andrew a genial host, and he was. But he was a businessman first and foremost, and his ready smile slipped away when he was not front-of-house.

He always stayed in the same place when he travelled south – a bed-and-breakfast boarding house in Harrow five minutes' walk from the Underground station. He could have stayed closer to the city centre, but his accountant was based there – going back to the days when he and his wife ran a pub in Northwood Hills, before they sold up and moved to live the country dream. Andrew's wife had berated him constantly until he finally gave in. She had been addicted to watching *Escape to the Country* type programmes and was like a dog with a bone about the idea. Country dreams . . . Country nightmare more like, Andrew thought. The trouble with quiet rural locations was just that. Too quiet, too little entertainment. So the locals made their own entertainment by keeping their noses in everybody else's business. A short distance from Lavenham was the ancient town of Long Melford, which had the longest street of antique shops in England. It also had two pubs that had topless barmaids working twice a week, and Andrew would dearly have loved to visit them. But he knew that news of that visit would surely fly back to Lavenham and he would never hear the end of it from his wife. As much as he considered himself a pillar of the community, she did even more so. Although she rarely worked, helping out in the pub, she sat on numerous committees and did endless charity work. Face was everything to her and Andrew had to play very, very carefully. But play he did.

In London. Where every variety of play was to be had. The B&B where he stayed in Harrow was frugal, basic accommodation, cereal for breakfast, a shared bathroom, but the place was cheap. The old woman who ran the house kept her rates low and her rooms full. Andrew Johnson liked it that way – he wanted to spend his hard-earned money on other things. More exciting things. The sort that would make the blood pound in his brain. The sort of entertainment he couldn't readily undertake in Lavenham.

Sometimes he saw the same girls, but not often. It wasn't about what was comfortable for Andrew Johnson. What was familiar and safe. For him it was about the new. But he always went for the same type of woman. Dark curly-haired women. Of medium height. And he always wanted them to dress the same way. This had posed a problem for him initially – as most working girls in the price bracket he liked to use didn't usually have the sort of outfit he liked them to wear. Schoolgirl uniforms, nurses', policewomen's. These were commonplace enough. Bought cheap from Ann Summers or online. Tools of the sex trade. But Andrew liked his women dressed like business-women. Power suits and suspenders. Attitude in Armani. High heels and haughty couture. But the wardrobes in the small rooms he visited above the staircases of Soho contained no such expensive items. And so Andrew had bought his own, at considerable expense.

He kept the clothes in a small locked suitcase in a locked cupboard in his windowless office, which used to be a storeroom, at the back of the pub, behind the kitchen. And he would take them with him when he made one of his 'essential' business trips to London. His wife, Marjorie, was a large, tall, blonde woman who would have fitted into one of his outfits as easily as the proverbial camel would have fitted through the eye of a needle. He would have said that he didn't know why he married her. But he knew exactly why. Without her money he would still be a second-rate salesman for a second-rate recruiting agency in Wembley specialising in accountancy personnel, where his entire client base was made up of people from the Indian Subcontinent. Andrew Johnson was not a racist by any means, as he was happy to tell anyone who wished to listen to him, but the one thing he didn't miss by moving to Suffolk was the world of dark-skinned faces that he had had to deal with every day. Suffolk was like England in the Fifties, and a foreign or ethnic face was something of a rarity, something to provoke comment. And the fact that the women he chose to play with were all white was not being racist either. How can a sexual attraction be racist? he thought. Given the things he liked to do, and dreamed of doing, he would have been more racist, in his opinion, had he chosen ethnic women. But he didn't.

The woman who was modelling his favoured outfit that evening was a tad chubbier than he usually liked. She was called Melody, according to the card on the wall at the base of the stairs, and the notice by the grimy bell on the door to the small flat. In reality her name was Natalie, and she was a single mother of two young children. She lived in Birmingham and commuted down to London three days a week. She earned enough in those three days to take the other four off.

At that moment, however, her hands were tied to the bedstead behind her. The silk blouse she had been given to wear had been opened to expose her breasts, which were cupped in a blood-red corset/bra combination from Agent Provocateur, that was a good size too small for her ample figure. The pin-striped skirt of the suit was pushed up around her waist. One of her high-heeled shoes had flopped from her right foot as it bounced uncontrollably as Andrew Johnson penetrated her. She would have grunted, maybe screamed as the weight of him landed on her soft belly. But the silky knickers he had supplied as well, had been removed and stuffed into her mouth. Her eyes bulged as much as those of the red-faced and perspiring man above her.

Then Andrew's eyes closed as he came, the tension in his thighs and knees relaxing as he collapsed his full weight upon her again, so that she feared she might well suffocate. He snatched the knickers from her mouth and used them to wipe himself.

'Jeez, you nearly crushed me to death,' said the woman beneath him.

Then Andrew Johnson opened his eyes again.

And there was no kindness in them.

Half an hour later he was waiting on the west-bound platform of the Bakerloo Line. Waiting for the train to take him to Baker Street, where he would catch his connecting Metropolitan Line train back to Harrow-on-the-Hill.

A small smile broke out on his face as he replayed in his mind what had happened in the flat. The look of fear in her eyes. The thought of it aroused him once more. He moved his hand surreptitiously down and stroked himself through his trousers.

The sound of a train clattering in the tunnel did little to distract him from his dark thoughts. Past and future pleasures imagined. He smiled again.

A hand fell on his shoulder.

4.

'I cannot tell you what was in the man's mind. I have had a jumper once before. A woman – she put herself in the path of my train. Her motion was such that it indicated no panic, no fear, but a resigned acceptance of her fate.'

'I see.'

'But this man, his face was not towards me, his arm was raised. Maybe in a farewell gesture. I would simply be speculating if I were to say what his motivations might have been.'

Detective Inspector Tony Hamilton nodded and made a note in his book. 'I was simply asking if you thought it was a suicide, or if you saw someone push him?'

The train driver was a tall man, in his early fifties, Tony would have guessed, with long, but neat, greying hair and half-rimmed tortoiseshell glasses perched on the end of a long, aquiline nose. There was something stork-like about him, Tony decided.

'If someone pushed him, I don't recall seeing it. My focus was straight ahead.'

'Ken here used to be an English teacher,' said Terry Randall, one of the two transport policemen who were assisting him with his enquiries into the suicide of an unknown man who had jumped in front of a west-bound Bakerloo Line train at Piccadilly Circus station. Constable Terry Randall, like the train driver, was in his early fifties, but was shorter, squatter and had a sour expression on his face that showed what he thought of the Metropolitan Police invading what he perceived as his territory. Back in 2006 Sir Ian Blair, the then head of the Metropolitan Police, had wanted a single police force in the capital. He had proposed absorbing the British Transport Police into his force, and this was agreed to by the then Mayor of London, Ken Livingstone, bringing it under the control of the Home Office. But it never happened and the two forces remained separate entities. The only difference being that constable was as high as the BTP's law-enforcing ranks rose. Any serious crimes and the Met would be brought in. Some constables like Randall resented it, but his colleague, Constable Emily Wood, didn't mind. She was in her early thirties, blonde-haired with a bubbly sense of humour, and she obviously liked the look of the tall, dark-haired detective.

'Couldn't face the horror of it, could you, Ken? And so became a train driver.'

'My doctor advised that I take a less stressful occupation some years ago,' agreed the thin man. 'I have always been interested in trains, electric and steam, and my pension was such that I could indulge my hobby and remain in full-time employment.'

'Is it easy to become a Tube driver?' asked DI Hamilton.

'Why's that, Detective?' asked Emily Wood. 'Thinking of hanging up your truncheon?'

Tony smiled at her. 'I'm a detective, remember. I don't carry a truncheon.'

The female constable quirked an eyebrow at him, suggesting she thought that might not strictly be true. He had to force himself not to smile as the driver answered his question.

'It's not easy, no. Vacancies are rare. To get on the handle isn't as easy as some people think.'

'On the handle?'

'It means driving the train,' said the male constable, a tad patronisingly.

'I thought they drove themselves mainly?'

'Only on the Victoria and Central Lines, sir,' said Emily Wood.

'That's right,' agreed the driver.

'Can I ask what difference it makes?' said Constable Randall.

Tony Hamilton gave him a flat look. 'No,' he said. 'You can't.'

'He means was my concentration focused elsewhere, so that I might not have seen clearly what happened.'

'And was it?'

'No, like I said. It happened very quickly – he hit into the window facing away from me, his right arm raised, and then he was down and under the wheels.'

DI Hamilton grimaced. 'I imagine that would be quite stressful for you.'

'You would be right, Detective. I may well reconsider my position. Once was bad enough; twice is . . .' He paused, looking for the right words. 'As you say, very stressful.'

The detective walked over to the table where a

small, battered suitcase had been opened and some items of clothing were placed in evidence bags.

'Nobody handled these?' he asked the Soco officer who stood beside the table.

'Just me.'

'Good.'

The detective turned back to Emily Wood. 'And there was no identification on him? No wallet? Nothing?'

'No, sir, just that card.'

She pointed to a smaller evidence bag. DI Hamilton picked it up and looked at the card. It showed a picture of a medieval man hanging by his one foot from a T-shaped tree. Red hose, blue jerkin and a yellow corona around his head. The Hanged Man.

'Tarot card, sir,' said Emily Wood.

'I can see that.'

'Major Arcana.'

'You know about this kind of stuff?'

'A little, sir. My mother is very into it.'

'What does it signify?'

'Do you think it is important?' asked her colleague.

DI Hamilton shrugged. 'I have absolutely no idea. It's what we detectives do, Constable. Find clues. See what they mean.'

'He killed himself. He jumped in front of a train. No one saw him pushed. And there were lots of people there. It's no great mystery.'

'I tell you what, Constable. Why don't you do your job and let me do mine?'

'I was just saying—'

'Well, don't,' Tony interrupted him. 'Just button it! Go on, Emily, tell me more.'

The constable grinned, as much at her colleague's scowling face as flirting with the detective.

'It's a Major Arcana card, sir.'

'Which means?'

'Well, there are two types of card in the tarot deck. Major and minor arcana. Bit like in an ordinary deck, with the court cards and the ordinary cards.'

'So what does the Hanged Man signify?'

'It's really to do with being in a hiatus, sir. A suspension, if you like. Spiritually. When the man is righted, everything will be different.'

'It was certainly different for him.'

'It certainly was,' she agreed.

'And there was just female clothing in the case?'

'Yes, sir,' the forensic officer nodded.

'So our John Doe was a transvestite?'

'Looks that way, sir,' added Constable Wood.

'Couldn't live with it, so he jumped in front of the seven-thirty Bakerloo Line to Harrow and Wealdstone.'

'I wouldn't be so sure,' said the scene-of-crime officer.

'Go on?'

'The underwear, sir. Female.'

'Yes.'

'Semen stains, by the looks of it. And blood, sir.'

'I see.'

'What does it mean?' asked Emily Wood.

Detective Inspector Hamilton flashed her a mirthless smile. 'I have absolutely no idea,' he said.

5.

May Bank Holiday . . .

Jason Kelling shifted into fourth gear and put his foot down. He was driving along the Western Avenue at one o'clock in the morning. He had been out clubbing, but hadn't exceeded the alcohol limit. He was very careful like that. He was exceeding the speed limit, though.

He felt the adrenaline pumping through his veins as the speedometer dial reached the 100 mph point. He leaned his head back and shouted, gripping the wheel tightly, feeling the car – a Porsche Boxter in midnight-black – still accelerating.

Ten minutes later as he tried to brake and couldn't, he was shouting again, this time the shout turning into a scream. The wreckage was strewn over fifty yards.

A week later, Jennifer and Jeremy Carling were seated at the kitchen table of their modest semi-detached house in Northwood Hills, west London. He was a retired milkman and she was a retired nursery-school teacher. They were both in their seventies.

A bottle of vodka was on the table, together with two shot glasses and a bottle of Jennifer Carling's newly prescribed sleeping pills. She had been diagnosed with clinical depression, and the pills were supposed to be a short-term measure to help her sleep while more thorough therapy was put in place for her. It was a short-term solution that provided a long-time answer.

They looked at the person who was standing in the doorway to the kitchen and, if they were hoping for sympathy in the eyes that gazed upon them, they were sorely disappointed.

'You can do it this way, or I can make it painful for you.'

'But why are you doing this? We don't know you. We've never met you. We never hurt you.'

The elderly woman's voice cracked as she burst into tears. Her husband patted her hand. Then he poured vodka into the shot glass and poured some pills into his wife's open palm. He looked up at the woman, angry now as he tilted the bottle into his mouth, then swallowed the pills with the vodka. His wife swallowed hers a few at a time, her throat constricting painfully as the harsh spirit burned her throat. The man took another shot of vodka and downed it in one, then glared at the figure in the doorway.

'Fuck you!' he said.

'No,' came the reply. 'Not me.'

Half an hour later and the couple were dead. Heads slumped motionless on the table. A card between them, face-up.

A tarot card. Major Arcana. The Lovers.

Part One

6.

The present. Friday, 19 December

Night-time in the city.

Seven-thirty. Friday evening. Inner London. The western edges. North of the river. The air had crystals dancing in it. The pavements sparkled with them, as if a dusting of magic had been sprinkled over them. The night sky had clouds half-covering the low moon. A moon that broke free, now and again, from the long, floating fingers of dark cloud that tried to snaggle it in their grasp, reel it back to them. But the moon shrugged them off, sailed free like a galleon under full sail. Further east, however, even darker clouds were massing and banking together, rolling ever westwards towards London, like a slow tidal wave.

On the streets of Oxford Street and Regent Street, of Piccadilly and Haymarket, the crowds still thronged. Couples and singles laden down with packages, gift-wrapped from Fortnum & Mason, from Selfridges and Hamleys. The golden light spilling from the ornate window displays in the shop fronts onto the faces of the happy shoppers. Office workers en masse, arms linked and singing. The air rich with a heady melange of sound, traffic, laughter, taxis hooting, the swirl and cacophonous dance of carol music competing with one another as doors were opened and closed.

Christmas.

A time for sharing and love. For wassailing and mistletoe, for mulled wine and mince pies. A time for peace and goodwill to all men – whatever their religion.

At least that was the theory. Some people, however, hadn't got the memo. Some people had other agendas – and goodwill to their fellow man was nowhere on their list. For in the hearts of some, even at Christmas (especially sometimes at Christmas), there is a black wickedness that defines humanity every bit as accurately as the charity in the hearts of good men and women.

Light and dark. Yin and yang.

Life and death.

Holland Park. Eight o'clock Friday evening

Jack Delaney sat on the edge of his daughter Siobhan's bed.

Her head was propped back on the pillow and her eyes were tired, threatening to close at any minute, but she blinked them determinedly, keeping herself awake.

Jack grinned at her. 'Why don't you just shut your eyes, my darling, and go to sleep. It's late.'

'Because you promised me a story. And I read in the papers that Detective Inspector Jack Delaney of

London England's finest Metropolitan Police force always keeps his word!' Siobhan said, gushing the words out with a defiant pout to her lips. A pout that reminded Jack so much of her dead mother.

Jack laughed out loud. And it was testament to the fact that the memories of his dead wife which his daughter conjured forth didn't put spikes of guilt and misery in his heart any longer. Siobhan had given a thick, Irish brogue to her words, sounding just like a wild, heathen child of Cork from his own youth. He'd schooled her in it, much to his late wife's annoyance and mock-scolding.

'I thought you preferred Kate's stories nowadays,' Delaney replied, teasing her.

'No, I always like yours best. It's just . . .' She trailed off and shrugged.

'It's what, darlin'?'

'It's Kate's house we're living in now. So it's only fair that if she wants to tell me a story, I should let her.' She frowned, as if puzzling over a matter of great philosophical debate, and Delaney laughed again. It was a rich laugh, full of life.

'To be sure,' he said, echoing her and putting on the *oirish*. 'Is it not yourself that has been off to scale the battlements and kissed the *Cloch na Blarnan*? Should it not be you the one as is telling the tales, I'm thinking!'

'What is the *Cloch na Barnan*?' asked Siobhan, all wide-eyed innocence.

'Ah now . . .' explained Delaney, although he was quite aware that Siobhan knew full well what it was. 'It's an ancient story,' he continued. 'The *Cloch na Blarnan* is what the unwashed, heathen devils on this side of the blessed channel call the Blarney Stone.'

'The Blarney Stone!' said Siobhan in feigned wonder. 'Is it magic?'

'Is it magic?' said Jack, his own eyebrows raising as if in mutual astonishment and his voice slipping into a softer, lyrical brogue. 'I like that! Why, is the pot of gold at the end of a rainbow magic? Is the music that the fairies' fluttering wings make magic? Are the wishes that come true on a falling star magic?'

'Yes.'

'Then you'd better believe it is magic, Siobhan. Very powerful magic indeed. One of the most important of all the magics.'

'What is it?'

''Tis said that whoever lays his lips on the cool surface of the stone will have bestowed upon them the gift of story, the gift of persuasion . . .' He paused dramatically. 'The gift, as they say, of the gab!'

'The gift of the gob?'

Delaney laughed again. 'Don't let Kate hear you using that expression, sweetheart.'

'Why not?'

Delaney grimaced. 'Let's just say that it's not one she's overly fond of.'

'Tell me more about the gift of the gab then.'

'Ah now, the magic of the Blarney Stone, you see.' Delaney pretended to consider the matter. 'Some say it's best described as giving you the ability to deceive someone without offending them!'

Siobhan made an O of her mouth. 'To lie, you mean?'

'Well now, *lie* – that might be too strong a word. Bending the facts to one's advantage maybe.'

'Tell me more about the Stone. Have you seen it?'

'No, I haven't. I don't need to. We Delaneys don't need to see or kiss it to have its magic work upon us.'

'Why not?'

'Maybe that should be a story for another night.'

'Tonight, tonight!' Siobhan wriggled impatiently.

Delaney seemed to consider for a moment, before sighing and relenting. 'Sure, and you'll promise to go straight to sleep when the telling of it is done.'

'Cross my heart and hope to die, if I should ever tell a lie. May my soul lay down to sleep, if a promise I do not keep!'

Siobhan made a cross with her finger over her blanket and smiled as Jack sidled closer to her.

'It all happened long, long ago. When a man called Cormac Laidir MacCarthy—'

'The same MacCarthy as MacCarthy's bar near where you were born, Da?' interrupted Siobhan. 'In Castletownbere.'

'The very same name, the very same family.'

'Will we go there one day?'

'Did I not promise it?'

Siobhan clapped her hands. 'And will we see the magic Stone there?'

'No,' Delaney shook his head. 'The Stone now resides in Blarney Castle in Blarney. Still in Cork, mind, but not where it came from originally.'

'Where did it come from then?'

Delaney looked at her for a moment before speaking. 'From Ballydehob!'

Siobhan gasped again, theatrically. 'The town where you were born!'

'It certainly is, but there's more to the legend than that.'

Siobhan settled back down on her pillow. 'Go on then.'

'Well, your great-great-great- to the power of something or other grandfather was a man called Liam Colm Delaney. And Liam was famous throughout the whole of Cork. As a fighter, as a poet and as a man who could charm the very birds down from the trees. But one day the worst thing that could ever happen to a man like him did indeed happen.'

'What was it?'

'He fell in love.'

Siobhan blinked, confused. 'Why was that so bad?'

'Because the woman he fell in love with, the very first time he ever clapped eyes on her, was called Aoibheann.'

'That's a pretty name.'

'It is, and Aoibheann means "beautiful". As in the heathen English word "heavenly". Aoibheann Aghna Finbar McCool was her name, and she was the only woman in the whole of Ireland who was impervious to Liam Delaney's charms.'

'What did he do?'

'He tried everything he could. He wrote epic poems, he sent fields of flowers, he pleaded and begged, but his honeyed words had no effect. She was as cool towards him as a Nordic snow-queen.'

'What happened?'

'Well, in desperation, Liam prayed to the goddess Cliodna for her assistance. Now Cleena, as they say in the English tongue, was Queen of the banshees of the Tuatha De Danann. She was the goddess of love and beauty, and ruled over the *Sheoques* or fairy

36

women of the hills of south Munster. And she answered his prayer.'

'She made Aoibheann fall in love with him?'

'It wasn't as simple as that. At the same time as Liam was petitioning for her intervention, so too was your man Cormac Laidir MacCarthy.'

'He was in love with Aoibheann too?'

'No, no. Not so as I know, leastwise. But Cormac MacCarthy was the very builder of Blarney Castle! The day after he prayed to the goddess Cliodna he was due to appear in court in a lawsuit that was like to ruin him entirely.'

'And was he innocent?'

'Ah no, that he was not. But the MacCarthys – stretching back, as they did, for many years as Kings of Munster and Desmond – were looked on favourably by the goddess. And they in turn always showed the Queen and her court of banshees the greatest respect. So Cliodna decided to answer both Liam's and Cormac's prayers at the same time. Kill two birds with one stone, as it were. She sent a vision to Liam Delaney to stand on the high hill overlooking the estuary at Ballydehob, where there now stands a fine bridge that used to bring the trains across.'

'I've seen the pictures,' said Siobhan, nodding enthusiastically.

'So your great-great-great-etc-granda, Liam Delaney, stood there at dawnbreak, as commanded. And as the spears of light broke over the horizon, sending golden flashes darting and rippling along the length of estuary, he saw a wondrous thing.'

'What was it?'

'A large raven burst from below the waters.

Exploding upwards in a flurry of feathers and sinew, his powerful wings beating and shaking from them the droplets of the Ballydehob estuary so that they hung in the air, sparkling like a mist of the finest diamonds. And then he swooped higher and higher, and Delaney could see that in his beak the raven held a big pebble. As he passed overhead, the raven opened his beak and let the pebble fall to Liam Delaney's feet. As instructed, Liam picked up the pebble, kissed it and then threw it hard out over the river. It hung in the air for a moment and then plummeted downwards. But before it could hit the water a loud caw was heard that echoed all through Ballydehob, and the raven swooped and caught the pebble in his beak once more and then, beating his powerful wings, headed north and east to Cork city and Blarney beyond.'

'What happened to it? What did it all mean?'

'It transpired that the stone had absorbed Liam Delaney's legendary gift of the gab. Taken it from him, in one fell swoop. That morning, on his way to court, Cormac Laidir MacCarthy was told to kiss the very first stone he saw. And as he set off across the wide green expanse of lawn, a pebble landed at his feet. He looked upwards but the bright sun dazzled his eyes so much that he could see nothing, but as he shielded his eyes he could hear the sound of giant wings flapping. He picked up the pebble and kissed it, put it into his bag, went to court and spoke like the greatest bard the world has ever known.'

'Did he win his case?'

'He did indeed! Guilty though he was, he lied like

38

an English politician and spoke with such eloquence, and with such honey in his words, that he was cheered and heralded when he won the case.'

'He had the gift of the gab!'

'Indeed. And when he stepped outside, his bag felt heavy on his back, so he took it off and opened it, and inside it he saw that the small pebble had been transformed into a large stone! And that stone he took and built into the parapet on one of the towers of Blarney Castle. And the legend goes that a little of the original magic lingers. So that all who now journey to kiss the Stone are gifted with an echo of the ancient spell of the goddess Cliodna.'

'And what happened to Liam Delaney?'

'Well now, it seemed his blessing was also his curse, because by kissing his stone he lost the power to deceive with eloquence.'

'So what could he do?' asked Siobhan.

'He could only tell the truth.'

'And was that so bad?'

Delaney smiled and ruffled his daughter's hair. 'Not at all. Because it turned out that Aoibheann Aghna Finbar McCool was in truth one of the *Sheoques* herself and so was totally immune to the blandishments of a mortal man like Liam Delaney. It was the truth that won her heart, and Liam Delaney never regretted losing the gift of the gab because he had a far better gift in return for it.'

'And what was that?'

'The gift of love.'

'Ahhh.' Siobhan smiled and clapped her hands. 'I like that story,' she said and snuggled into her pillow, her eyes blinking as she fought to keep them open.

'Go to sleep then, my little angel,' said Delaney, smoothing her hair neat again.

'But I thought you said we Delaneys didn't need to kiss the Blarney Stone to have the gift of the gab.'

'We don't.'

'But if Liam Delaney put the gift into the Stone, why is that, then?'

'Because we are direct descendants of Liam Delaney and Aoibheann Aghna Finbar McCool. Herself a fairy of the magical hills of the ancient Kingdom of Desmond, and favourite cousin to the goddess Cliodna. And when the goddess saw how happy Liam had made her cousin, she gifted the magic back to his children, and so it has passed on through all the generations to his descendants.'

'Does that mean you still have the gift to deceive without offending then, Daddy?' Siobhan asked, stifling a yawn.

Delaney smiled again. 'Ah no, in that respect I take after our great forefather Liam Colm. I am only capable of telling the truth.'

Siobhan smiled peacefully, and as her eyes closed she was asleep almost before they did so. The smile stayed on her lips.

However, Jack Delaney wasn't smiling.

He was thinking about the last question his daughter had asked him, and what he had to do the next morning.

Thinking he had more in common with Cormac Laidir MacCarthy than he ever did with his smooth-talking, invented ancestor.

7.

Geoffrey Hunt was feeling every one of his sixty-eight years.

He was a tall, thin man with a full head of once-dark hair that had gone iron-grey early in his fifties. His hair was silver now, shining, as he stood bathed in moonlight in front of the butler sink in his kitchen. He was looking out through the leaded-light window into his garden beyond. Staring into the middle distance, his grey eyes sad. Unblinking.

A round platter of a moon was shining as brightly as it had done for a long while. Geoffrey was wearing red tartan pyjamas, but no slippers, and he shivered as he looked upwards. His long, narrow feet should have been frozen on the bare stone of the kitchen floor, but when he shivered again it was not from the cold.

Unaware that he was doing so, he made a sign of the cross on his chest. Then rubbed his hands. His arthritis seemed to have become progressively worse over the last few months. It was always bad when the weather was cold, and it had indeed been very cold of late that winter. Bitingly cold. But this aching seemed

41

more than just that. The pain was eating into his bone marrow and not just his joints. He looked down at his hands, thin but swollen, the knuckles like small deformed walnuts on his twig-like fingers.

He rubbed one hand over the other again as he looked at the moon and winced.

'Geoffrey, what are you doing out here? Come back to bed.'

He turned round, startled to see his wife standing in the doorway to their kitchen. She was just a few years younger than him, but she looked younger than that, even though her hair was pure white and the concerned expression that she wore on her face had settled into permanent lines from familiar usage. She had pale-blue, innocent, almost child-like eyes. Eyes that were large with concern. She was dressed in a pale-green dressing gown with matching slippers and held her arms wrapped around her body to comfort herself against more than the cold night air.

'It's dark, Geoffrey,' she said again, 'and it's freezing down here.'

'Yes,' he nodded, but didn't seem to register what she had said.

'You could at least put something on your feet – where are your slippers?'

'I don't know, dear. Probably upstairs. Why don't you get back to bed?'

'I can't sleep, with you down here.'

'I won't be long.'

'But you haven't even got your slippers on, you'll catch your death of cold!'

Geoffrey nodded at the window. 'Another full moon.'

'I can see.'

Geoffrey Hunt looked back at his wife and blinked. 'It would have been his birthday tomorrow, Patricia,' he said.

His wife crossed over to him and wrapped her arms around his frail body.

'I know,' she said, and then again, 'I know. I didn't mention it. I thought you didn't want to talk about it.'

Geoffrey nodded as he stroked her hair and looked up at the full moon. He shivered again and Patricia took his hand.

'Come to bed now. There's nothing we can do. There never was.'

'I wish I could believe that.'

'It's true.'

Geoffrey nodded, but his eyes belied the gesture. He stroked his wife's hair gently, kissed her on the cheek and let her lead him from the kitchen.

8.

Edgware Road. Ten o'clock, Friday night

The whisky was doing the trick now.

It always did, when he could get enough of it. And that was bloody rare. Sodding London! Too many fake immigrants with dogs and babies messing up the game. Only for him it wasn't a game. People took him for a scammer too, though. Bloody Eastern Europeans – he'd spit on them. He'd blood their noses! Them and the bloody *Big Issue* nonces. Spoiling it for Bible. Spoiling it for all the real people. The civilians didn't know better now. They couldn't tell the Pharisees – the separated ones – from the Pharaohs, and who was to blame them! But it was he and the rest of them who suffered. Separated, right enough. They might be beloved of God, but you couldn't tell it on the streets of London.

'For I tell you,' he shouted and waved his grimy fist in front of him, the people on the streets parting around him like waves before a prow, 'that unless your righteousness exceeds that of scribes and Pharisees, you will never enter the kingdom of Heaven!'

He slumped against the window of McDonald's

and took a ragged breath. There was a buzzing in his head building now, and he half-mumbled, half-sang along to the rhythm of it. He moved his head slightly from side to side as he did so, bloodshot eyes peering through nearly closed eyelids. He liked it when his head buzzed. It blocked out his thoughts and his feelings, such as they were. Truth to tell, Bible Steve, as he was known on the streets, didn't feel a great deal any more. Except cold. The last couple of winters had been brutal, and this one looked like it was going to be no better, before it was done with him. Maybe would do for him, because the worst of it still lay ahead, if he was any judge. He tilted his head and looked up at the night sky, his singing turning into a gurgle as he took another sip of medicine and grunted as he stumbled further down the road, heading in the direction of Marble Arch. The snow that had been promised all week might come at last. Which at least meant it would be warmer than it had been for a good long while. Last week it had been too cold to snow, people had said – a ridiculous thing, but seemingly true. And cold it had been right enough, cold so that friends of his had died right there on those very streets. Frozen solid and immobile where they lay in doorways and alleys. Curled up like rimed leaves, their eyelashes white and brittle, their lips blue.

Not that Bible Steve had friends, as such. Just people like him. Living rough. Inner-city flotsam and jetsam. Human beings washed up on the tide of indifference, to seek shelter where they could and oftentimes finding none. Their bodies like the frozen statues in Narnia, only no shaggy lion's breath was going to bring them back, thought Bible Steve. Then he blinked and the notion had gone from his mind. He shook his head again angrily and grunted, looking behind him suspiciously as if some thief of thoughts had stolen his memories.

'Wassat?' he said, but there was no reply. Steve looked forward again, but no one was there, and the person who had been speaking to him in his thoughts was from a time long before. A lifetime ago.

He shivered his shoulders a little to generate some warmth and took another hit from his bottle.

The whisky helped. The whisky always helped Bible. Some said it made him violent, but if it did, he could never remember anyway. Maybe it was the wild Celtic ancestry in him as much as the rough liquor? Sometimes he did feel himself getting angry for no reason, rageful. The buzzing in his head turning from a melody into a storm of locusts, their wings chittering and chattering. It would come out of the blue, the anger building in him like steam in an engine, so that he would explode if he didn't do something. Maybe that was why he drank? Maybe that was why he turned to the stuff in the first place? Did it dull the rage or fuel it? He couldn't remember. What he did know was that the alcohol made him oblivious, untouchable, eventually blissfully unconscious. He held the cold bottle to his lips once more and felt the harsh liquid burn down his throat like a cleansing fire. He coughed and shivered, the shiver turning into a trembling that he couldn't stop. He dragged the rough fibre of his coat sleeve across his mouth and sat down on the pavement, his back propped against the cold brick of an empty building.

'Vengeance is mine, sayeth the Lord,' he said and took another sip of whisky, but it did nothing to stop the tremors of his battered body, and even less to stem the darkness that was building now in his mind. 'Vengeance,' he said again. Then he looked up at the moon and shook his fist at it. 'Vengeance!' He shouted it a third time and then stumbled to his feet once more. 'An eye for an eye, a life for a life!'

9.

White City Police Station, west London. Ten-fifteen, Friday night

Dr Laura Chilvers was a striking-looking woman.

She was just under five foot nine inches tall in her flat-heeled shoes. She had her hair cut in a platinum bob, with a muscular, fit, but womanly figure; she wore little make-up, but didn't need to. She had a luminescence to her skin and a natural beauty that shone. Her eyes were Nordic blue and her smile dazzled. When she walked into or out of a room all eyes turned on her. If she was aware of it she made no sign. Few men dared to ask her out and, if they did, they were wholly unsuccessful. Laura Chilvers was gay. One hundred per cent all-the-way sister. The *waste* of it was often the subject of frustrated speculation by most of the male policemen at the station (never the bastion of political correctness), over their breaktime cups of tea and bacon sandwiches. And by quite a few of the women too, but not all.

As it was, Dave Matthews, a happily married man, just smiled warmly at Laura when she handed some paperwork over to him as he stood behind the custody desk. 'Busy night again,' he said.

48

'Friday as well,' agreed the police surgeon. 'Which means it is only going to get worse. A lot worse.'

'How late are you on?'

'Couple of hours, then off.'

'Home to bed?'

Laura circled her fists and shimmied her hips a little. 'On a Friday night? You've got to be joking, Sergeant!' she said. 'Friday night is down-and-dirty night, it's clubbing night. You better believe I'll be seeing the dawn in.'

'Who's she, then? The new girlfriend?'

'That's funny, Dave,' she said, deadpan. 'You're not a clubbing man, I take it?'

'What, with these bunions? Why do you think they put me behind a desk so often? Too many years pounding the streets. Tough on crime – tough on feet!'

Laura laughed. 'Rubbish! You play rugby for the Met. I bet you could still work the dance floor.'

'I wouldn't be putting your mortgage on it. The last disco I went to was at school when I was sixteen and copped off with the future Mrs Slimline. You couldn't pay me to dance.'

'You wouldn't want to,' said Kate Walker, laughing, as she came into the custody area holding three mugs of tea. 'You didn't see him at the talent contest a few months ago.'

'This the one when Smiling Jack Delaney did his Johnny Cash impression?'

'That's it.' Kate smiled herself at the memory. 'Dave here was trying to bust some moves on the dance floor. Ended up busting the table he landed on!'

'I was not dancing, I was being jostled by a group of overexcited WPCs! Quite a different matter.'

Laura laughed as her mobile rang. She fished it out of her pocket and answered it. 'Laura Chilvers?' she said and her smile vanished. 'No! I can't do that. Look, I'll see you later, okay?' She snapped the phone shut.

'Problems?' asked Kate.

'Nothing I can't sort.'

She turned and walked over to one of the police surgeons' offices.

'What about your tea?' Kate called after her, but Dr Chilvers waved her hand dismissively and closed the door as she went into her room.

Kate Walker looked at Dave Matthews and raised an eyebrow.

The sergeant shrugged. 'Wrong time of the month?'

Kate laughed. 'If I didn't think you were being ironic, Dave, I would tell Laura you just said that. I reckon she'd do more than jostle you!'

The sergeant held his hand up in mock-surrender. 'No, thanks, I wouldn't want to get on the bad side of that one!'

'Or me,' said Kate, throwing him a look.

'There's something about Dr Laura Chilvers,' the desk sergeant continued. 'I reckon, push comes to shove, she could handle herself pretty well.'

'Best you don't find out then!'

The sergeant nodded thoughtfully as Kate headed to her office. Then took a sip of his tea and looked over at Dr Chilvers' closed door. He'd seen the look in her eyes as she took the call. And it wasn't a kind

50

one. There was trouble coming for someone tonight, he reckoned.

And he was right.

10

Bible Steve took a look at his bottle of whisky, half-empty now.

He held it to his lips and poured himself another small glug, felt his body shiver uncontrollably once more as the rough alcohol burned his throat. He looked to his side at the young woman who was sitting next to him. She was five foot six inches tall, with long, blonde hair, a stick-thin body. Innocence in blue jeans. Her skin was stretched tight over the bones of her face with fine, translucent veins showing through. She could have been an anorexic or a supermodel.

She was neither.

She had been abused by her father, an unemployed sheet metal worker, since she was twelve years old. Her mother, an undiagnosed manic depressive self-medicating on meth amphetamine, had added physical to the sexual abuse and she did what tens of thousands of children a year did. She ran away from home.

The young woman sitting next to Bible Steve would have rather walked in front of an Intercity express train than return home. She had come to London when she was fifteen, lived rough on the streets for two days before falling into prostitution, shoplifting and petty crime. Recruited into it by a girl a year younger than her and already six months into the life. She had had two abortions from back-street *clinicians* and had recently been released from Holloway prison, serving a year of a two-year sentence for fencing stolen goods, amongst other charges. She had been out two months. Two weeks out and she had left the supervised accommodation she had been provided with and was back on the streets. She was an alcoholic and drug-dependent. She was in her early twenties. An old hand. She had the mind of a child. Her name was Margaret O'Brien but anyone only ever knew her as Meg.

Bible Steve looked at her for a moment more, squinting his bloodshot eyes again. 'Whoever was the father of disease, an ill diet was the mother!' he roared and handed her the bottle. The girl muttered some thanks, her words slurred, her eyes unfocused. She took a sip and would have let the bottle slide from her grasp as she slumped backwards, but Bible Steve took it from her and held it towards a couple sitting on the other side of him. All four of them huddled together and against the wall for the warmth coming from the heated building.

'Give, and it will be given to you. A good measure, pressed down, shaken together and running over, will be poured into your lap. For with the measure you use, it will be measured to you. Luke 6,37–38,' said Bible Steve, grinning and revealing teeth rotten with neglect.

The older woman took the bottle gratefully, drank some, coughed and handed the bottle over to her husband. They were in their fifties and had been homeless for over a year. Unemployment, debt, gambling, loan-sharks. Theirs was not an unfamiliar story. Rare, however, that they had stayed as a couple and moreover had stayed together on the streets. The winter was going hard on them. You could see it in the cracked skin of their ravaged faces, and the hopelessness that dulled their eyes. The man took a drink of the whisky and handed the bottle back.

'You're a good man, Bible,' he said.

Steve took the bottle, scowled as he looked at its diminishing contents – barely one-third left now – and had another small slug. He dragged the back of his coat sleeve across his mouth. 'That, sir, I am not,' he said. 'The Lord has looked upon my blackened soul and He has seen that it is not good.'

'I don't know about the Lord, but there's not many as would share whisky,' said the older woman.

The younger girl snuggled into Bible Steve and he put his arm around her and roared again. 'But if at the church they would give us some ale. And a pleasant fire our souls to regale. We'd sing and we'd pray all the livelong day, nor ever once wish from the church to stray!'

'Too fucking right!' said the young girl and Bible Steve pulled her in tighter to him. 'Cuddle up, my lovely, old Bible'll keep you warm. Warm as toast,' he said. 'Warm as buttered crumpet.'

The woman nodded, her eyes half-closing again.

'I'll make Christians of the whole heathen, ruddy lot of you,' he said. He stood up, the girl's face falling into his crotch. He held it there for a moment or two.

'Business first though,' he said. 'Nature calls.'

The hairy man put a hand to the side of the rough brickwork to steady himself, he had to blink for a moment or two to remember where he was. All memory of the last two hours had vanished from his mind again as soon as he stood.

This happened to him often. Whole hours of blankness, days sometimes. He remembered early evening. A drunken Japanese tourist had handed him a twenty-pound note some hours ago when he had asked for any change. A mistake by the tourist, presumably, being unfamiliar with the currency, or else to impress the loud and overly made-up women who accompanied him and his business colleague.

Hired women no doubt, Bible Steve thought at the time. But if you were to ask him now what he thought he wouldn't have been able to remember where the money he had spent had come from. Strong lagers and a bottle of whisky. He had passed a slug or two of the whisky around, but not much and the bottle was severely depleted. He looked at it, confused, and down at the people he had been talking with.

'Have you been at my whisky?' he snarled.

But the other three were huddled into each other and didn't reply.

Bible Steve patted the young woman on the head. 'I'll be back in a minute, darling. Don't worry, Bible'll see you all right. He'll see you snug,' he said with a wink.

He took his hand off the wall and staggered a little further down the alleyway. Bright light spilled from a lone restaurant further ahead.

The Lucky Dragon restaurant. Cantonese. Bible

Steve staggered towards it and put his hand on the glass, peering in as he fought to keep steady. The nearly finished bottle of whisky swayed in his left hand as if to counterbalance.

He didn't recognise the figure staring back at him, reflected palely in the glass of the restaurant window. It had the face of a wild-haired and heavily bearded man. A French rugby player came to his mind. But he couldn't remember his name. This man's hair, though, was lank, greasy and matted. The beard covering most of his face was like a tribal shaman's mask. He had on a battered and soiled army greatcoat with layers of equally filthy clothing beneath. His eyes were like coals. Sore, cracked and flickering with residual heat, but near to winking out as his eyelids closed. He shook his head and growled. He peered in the window, scowling at the diners within, who regarded him with an equal mixture of horror and disgust. An elderly Chinese woman shook her hands, gesturing at him as if to shoo away a large rodent.

Bible Steve blinked again and then snarled and banged on the window.

'A corruption! A plague!' he shouted. His native tongue broader now than earlier that day. His voice raspy with the rawness of the whisky and his outrage. 'And the Lord says that he who eats with the pigs shall be as swine. Consumption and damnation is your bill. And ye shall pay it in punishment and in death!'

He banged on the window again. The Chinese woman leaned out from the doorway and shouted at him.

'I call police! I call police! You go now.'

Bible Steve looked across at her and belched. 'Madam, I shall gladly go now, as per your instructions.' He belched again.

He looked down at the bottle of whisky in his hand, now empty, and tossed it imperiously to one side. Then glared at the woman once more. 'As per your commandment, so mote it be!' He fumbled with his trouser zipper and pulled out his member. 'If you want me to go I shall go. And great shall be the mic . . . the mic . . .' Bible Steve said, struggling to find the word and then grinned showing a full set of yellowed teeth. 'Great shall be the micturation!' he said and began to urinate powerfully on to the window, splashing down onto the pavement. The Chinese woman hopped, horrified, back into the restaurant, flapping her arms and shouting like a startled crow.

Bible Steve looked down and grinned again. 'And the Lord looked down at the waters that came to pass and he was pleased,' he said before falling backwards to crash unconscious on the floor, a river of piss still flowing toward the kerbside.

A short while later and in the distance was the faint sound of an ambulance siren. But Bible Steve didn't hear it. He was snoring like an elephant, and the buzzing, for a while at least, had stopped in his brain.

Above him clouds scudded past, revealing a full moon that hung even lower and fatter in the sky now, its pits and craters clearly visible to the naked eye. Yellow, seemingly, like ancient wax, swollen and pregnant with omen.

The Chinese woman looked up at it and made

another gesture. Warding with her fingers and muttering under her breath. She looked scared.

She had every good reason to be.

Dr Kate Walker lifted the eyelid of the man lying supine on the cot in the holding cell and shone a small torch in his eye.

The man's pupils contracted but he continued to snore. Loudly. She looked over at 'Slimline' Matthews and shook her head.

'Sleeping Beauty here won't be round any time in the near future.'

'Not surprised.'

'Get someone to look in on him in the morning.'

'The amount of booze he had in him, probably take a day or two before he's fit for questioning. It wouldn't be the first time.'

'You know him?'

'Oh yeah. Keith Hagen's been a customer of ours since he was fourteen years old,' said the sergeant as they walked out of the cell. He closed the door behind them none too gently but the snoring could still be heard.

'And how old is he now?'

'Twenty-two.'

'Really? He doesn't look older than eighteen,' said Kate, surprised.

Dave Matthews shrugged. 'I guess some people

have all the luck.'

'It's the kind of luck that won't see him making thirty.'

The sergeant shook his head as they headed towards the custody area. 'I'm not so sure. The thing is, he only does it now and again. Most of the year he's as good as gold. Works for the post office, volunteers at a local charity shop most Saturdays.'

'So what sets him off?'

Dave Matthews jerked his thumb to the moonlight shining through the front window of the police station. 'The full moon. Brings all the loonies out.' He twiddled his finger round his temple in case Kate had missed his point.

Laura, who was putting a report behind the reception desk, turned round and frowned at him.

'Not a term we in the medical profession entirely endorse, sergeant.'

Kate walked across and looked out of the window at the night sky. The moon hung clear for a moment or two, as it had all evening, and then clouds began to drift around it, quicker than she would have thought, and soon the moon was wrapped and hidden and the night was dark.

'They reckon we're due snow any time now,' she said.

'Shouldn't wonder,' the sergeant grunted, looking none too happy at the prospect.

'Not looking forward to a white Christmas, Dave?' asked Bob Wilkinson cheerily for a change. 'Not going all "bah humbug!" on us, are you?'

Dave Matthews' scowl deepened. 'We're spending it at the in-laws'.'

'Ah,' Bob nodded sympathetically.

'*Ah*, indeed.'

The telephone on the front desk rang and PC Wilkinson snatched it up.

'White City Police Station?' he said and listened for a moment or two. 'Okay, Peggy. Show me as attending.'

He hung up and nodded to Dr Laura. 'You're with me.'

Laura looked at her watch. 'I'm off soon. Can't you go, Kate?'

'Sorry. I'm off shift, and I've got a pile of paperwork to process before I can get home.' Kate shrugged apologetically.

'It's only Edgware Road,' said Bob Wilkinson to Laura. 'Come on, Doctor, the sooner we go, the sooner we'll be back.'

12

A short, fast ride later and Laura Chilvers and Bob Wilkinson were walking down Edgware Road.

There were plenty of people out on the streets. London doesn't stop for the cold; it doesn't stop for anything, particularly at Christmas. The restaurants were packed with office parties, and the sound of their celebrations spilled out into the street as doors were opened and closed. A lot of sore heads in the morning, if the raucous laughter and the unsteady balance of people leaving and waving drunkenly for taxis were anything to go by, in Laura's considered, professional opinion. She stepped aside as one drunken man in his twenties staggered out of McDonald's and lurched by, clutching a hand to his mouth and hurrying to the kerb looking like he was about to be violently sick. She left him to it. Taking the Hippocratic Oath didn't mean she had to rush to the aid of every binge-drinking idiot in London. She'd be working round the clock from here to Michaelmas if she did.

Bob Wilkinson was chatting to her as they made their way down the road, moaning about something or other as usual, but she wasn't really listening. She was thinking about partying herself and the night ahead that she had planned. A new, fashionable fetish-club was opening in the West End and she was looking forward to paying it a visit. A young woman she had met last week at a gay bar in Soho had invited her. Laura had coolly told her she might be there, she might not! The woman was clearly the submissive type, but absolutely gorgeous, and Laura liked to play mind-games, as well as the other games. Mind-fuck them first, she thought to herself, and she was happy to take the dominant role if that was what was required. It wasn't always her thing, but if the mood took her she'd get into it as much as any of the serious players. S&M was more about the mental than it was about the physical – something women understood a lot better than men in her experience. Laura didn't consider herself a sadist as such, but she liked giving sensual pain if it was consensual. Not the kind of all-out beatings that some women she had met wanted. The kind that draws blood, leaves serious bruising; she couldn't even watch that, at some of the clubs and private parties she had been to. She was a doctor after all and the Hippocratic Oath definitely did go against that kind of thing! She smiled to herself at the thought.

'What?' Bob Wilkinson asked her as he stopped walking and looked at her curiously.

'Nothing,' she said, keeping the smile on her face. She couldn't imagine what the perennially cranky police constable would make of her thoughts, or her plans for that night. She certainly had no intention of telling him. Her private life she kept exactly that. And when she did attend the kind of clubs like the one she was going to later, she always wore a mask and went incognito. A sexy mask, mind. She was not only a doctor but a police surgeon, after all, not the sort of thing she wanted to be public knowledge. Fetish wasn't quite the *new gay* yet. Hell, gay wasn't even the new gay in the Metropolitan Police. She had lost count of the number of women who had hit on her. Some of them married, some with boyfriends, others not. But a lot of them asking her to keep it strictly between themselves. There were some women who were out and proud, of course. Chief Inspector Diane Campbell and her gorgeous girlfriend, who worked in the evidence area back in White City, for one. But a lot of gay women – and men come to that – kept that part of their life separate from work and, in all honesty, she didn't blame them. It was a lot easier for her to come out as a student going on to be a doctor than it was for a cadet over at Hendon.

'Down here,' said PC Wilkinson, snapping her out of her thoughts and heading her off the main drag down a small cul-de-sac of a lane. There were a few shops, closed for the night now; some offices where homeless people were huddled together with their backs against the wall, taking some small comfort, she assumed, from the heat emanating from it. She looked up at the night sky, heavily swollen with snow, and wondered why they didn't make it to one of the homeless shelters. Maybe they would later. She fished in her pocket and came up with a couple of pound coins. She threw them onto the blanket laid out in front of a young woman seated with a man and another woman, both much older than her. The girl looked up at her. She had the face of an angel, Laura found herself thinking. A malnourished, haunted-eyed angel. Homeless girl by way of Margaret O'Brien. But the girl's eyes were unfocused as well as enormous and sad, the pupils dilated and huge. God knows what cocktail of booze and pills she was on. Laura wanted to stop and speak with her but the girl mumbled some thanks and closed her eyes, unable to keep them open, and leaned up against the older man next to her.

Bob Wilkinson pointed ahead some twenty yards further on to the Chinese restaurant. An elderly Chinese woman was waving angrily at them. In front of her restaurant window a homeless man lay sprawled on his back, a broken whisky bottle on the pavement near him, his arms outstretched. Cruciform. A hobo Christ nailed to a London side-street.

'He piss on window,' the Chinese woman was saying as they approached, still waving her hands around. 'All the time he come and piss on window, and police do nothing!'

'Yeah, well, we're here now, missus,' said Bob Wilkinson, trying to be placating, but his gruff tone did little to assuage the indignant old woman.

'Yeah, you here now!' she continued, spluttering with rage. 'Then you let him out, and then he come and piss on my window. People eating dinner here! How you like him to come and piss on you when you having your roast beef and gravy?'

Bob looked down at the man lying near his feet for a moment, and then back up at the woman.

'I don't think the wife would approve,' he said.

Dr Laura Chilvers knelt down and put her hand to the unconscious man's neck. She felt for a pulse, somewhat unnecessarily, for at that moment he made a wet, slapping sound with his lips and grunted. His eyes remained firmly closed, however, and his stretched arms still stayed wide and immobile. Laura looked up at the sky again. Maybe he was welcoming aliens from space. It wouldn't be the first time a mentally ill person had ended up on the street. Not by a long chalk, and certainly wouldn't be the last.

She looked down at the man again, wondering what his story was, and then shrugged and nodded up at Bob Wilkinson, who stood with a couple of tall, uniformed police constables that she didn't recognise.

'He's alive at least, I can tell you that much,' she said. 'He's got a steady heart rhythm. Lungs seem to be functioning fine too.'

Bob Wilkinson glanced across at the now-broken and empty bottle of whisky and grimaced sourly. 'Take more than a cheap bottle of Scotch to kill Bible Steve, I reckon,' he said.

'You know him?' asked Laura.

The sergeant nodded. 'Don't know his real name. I'm not sure even he does any more. Everyone calls him Bible Steve. He's always quoting the scriptures or preaching at people. When he's not falling down drunk, that is, or pissing on Mrs Lucky Dragon's window.'

Laura glanced back at the man sprawled on the pavement. He looked like an actor, she thought, but couldn't remember who he reminded her of. Hard to tell under all the grime and the greasy, matted hair. Maybe an older version of Mickey Rourke in *The Wrestler*, when out-of-his-face on booze. Maybe Oliver Reed in his hell-raising heyday. This man's hair was dark at one time, she could see, but it was mostly grey now, tangled, long. Impossible to tell what he would look like when he was shaved, shorn and cleaned up. Either way she knew for certain he wasn't Oliver Reed and was pretty certain he wasn't Mickey Rourke nor likely to be getting a call from Hollywood any time soon. Cricklewood maybe.

'Bible Steve we'd call a bit of a nut-job,' continued PC Wilkinson. 'But what you medical types would probably classify as having mental difficulties.'

Laura didn't smile. 'Whatever he is, he shouldn't be left out unconscious on a cold night like this. Is he violent?'

'Not particularly. Harmless enough most of the time. But when he's had a drink in him, he has been known to swing his fists. No different from most of them on the streets, when they're out of it on drugs or booze.'

'He's pretty much dead to the world now, but you better get him back to the station. So he can't harm himself. Or anyone else, come to that.'

She stood up and sprayed some antibacterial, disinfectant into her left palm and rubbed her hands together.

Bob Wilkinson gestured to the two uniforms to pick up the sleeping man, his nose wrinkling. The drunk continued groaning, muttering half-formed obscenities, his hands twitching, but he didn't waken. PC Bob Wilkinson scowled and looked down at the homeless man as they manhandled him to his feet. 'And for God's sake put that thing away, and zip him up.'

13

Dr Laura Chilvers had only been back at the station for a short while, but had had to see to a couple of forty-year-old businesswomen who had got into a fight in a male lap-dancing club over one of the dancers, and needed minor treatment before being booked; a nineteen-year-old woman who was cycling the wrong way up a one-way street dressed only in her underwear, a feather boa and a Santa Claus hat on her head; and a seventy-year-old retired army general who had become convinced after several bottles of Dom Perignon that he was living in the nineteenth century and that the head concierge at Claridge's was a Russian cavalry officer, he'd led his own Charge of the Light Brigade with an empty luggage trolley and had fractured one of his shins.

Laura was coming round to Bob Wilkinson's way of thinking as he led her to one of the holding cells. Nut-jobs. The guest in number-two cell was awake, according to the sergeant, and she could hear it for herself as the sound of his drunken shouts reverberated from the locked room.

'Lord, you have assigned me my portion and my cup; you have made my lot secure. The boundary lines have fallen for me in pleasant places; surely I have a delightful inheritance. I will praise the Lord, who counsels me; even at night my heart instructs me. I have set the Lord always before me. Because he is at my right hand, I will not be shaken!'

Bob Wilkinson opened the door and held it wide for Laura Chilvers to enter. 'All right, calm it down, Bible,' he said. 'You're not in Kansas now.'

Bible Steve stood up from the bench-bed, casting his eyes heavenwards and spreading his arms wide, and shouted, 'It is God who arms me with strength and makes my way perfect. He makes my feet like the feet of a deer; he enables me to stand on the heights. He trains my hands for battle; my arms can bend a bow of bronze. You give me your shield of victory, and your right hand sustains me; you stoop down to make me great. You broaden the path beneath me, so that my ankles do not turn.'

Lowering his arms, he looked at the doctor, then squinted his eyes. 'I know this harlot!' His finger jabbed towards her chest and Laura took a step back.

'No, you don't, Bible. She just moved down here.'

'She is a Jezebel! Satan's spawn.' He continued to point, saliva running into his beard.

'She's a police surgeon from Reading,' said PC Bob Wilkinson.

'I think you must be mistaking me for someone else,' said Laura Chilvers patiently, and smiled at him, trying to calm him down.

The drunken man clasped his hands over his ears. 'That voice,' he said, almost reverentially. 'Are you my angel?'

'No, like the constable said,' she replied, 'I'm just a police surgeon.'

He opened his raw eyes and looked at her, tears welling up now. 'Are you my guardian angel?' he asked.

'I'm nobody's angel!' she said. 'He's still drunk, Sergeant. Get him some tea and I'll check back later.'

'What about—' the sergeant started to ask her, but Laura was already moving away, her heels clacking on the stone floor.

14.

Patricia Hunt stood by her bedside window looking out, just as her husband had done earlier in the evening, at their garden below her.

It was late. Past midnight. A few hours into a new day that she was dreading. Had been dreading for years, even though she didn't know what the day would bring. But, just as her husband felt the ache of arthritis in his bones, so in her bones she knew that their time was coming. Sometimes you can run for ever, but justice is always there ahead of you. Waiting patiently for you.

Her husband behind her mumbled something and turned over in his sleep. He would be awake soon, she knew that. And if he did manage to get to sleep again, it wouldn't be for long. It was the same for her. Neither of them had been able to sleep properly for days now. The strain of it was carved into their faces, like bark on a tree.

Outside the snow had finally come. There was no wind to speak of and so the snow seemed to fall in straight lines. Like an illustrated picture from a Victorian children's book, she found herself thinking. Mysteries in the Secret Garden. There was moonlight shining through the cloud now, and the frost on the

71

ground had hardened so that the snow was settling. There was an oak tree in the corner of the garden with a flowerbed beside it and a high hedge running around all sides. A stone slab was laid into the lawn in the opposite corner to the oak tree, and an ornamental birdbath sat in its middle.

Beyond the hedge, in the distance, Patricia could make out rooftops gradually whitening as the snow settled, and in the midst of them a tall spire rose. The weathervane atop it was unmoving. Patricia gazed at the spire for a while and then looked back down at her garden. The snow had completely covered the green of their lawn now. She looked at the birdbath. And thought about what was buried beneath it.

'Come back to bed,' her husband said.

15

Laura had locked the office door and was changing into her outfit for the evening at the new club – putting on a pair of stockings with black suspenders before slipping into a pair of cami-knickers. A short black leather skirt, with a matching stud-fronted, plunge-style basque and a black leather jacket over it. Dominatrix by Gucci. She'd sort her hair and make-up later. Meanwhile she slipped a pair of killer heels into her large shoulder bag together with a small riding crop and a Catwoman-style mask. Time to party.

She put a full, almost shoulder-to-heel leather overcoat on top of her outfit, buttoned it up and put a Russian military-style fur cap on her head.

She turned the lock in the door and went into the reception area, sticking her head around Kate Walker's door to say goodbye, but she had already left. As she headed for the exit, the desk sergeant, Dave Matthews, called her back.

'Hold your horses a moment, Dr Zhivago.'

Laura turned back, not particularly amused as she saw that he was with another PC, leading the drunk they had collected earlier from the Edgware Road. Bible Steve. He was a lot quieter now and quite passive as the young constable walked him forward.

Laura looked pointedly at her watch. 'I'm out of here, Sergeant.'

'Just take a minute. The cells are full back there.'

'Are you going to charge him?'

'You bet! I want him charged and out of here as soon as.'

Laura's nostrils quivered. 'I can see why.'

Bible Steve looked up at her. 'I am here, you know!'

'No doubting of that, Mr Bible.'

'What are you going to charge me with?'

'Putting people off their sweet-and-sour pork balls,' said Dave Matthews, and Laura laughed despite herself.

'I did nothing of the sort!'

'Wagging the weeny at the window, Bible. It's not the sort of entertainment the diners at the Lucky Dragon were expecting. I don't know . . .' The sergeant wagged his hand himself. 'Maybe a fortune-cookie.'

'The call of nature must be answered, Sergeant. No man can ignore it.'

'You could have gone down the alley, Bible. Spraying the shop window like a territorial Great Dane – it's hardly being discreet, is it?'

'I was making a protest. My Christian duty. This city is rife with its worshippers, like an apple rotten with worms. They dine as others starve so that the seventh prince of Hell be worshipped!'

'I haven't got time for this, Dave,' said Laura.

Bible Steve held his hands aloft again. 'Lay not up for yourselves treasures upon Earth, where moth and rust doth corrupt, and where thieves break through and steal. But lay up for yourselves treasures in Heaven, where neither moth nor rust doth corrupt, and where thieves do not break through nor steal. For where your treasure is, there will your heart be also. No one can serve two masters, for either he will hate the one and love the other; or else he will be devoted to one and despise the other. You cannot serve both God and Mammon.'

'Right,' said Laura with a sigh and looked at her watch.

'*Matthew six, nineteen to twenty-one,*' said Bible Steve.

'Shut it now, or I'll put you back in the cell and leave you there till Christmas. *Sergeant Matthews, White City nick,*' said Slimline Dave.

Bible Steve lowered his hands and looked at Laura. 'Lead on MacDuff.'

'This way.' Laura gestured for the constable to bring him to her office. As they walked towards it, Bible Steve turned and looked at her.

'I know you,' he said.

'No, you don't.'

Bible Steve looked across at the constable. 'She interfered with me, the last time I was here.'

'She wasn't even here the last time you were brought in, Steve.'

'Interfered, I tell you!'

Laura opened the door to her office. 'In here.'

Bible Steve saluted and followed her in. The constable nodded to her. 'I'll be just outside, if you need me.'

'Thanks, I am sure I'll be fine.'

Back inside her office, Laura checked his eyes, his pulse. Then looked at his hands, which were bruised, scarred and had dried blood on both sets of knuckles.

'How did you hurt your hands, Steve?'

Bible Steve spread his fingers wide. 'But I hae dreamed a dreary dream. Beyond the Isle of Skye. I saw a dead man win a fight, and I think that man was I.'

'The Bible?'

'The Battle of Otterburn, mid-sixteenth-century.'

'Are you a time-traveller?' asked Laura gently, as she cleaned his knuckles up as best she could with a tissue and surgical spirit.

The bearded man nodded his head. 'I have been.'

'And how did you hurt your hands in this millennium?'

Bible Steve looked down at his hands again and made fists of them. 'Doing the Lord's work,' he said.

'Fighting?'

He nodded. 'The good fight, yes.'

'Who were you fighting with?'

'I fight the Devil, Doctor. Where I find him.'

'On the streets?'

'The Devil is in the hearts of men,' he said angrily and glared at her. 'In the hearts of men and women and in the corruption of children!'

Laura looked at him, concerned. 'Have you hurt children, Steve?'

Bible Steve shook his head, then tilted it to one side. 'I am just a vessel. No more than that.'

Laura put the cap on top of the bottle of surgical spirit and placed it to one side. She would have stood up, but Bible Steve grabbed her hands and pulled her towards him, an intent look in his red, sore eyes. 'I know you, don't I?' he said again.

Laura shook her head and took her hands out of his. 'No. Like I said. I met you earlier, on the street, and when you were in the cell. You were drunk. You still are.'

'No. I know you!' he said for the third time, in a hoarse croak. 'You are my angel. My guardian Angela!'

He stood up and reached out for her, turning his huge hands into claws, and Laura stepped back, her eyes wide. Horrified.

16.

Laura stepped out from her office, nodding to the constable, and hurried across to the desk where Sergeant Matthews was filling in a form and watching two uniforms lead a drunk Santa Claus to the holding cells. He sighed and put the form to one side.

'What's the verdict, Doctor?'

'He's sober enough now, I guess. If not entirely lucid.'

'Bible Steve is never entirely lucid.'

'Probably not, no.'

The sergeant looked across as the constable led the man in question out of the police surgeon's office. 'So I can charge him and release him?'

Laura held up her hand to the constable, signalling for him to wait, and leaned in to speak quietly with the desk sergeant. 'He's sober enough to be charged and released, but why don't you keep him in for the night?'

'Why would I do that? Is he ill?'

'Not physically, no.'

'I'm jammed up here, Laura.'

'I know it's against procedures, but a night out of the cold isn't going to hurt him.'

Bible Steve called out to them, 'I just want my own bed, Officer. Take a page or two of the Good Book. God's love keeps us warm. Nourishment, not punishment.'

'He hasn't got a bed, Dave.'

'Neither have we – like I say, we're jammed up here and the night is far from over.'

Laura looked at her watch. 'Yeah, and it's time I was out of here.'

'We'll drop him off at the shelter. We always do.'

'You're a good man, Sergeant Matthews, and I'll kill any man who says otherwise!' shouted Bible Steve.

The sergeant nodded to him. 'Please don't. And remember, sweet-and-sour pork balls are off the menu tonight!'

Laura adjusted her hat and headed for the door.

'Bless you, my child!' the homeless man called after her.

But Laura hurried on, the door closing behind her.

'Take care, darling,' Bible Steve said softly.

17.

London, off the Edgware Road. 3 a.m., Saturday

The streets of London were mostly quiet now.

In the distance, the sound of music playing from a club that was staying open until five in the morning. Lou Reed singing about shiny boots of leather, but faintly. Audible when the club doors opened for people to leave. There was little or no traffic on the roads, which were covered with thick snow. Large flakes of it that continued to fall, filling the air. Any footprints in that snow in the little side-street had long been filled in.

Bible Steve looked upwards, his eyes wide with wonder as the snow fell on his upturned face. He reached a hand out and clutched it, as if the dancing snowflakes were little bits of magic he could catch in his palm. He watched as they melted on the back of his hand and a tear trickled down his cheek. He wiped the sleeve of his coat roughly over his eyes, as he did hundreds of times a day, then thrust his hand into his pocket and pulled out a can of strong lager. He pulled the ring-pull, took a long drink and then belched.

'Onward then, ye people,' he sang loudly. 'Join our

happy throng, blend with ours your voices in the triumph song. Glory, laud and honour unto Christ the King, this through countless ages men and angels sing.'

He waved his can of lager to conduct an invisible choir, and his voice grew even louder.

'Onward, Christian soldiers, marching as to war, with the cross of Jesus going on before . . .'

And then his voice faltered and his eyes widened. But not with wonder this time. He shrank back against the brick of the wall that he was leaning against and raised a protective arm.

'You keep away from me,' he said, his voice trembling with fear. 'You keep away from me!'

Part Two

18.

Hampstead, north-west London. 6.30 a.m., Saturday

Jack Delaney yawned and got out of bed. He peeled back the edge of the curtain and peered through the window; it was still dark outside.

Dark, but still snowing heavily in London and had been all night, by the looks of it. As his eyes adjusted to the light, he could see the garden thick with it. Five days away from Christmas now, and the capital was blanketed in snow. The bookies would be paying out big time this year, he thought to himself, as he slipped his feet into a pair of sheepskin slippers that Kate had bought for him. He hadn't worn slippers for years. Thin end of the wedge, he had told her; but a nice wedge, he conceded.

He could hear her snoring gently behind him. The corners of his lips slipped into a smile as he listened to her. Kate denied she ever snored, and truth to tell it was more of a sighing sound, and a gentle smack of her lips, than a proper snore. It was a peaceful sound, a contented one, but Delaney was a light sleeper, unless he had had a skinful of whiskey of course, and then he slept through pretty much anything. But it was getting rarer and rarer for him to tie one on nowadays. The last few months had changed him. That much was for sure. He'd put the past back where it belonged and was concentrating on the present, on the future. At least he was trying to. He knew he was a changed man, and a lot of that change had been down to the good lady doctor who shared his bed.

He looked out at her back garden again. A picture-postcard scene. Hampstead in winter. It could have been 100 years ago, 200. Kate owned the whole house, but rented the upstairs flat to a gay couple, Patrick and Simon, a pair of musicians with the London Philharmonic Orchestra. Violinists. They spent most of their time away and so she hadn't bothered parcelling the garden into two lots, as her tenants were quite happy not having the use of it – if it meant they had to pay less rent. It suited Kate fine, and she and Delaney had talked about not letting the flat out again, if the musicians decided to move on. At some stage, in the hopefully not-too-distant future, they had discussed selling Kate's house and buying somewhere out in the country. The Chilterns maybe, or somewhere else equally rural out near Oxford.

The garden was long and narrow, but beautifully laid out. Not that you could tell at the moment, with the thick snow covering every surface like the frosting on a wedding cake. Jack smiled to himself again, as the image came to his mind. Kate and he had never actually discussed the idea of getting married. But others had. Particularly down at White City Police Station. It was becoming something of a standing joke.

The main line of questioning on the marriage issue, however, came from his daughter Siobhan. Seven years old, going on twenty! More of an interrogation than a questioning, come to that. Jack had thought she might have been against the idea, seeing as her mother had died when she was still young. Jack had carried the guilt of her death around like a small child carries a comfort-blanket. But meeting Kate had changed all that. It had changed everything. And for the better.

He looked back over his shoulder and squinted through the gloom to look at her. Her dark and gloriously curly hair was piled around the pillow that supported her head. He resisted the urge to cross over and smooth it. She had got in late last night and he didn't want to disturb her. She deserved a lie-in now and again, and she wasn't rostered on at the police station or at her general practice at the university until later.

He looked back out at the garden again and pulled the curtain shut. He'd talked with Kate about digging a fish pond when spring came and the ground was soft enough. But she had pointed out that they had a baby on the way. Maybe later, when the new addition to the family was old enough for it to be safe, but for now maybe a small fish tank for Siobhan would suffice.

Downstairs he yawned, stifling the noise with his hand, pushed the button on Kate's DeLonghi Prima Donna coffee machine and waited for it to work its magic. He had dressed in a coal-black woollen suit that Kate had bought him. A white shirt with a new dark-blue silk tie.

He caught sight of himself reflected in the glass of the window looking out over the sink into the lawn. He didn't recognise himself from the wreck of a man he had been only some few months ago. A shambling, borderline alcoholic on the verge of coming apart at the seams. His jaw was clean-shaven, his dark hair was cut and brushed, his deep-blue eyes were clear and intelligent. Even his black shoes were polished to a military shine.

He looked like he was going to a wedding or a fashion shoot for a men's magazine cover . . . or what he actually was going to be doing, later that morning.

Appearing in court.

Seemed that some of his past wouldn't stay buried after all.

19

Dongmei Chang was in a foul mood as she came out of Edgware Road station.

Her first name might well be a translation of Tung Mei which translated as 'winter plums' for some, but the truth was that she hated winter. And always had. To her it meant 'younger sister from the east' and she would have dearly loved to return east. To Hong Kong, where she was born. But Dongmei was in her late sixties now and resigned to the fact that she would never be going home. She had been in the United Kingdom since 1962, when she had been brought over to marry a man her father had chosen for her. He was starting a Chinese restaurant and, although she didn't love him when they first met, he was older than her and he wanted her respect and obedience more than her love. It wasn't an unusual concept to Dongmei, for she had seen her elder sisters married in a similar fashion. Daughters were business assets in her family. But she and they worked hard, and the business prospered in a modest way, and over the years she came to love her husband in her own way.

He had died ten years ago from a brain embolism suffered during celebrations for Chinese New Year in

Soho. They had never been blessed with children, and her husband had refused her requests to seek medical help, so she had carried on the restaurant on her own, staffed mainly by family members who came over from China in generational waves. Trained up for years and then moving on, setting up their own restaurants in different parts of the country. Nobody could afford to buy or rent in London now. Dongmei Chang held the deeds to the building, however, and had been advised to sell up and retire many, many times. But the restaurant was more to her than just a business. She had toyed with the notion of selling up immediately after her husband had died, but even though she wanted to go back home to Hong Kong, she knew that it no longer existed. It wasn't just that it was now under communist China's governance, but everything about it had changed. She had left it half a century ago and there was nothing there for her now, and there was nothing here for her either if she sold the Lucky Dragon. And so she hadn't.

Some mornings, though, the thought did still tempt her. And it certainly tempted her again that morning. Even though it was still dark, her train from Paddington, where she lived in a small apartment that she also owned, was late and subsequently packed full of early-morning commuters. Nobody had offered her a seat, so she had been jostled and bumped all the way on her admittedly short journey.

The rest of her staff and family wouldn't be in until later, but she had come in early to do the book-keeping. She didn't trust handing her accounts over to a family member to prepare for her accountant. Her financial business was just that – hers.

She was muttering to herself as she came out of the station. There are two Edgware Road stations in London, for some reason, neither of them connected and about 150 yards apart. Dongmei Chang used the Marylebone Line one, next to the flyover on the corner of Edgware Road, Harrow Road and Marylebone Road.

She was still muttering as she made her way down Edgware Road to her restaurant. She had been in England for more than fifty years now, but still thought and spoke in Chinese. She could speak a little English, but didn't care to. The snow was heavy underfoot as she turned into the side-street, and she had her eyes focused on the pavement. The flakes were swirling in the wind, lighter now, but enough to make her eyes water. As she fumbled for the keys to her shop she didn't at first notice the shape lying against the wall, a heavy coating of snow on it. But when she got nearer and looked more closely, she could see it was a man. As she bent down to look even closer, she could see the thick mat of dried blood on the man's skull, and the red staining of it on the snow beneath and around him. And then she gasped with shock, clasping a hand to her chest, which had suddenly become impossibly tight and painful, and collapsed in a gentle heap to lie beside him on the snow-crusted pavement.

20

Geoffrey Hunt stood up and rubbed his right hand at the base of his spine, arching his back and tilting his head skywards.

From the warmth of their kitchen his wife, Patricia, watched him as he did so. After a moment or two he bent over again and continued to shovel the snow that had covered the path running along the side of the garden, down to the summerhouse that Geoffrey used as an office. Fair weather or foul, he always spent an hour or two in there writing.

For some twenty years, since he had retired, Geoffrey had been writing stories, as well as mystery and romance novels, and sending them off to magazines and publishers. As yet he had had no luck, but he hadn't given up hope. At school he had always wanted to be a writer, a novelist, but things had turned out differently for him. He knew better than most that the plans men make when young are sometimes as resistant to the forces of change as a stick tossed into a river.

Patricia watched him as he worked, methodically clearing the snow, although she knew full well the pain would be shooting through his body. Snow was no friend to arthritis. She knew very well too that his body was stooped and burdened with more than the manual effort and the inflammation in his joints.

She looked at the calendar on the wall. At today's date circled in red, and at the flowers he had placed on the table beneath it.

Flowers that would never be placed in any cemetery.

Diane Campbell stood by the window of her office, looking at some uniformed officers who were hard at work shovelling snow from the car park.

Grit had been ordered, but as yet there was no sign of it. No doubt there would be a national shortage of the stuff, like last year. The uniforms had a Sisyphean task, she reckoned, as she watched the fat flurries of snowflakes swirling in the air around them, settling on the ground and freezing. Another cold, hard winter on the books.

She took a sip of her coffee and grimaced; she hated the instant muck that passed for it at White City nick, but she needed something. What she really wanted to do was throw the window open and fire up a cigarette. But she couldn't. Not because it was illegal now in public buildings – Chief Inspector Diane Campbell didn't give a damn about that. But she couldn't fire up a cigarette because her boss – a jobsworth if ever there was one – was standing by her desk fixing her with a serious look designed to intimidate her. She would have smiled, Diane didn't do intimidated, but her political sensibilities kept her face neutral. Jack Delaney didn't have a political bone in his body, so for his sake, she'd play the game with her boss. That morning at least.

The man in question, Superintendent George Napier, was an imposing figure. Tall, ebony-skinned, and dressed with military neatness and precision in his full uniform. Most people quailed beneath his critical scrutiny; but Diane Campbell wasn't most people.

'I'm sure everything will be fine, sir,' she said and looked out at the car park again. Still no sign of Delaney's ancient Saab, and George Napier had expressly told her that he wanted the detective inspector to be in first thing.

'Everything had better be better than fine!' said Napier and looked angrily at his watch. 'And where is the bloody man?'

Diane reckoned if she had been given a pound for every time she had been asked that question about Jack Delaney, she could have retired five years ago and set up an antiques shop in Norfolk. Not that she knew anything about antiques, mind, but her partner – who worked downstairs in the evidence store – did. And what made her happy usually ended up making Diane happy. She smiled slightly at the thought, remembering how she had been woken earlier that morning.

'Something amusing you, Diane?' snapped the superintendent.

Diane shook her head, putting on the kind of serious expression her boss expected. 'No, sir. Just pleased at the prospect of seeing justice done. Finally.'

'Justice would have been done if the man who stood on Robinson's neck had done a proper job of it there and then. Saved the taxpayer a great deal of wasted time and money.'

'True.'

Napier tapped his finger on his colleague's desk. 'But your man Delaney has a history of cock-ups, Diane. This trial better not turn into another one or I will have his arse on a plate and served back to him.'

'You're mixing your metaphors, sir.'

Napier looked at her straight face. 'Are you being flip with me, Diane?'

'Not at all, sir! Sorry, I'm a bit anal about grammar and the like. Drives my PA mad.'

Napier nailed his finger on her desk again. 'I mean it. This goes pearshaped and he's gone. My word on it!'

'Michael Robinson is guilty, sir. We all know it.'

'The press don't share your level of confidence, Chief Inspector.'

'With respect, sir, some of the press don't share the same gene pool as the rest of the human race.'

'Like I say, Diane. This is not the time for levity. Michael Robinson spent nine months in hospital. The fact that he didn't die is considered a medical miracle.'

'I am aware of that.'

'Do you need me to list the broken bones?'

'No, sir.'

'The crushed larynx.'

'I know the injuries he sustained.'

'Injuries. The man spent weeks in a coma, five months before he was able to walk properly again, and damn near a whole year before he was fit to stand trial.'

'He's certainly able to do that now, sir.'

'Isn't he just!' Napier slammed a copy of that

morning's *Times* on the Superintendent's desk. The headlines reading, POLICE ON TRIAL AS MICHAEL ROBINSON COMES TO COURT.

Diane glanced briefly at the paper. She'd already seen it and the others, including the more aggressively accusatory red-top banners.

'I would point out that the assault on Michael Robinson took place under the aegis of Her Majesty's Prison Service, sir. The Metropolitan Police had no culpability whatsoever.'

'Jack Delaney is not culpable, you damn well mean! After all, the man is as pure as driven snow, isn't he?' Napier added sarcastically.

Diane looked at the piles of snow being shovelled from the car park and resisted the urge to smile again; winding her boss up was one of the small pleasures she took delight in, but, as he had said himself, this morning was not the time for it.

'I wouldn't go so far as to say that,' she said instead.

'No! But I'd go so far as to say the man is a bloody liability!'

'To be frank, sir, I don't know why you allow the press to agitate you so much. It was a righteous arrest.'

'Righteous? What are we – in the United States of Bloody America now?'

'It was a sound arrest. The CPS would never have allowed it to get to court, if it hadn't been.'

'And yet Michael Robinson is swearing he was fitted up. Fitted up by Detective Inspector Jack Delaney.'

'Well, he would say that, wouldn't he?'

'Maybe he would. But he is also saying now, to whoever will listen to him, that the person who attempted to murder him said he was doing so at the behest of your Irish bloody troublemaker. We are talking conspiracy to murder here, Diane.'

'Jack Delaney would never be a party to that, sir.'

'And are you absolutely sure of that?'

Diane Campbell looked at her boss without answering. She didn't trust herself.

21.

Dr Kate Walker closed the passenger door of the car and nodded to DC Sally Cartwright who had driven the pair of them out of town to the churchyard near to the QPR football ground, a half a mile or so from White City Police station.

The DC had called Kate earlier that morning, waking her from a dream: she and Jack were having a barbecue in her back garden. It was summer, and the sun was as hot as she could remember. She had looked puzzled at the pond in her garden; the York stones that had been laid around it were green with moss. And the fish in the pond were large carp, their reds and golds flashing in the sunlight. A voice behind her, and she turned round. There was Siobhan, only she wasn't seven any more – she was in her early twenties and was dressed in a beautiful wedding gown. And behind her were four bridesmaids, her daughters, ranging from seven years old to thirteen. Hers and Jack's daughters. All with his curly black hair and bright blue eyes. The youngest one ran up and took her hand.

'Come on, Mummy, we'll be late,' she had said.

'Where's Jack?' Kate had asked, and Siobhan had looked at her, tears welling in her beautiful, big eyes.

'Oh Kate,' she had said. 'Don't you remember?'

Then the sound of a police siren that pierced the hot summer air. And the siren had become the sound of a bell, her bedside phone ringing, and Kate had started awake. Her heart thumping in her chest and her mouth dry. She snatched the phone up and it took her a moment or two before she could steady her breath and speak. It had been Detective Constable Sally Cartwright.

'Not the wake-up call I had in mind first thing this morning,' she said, yawning now into a gloved hand and tightening her jacket as she walked beside the constable into the churchyard. The gravestones visible in the cemetery attached to the church sent goosebumps down her back as she remembered her dream.

'Sorry, Kate. Like I said on the blower, I couldn't get hold of Dr Chilvers and David Riley called in sick. So it was down to you.' She shrugged apologetically.

Kate looked up at the sky, still thick with snow clouds, although it had actually stopped snowing, for a time at least. 'At least this time David Riley was being genuine and isn't at a golf-society match!'

Sally shook her head, chuckling. 'I wouldn't put it past him. Strange breed, golfers. Probably play with red balls or something. Sorry again – I know you were on a late shift last night.'

'It's not your fault and at least it wasn't an all-nighter,' said Kate as she unlatched the gate and they walked into the church grounds. 'But I had a pile of paperwork to catch up on, and I don't want anything hanging over me with Christmas coming. I want to have the decks totally clear. Have a proper holiday this year.'

'I know how that works. How was the inspector this morning?'

Kate shrugged ruefully. 'He left before I got up, was sleeping like a baby when I got in.'

'Not too worried about the court case then?'

Kate rolled her eyes. 'You know Jack!'

Sally returned the grin. 'That's true. Personally I hope they lock the door on that sick, fucking bastard Michael Robinson and throw away the key!'

Kate looked across at her, surprised to see the anger flashing in Sally's usually cheery eyes. And she was pretty sure she had never heard the detective constable swear before.

Sally picked up on the look. 'Sorry, Kate, pardon the French. But what is it with the name Michael? When I remember what nearly happened to me . . .' she said by way of explanation, then shook her head to interrupt the thought, as if to chase the memory away. 'But nothing did happen to me,' she continued with a small nod, 'because of Jack Delaney.'

'He does have his moments.'

'He does that.'

Kate patted Sally on her shoulder as they walked up to the waiting uniforms.

Some months earlier Sally Cartwright had been kidnapped by a mentally ill man. His name was Michael Hill and he was a police forensic photographer. He was off his medication and, together with his psychotic sister Audrey, they had gone on a killing spree. Sally had gone on a date with him, and when he realised that she was getting close to discovering his involvement in the killings, he had drugged her and taken her to his aunt's empty house.

She had woken to find herself chained to a wall, wearing only her underwear, in a cellar hidden in the house. The walls were thick stone and no amount of shouting would help. As she struggled to break free of the manacles holding her to the wall, she remembered what mutilations had taken place to two previous women's bodies at the hands of this mad man. She didn't let him see her terror at the time, had fronted up to him in a way she wouldn't have believed possible. Those kinds of perverts got off on power and control – she had gleaned that much from her studies at Hendon Police College. So Sally had shown him no fear, had mocked him in fact. But she had had nightmares about it ever since. Waking and starting bolt upright in the middle of most nights. Her skin clammy with sweat, a scream unuttered on her lips. But the scream was there, always there. She reckoned if she ever let it go, she wouldn't be able to stop. She would hold a hand to her mouth, bite on her knuckles, shiver at the thought of what might have happened if Jack Delaney hadn't rescued her.

Sally smiled back gratefully at Kate as the older woman took her hand off her shoulder. 'Yeah, for a miserable old bastard he's not too bad sometimes, is he?'

'Less of the old,' said Kate. 'He's the father of my unborn child, remember, and I'm not much younger than him!' Automatically her hand went to her stomach as she turned to the uniformed officer who had come across to meet them as they neared the top of the path. 'Hey, Danny,' she said. 'So what have you got for us, this cold and snowy December morning?'

'Probably nothing,' he said, then flashed a nervous smile at Sally Cartwright. 'Morning, Detective Constable.'

Sally flicked him a brief nod. She had gone out on a date with him before she had agreed to go out for an Indian meal with Michael Hill. Playing them both off against each other. A stupid thing to do, in the circumstances. PC Danny Vine had been walking on eggshells around her after what had happened, but he had still made it clear he was interested. But Sally wasn't about to rush into anything romantic any time soon, and she had decided that if she were to get into a relationship with a man again, it certainly wouldn't be with anyone she worked with. Been there done that. Bought the T-shirt.

She looked over Danny's shoulder. They were some thirty feet from the church, which had been built some time back in the nineteenth century, early in Queen Victoria's reign, and stood in its own fair-sized plot. There was scaffolding running all the way around the building; clearly some extensive reno-vation was taking place. In real estate terms, given its location, the place was worth millions. Sally wondered what the planning permission guidelines were for old churches. She had been looking into getting a mortgage on a small flat and realised she couldn't even afford a garden shed in west London, nowadays.

Danny Vine jerked his thumb back at the church. 'It's been deconsecrated apparently. Built on the site of a plague pit.'

'Nice.'

'Back in the fourteenth century. The plague, I meant, not the church.'

'I kind of gathered that, Danny,' said Sally. 'I'm a detective. I'm supposed to notice details like that.'

'Yeah, sorry.'

'They're knocking the building down?'

'They are. Dangerous subsidence. Can't really fix it without clearing the area. So they are going to do that and build a block of apartments.'

Sally looked over at the cemetery. 'Nice view.'

Danny shrugged. 'They're going to plant trees around.'

'What's the trench for?' asked Kate Walker. 'If they're demolishing the building.'

'They're putting in some power cables. Heavy-duty. They're not knocking it down in one go. Just taking it apart bit by bit. Some very valuable architectural salvage there.'

The trench had been dug in the ground, leading from the side of one of the flying buttresses of the building and heading for the road. Outside the trench stood the other uniformed officer and a couple of builders, judging by their outfits. Two spades lay on the ground beside them. They didn't seem too bothered by what they had discovered. One was eating a sandwich and the other was having a mug of tea. A thermos flask was propped up by an open canvas bag alongside their discarded spades.

'It's probably just an animal bone. A family dog buried here years ago?'

'A pet buried on hallowed ground. Doesn't sound likely,' said Kate as she stepped into her forensic bodysuit and pulled the zip up and the hood over her rich, dark hair.

Danny Vine jerked his thumb back at the vicarage. 'I was thinking the vicar's pet maybe. Who knows, back in the last century sometime. It certainly looks old.'

'Is this hallowed ground anyway?' asked Sally. 'It's not the cemetery, quite a way from the church.'

Kate shrugged. 'I don't know. Not my area. Ask Jack, if you see him. Used to be a choirboy, you know.'

Sally laughed. 'Now that I do find hard to believe.'

Danny gestured at the trench again. 'You think it's an old bone?'

Kate nodded with a wry smile. 'Why don't I find out,' she said, as she snapped on a pair of latex gloves. She swung her evidence kit over her shoulder and used the short, three-step ladder that had been put up to climb into the trench.

The workman watched disinterestedly as she made her way along the frozen mud of the trench towards them to where they had stopped digging. Both men were in their forties with wide shoulders and short grey hair. They were dressed in black trousers with silvered reflective cloth around the lower part of them, and thick donkey-jackets. They looked like brothers.

'You stopped as soon as you discovered it?' she asked them.

The taller of the two stepped forward. 'Well, it's a cemetery, isn't it?' he said belligerently, as if Kate had made some kind of accusation. He was Irish but his accent had none of the charm or, sometimes, softness of Jack Delaney's.

104

Kate looked around. 'Not this part of the grounds it isn't.'

The man shrugged. 'Anyway. Standard procedure.'

'You dig up a lot of bones?'

'It happens. Usually animal.'

The other man stepped forward, his accent the same. 'We're told to stop with the dig, you see, if bones come up.'

'Good job too. Let's see what you've found, then.'

Kate bent down and, using a fine-haired brush, swept a light falling of snow away from the exposed bone. It was about three inches long, seemingly brown with age, and pitted. The earth around it was hard with the cold and she brought out a stiffer-haired brush and slowly started to clear the soil.

'How long do you think it's been there?' asked Sally Cartwright.

'It's not recent,' Kate replied. 'I can tell you that much. Could be years, could be decades. Could of course have been moved and planted here at any time.'

'Why?'

Kate looked up at her. 'I have absolutely no idea, Sally. You should know as well as I do that people do things for all kinds of reasons.'

'True.'

'Let's see what we've got first.'

'Is it human bone?'

'Not sure yet.'

Kate brushed some more of the mud away and then gestured to Sally: 'There's a camera in my bag, get down and get some shots.'

Sally fished Kate's camera from the bag, a Canon

105

she had bought herself as an early Christmas present. It took very high-quality stills and extremely good, high-definition video footage. Kate wanted to capture their first Christmas together, and figured it was worth the expense. Sally climbed down into the trench with Kate and handed it over to her.

'What have you found?' she asked.

Kate pointed at the piece of bone that was more visible now through the earth. 'Hang on, I'll set it up for you.' She took the camera from the young detective constable, took the lens cap off and altered some dials. 'Okay, focus here,' she said, showing Sally the various dials. 'Just hold the shutter halfway and it will do it automatically, then push it in for the shot.'

'Okay.'

'And push this button here for video and, as you're filming, take some shots in the normal way and it will record both.'

'All right, Kate. I got it. What have you seen, then?'

'Looks like metal here.' Kate knelt down again and brushed some more dirt away while Sally filmed. 'Not quite sure what yet.'

After a few moments a small sliver of rounded metal became visible. 'Take some photos here,' she said.

Sally crouched down and fired off a number of shots.

'Okay, Sally. That will do for now,' said Kate. They both stood up and Kate took back the camera. 'I think my work here is done,' she said, putting the lens cap back on.

Sally Cartwright looked down at the sliver of metal on the bone. 'What is it then?' she asked.

'In the unlikely event that the vicar's family pet wasn't a watch-dog, I am guessing we are dealing with human remains.'

'Why?'

'It's a watch, Sally. On a human wrist bone. I am guessing the rest of whoever it is is attached also. I don't want to contaminate the site. The forensic pathologist needs to take over from here.'

'Outside my pay-grade then,' said DC Cartwright, fishing her mobile phone out of her pocket.

'Mine too nowadays, can't say I miss it.'

The workman gestured with his sandwich at the exposed bone. 'Murdered, you reckon?'

Kate looked at him coolly. 'What I reckon,' she said, 'is you won't be finishing this job for a little while yet. You had better phone your bosses.'

The taller man shrugged and pulled out his mobile phone.

'No skin off mine,' he said.

'More than you can say for him,' said the other man, looking down at the exposed bone and taking a last bite of his sandwich.

Laura Chilvers groaned and rolled onto her side.

She immediately regretted it. Her groans became deeper, visceral, and she was clearly in great pain. She breathed heavily but didn't dare to open her eyes. She moaned like a hurt animal and held her hand to her dry lips. She tasted blood. Her eyes flew painfully open. Her stomach convulsed and she nearly retched, dry-heaving as if she was choking. But after a moment or two, she stopped and gulped some air into her lungs. She closed her eyes again. It was pitch-dark but somehow the lack of perspective, and any awareness of where she was, made her head spin and the nausea rise in her throat again. She took a couple of deep breaths to calm herself and ran her other hand over her body. She was naked apart from a pair of ripped cami-knickers. She rubbed her sore hand over the smooth, silky fabric of them and groaned again.

She took some more deep breaths and put her hand to one side and almost sighed with relief. She could feel the familiar outline of her radio alarm clock on her bedside cabinet. She was home at least, and in her own bed. She knew that much, if little else. She reached tentatively around her, but no one else was there. She contemplated switching on the light but thought better of it. The throbbing in her head was getting worse if anything. As if someone had taken an ice-pick and was tapping away on it, the pain spiking through her head like a pulse. It was a pulse, of course, she knew as well as anyone what the brain did when exposed to too much alcohol, too many drugs.

Christ, she couldn't remember what she had taken. Couldn't remember anything much at all. Had her drinks been spiked? She was certainly displaying the symptoms of having taken Rohypnol. She had had the rape-kit out far too many times not to recognise the symptoms.

She rolled over to her side once more, cradling the pillow under her head, and tried to remember.

Think!

Late night. Flashes of memory were coming back.

She had been looking through her office window as the snow had started to fall. She had locked the door, pulled the curtain across and changed her clothes. Her hand went to her thigh again. She remembered stripping completely out of her work clothes. Looking at herself in the mirror and admiring her taut and toned body. She had put a hand to her chest, her nipples stiffening as she ran a nail across her right breast.

She remembered turning round and looking at her bottom. She worked out every day at the gym, or at home, and she was not displeased with the results. She didn't consider herself a narcissist but treated her body like a temple. A temple of pleasure. Her Scandinavian heritage coming into play probably.

She had moved her hand around and cupped her bare sex, smiling as she did so. Knowing that Slimline Dave Matthews was just beyond the locked door with DC Cartwright. What would they make of her? she had wondered. She had laughed and opened the small case she had brought with her, snapping open the locks and taking out a pair of deep purple, silk cami-knickers.

In her bed she ran her hand over her bottom again, gasping involuntarily as her fingers lingered over the thick welts. She moved her hand upwards. Welts criss-crossed her back, her buttocks, her upper thighs.

She reached out to her bedside cabinet, and found a glass of water. Her eyes had adjusted a little now and she could just about see it. She opened the drawer, fumbled for a couple of ibuprofen tablets from the pressed foil and swallowed them. Then took a long drink of water. She breathed a little, took another gulp, replaced the glass and lay back on the pillow, closing her eyes. Remembering.

Disjointed images flashed into her mind. Strobe lights. Sounds. Distorted music. The music was a physical thing. Sensual. The light and sound surrounded Laura. She felt like a goldfish in a surrealist fish tank. The other clubbers shimmering around her like a shoal of shiny creatures. Decked out in leather or rubber or PVC. Dominatrixes, slave outfits. Police-women, schoolgirls, masters and schoolboys, maids and mistresses. One woman walked past wearing a ring-mistress outfit complete with red shorts, top hat and long whip. She looked like Amanda Holden, but Laura guessed she wasn't. She looked down at the glass she held in her hand. A large shot of Absolut vodka over ice. She swirled the glass, just about hearing the clink and tinkle of the ice over the heady music and the loud chatter surrounding her. She tilted her head back and downed the shot in one.

'Prosit!'

The man beside her at the bar was in his thirties and smiling at her. He was wearing tight, black leather shorts and that was all. He had hairless, sun-bronzed skin and short cropped white hair. His excitement was all too evident.

She looked him up and down. 'Fuck off!' she said.

'Was just going to offer you a drink,' he replied.

'Now!' said Laura and turned her back on him, holding out her shot glass to the barmaid, who was dressed as a Bavarian waitress from a beer cellar. 'Hit me!' she said.

'I thought you'd never ask.'

Laura sighed and turned back to the man. 'Run along and play with someone else. I don't do men.'

'Pity.'

'Not for me.'

She turned away and sipped on her new drink. Swirling the ice and remembering what the homeless man had said to her. Her hand shook as she finished the drink and held it out again.

'Hit me again, Heidi.'

After a while she lost track of time, and Laura felt the warm, familiar buzz. But it hadn't taken the edge off her thoughts, it had intensified them. The vodka didn't seem to be doing the job. She picked up the short riding crop she had laid on the bar and held it tightly in her grip.

She became aware of another presence beside her and turned round. It was the woman she had met the week before, Nicola French. Petite and blonde with fine porcelain-like skin and large, expressive baby-blue eyes above her chiselled cheekbones. Her lips were painted the colour of strawberries with a glossy sparkling layer added. Laura felt like sinking her teeth into them and biting them. The woman was dressed like a Roman slave girl. Her hair was coiled in plaits, a gold chain around her thin neck. A silky, diaphanous shoulderless gown gaped open and revealed her breasts. Breasts that had had the nipples painted and glistened like her lips. The skirt of the dress fell just below her waist. She wore high-heeled, golden sandals on her feet and a chain around her waist.

'Sorry I'm late,' she said.

'You will be, Nicola!' said Laura, noticing the nipples on the younger woman's breast harden.

'I'll make it up to you?'

'Do you like to be disciplined?' asked Laura, stroking the tip of her crop against Nicola's breasts.

'Yes,' said the younger woman with a breathless sigh.

'Yes, what?' barked Laura and flicked the tip against her nipple.

'Yes, mistress,' she said. 'If it please you.'

'Tonight just might be your lucky night then,' said Laura as she slipped her left hand under Nicola's mini-skirted dress.

'Thank you, mistress.'

Laura leaned in and whispered in her ear. 'You are not wearing any panties, Nicola,' she said.

'No, ma'am'

'Good girl. But that is very, very naughty!' The woman gasped as Laura worked a finger into her. 'I think you are going to have to be punished, very, very severely.'

'Yes, ma'am.'

'Shush.' Laura removed her hand from under Nicola's skirt and put her finger in her mouth. 'From now, on you speak only when I give you permission.'

The younger woman's eyes dilated with desire and excitement. Something was dancing in Laura's eyes too. But it was a desire of a completely different nature.

'Come with me then,' she said and led Nicola away from the main room.

Laura took another glass of water, squeezing her eyes shut trying to remember what happened next.

She swung her legs over the bed and held her head down, not noticing the tears that splashed onto her red and welted thighs.

23.

Detective Inspector Jack Delaney blew on his mug of tea and took a sip, stamping his feet up and down a little, and tapping his heels on the side of the kerb to knock off the snow.

'Any chance of getting that bacon sandwich before Easter, you reckon, Roy?' he asked.

'You're a real miserable sod in the mornings, Jack. Anyone ever tell you that?' Roy, the ruddy-faced owner of the burger van, called over his shoulder.

'And make sure it's crispy.'

'Well, do you want it now or do you want it crispy?'

'Just get on with it.'

Roy gave him a quizzical look. 'You're not worried about this court case, are you?'

'Do I look worried?'

'Hard to tell with you, Jack, you always look as happy as an Irishman chewing on a lemon.'

Delaney would have responded, but his mobile phone trilled in his pocket. He fished it out and flipped it open, looking at the caller ID, but not recognising it.

'Delaney?' There was a wheezing sound on the other end of the line. 'Still economical with your words, I see, Jack?'

114

'Who is this?'

'It's an old friend, don't you recognise me, Detective Inspector?'

The man had a raspy, low voice and Delaney nodded. 'Michael Robinson.'

'In the flesh, large as life. So to speak.'

'What can I do for you?'

'Just wanted to tell you I'm looking forward to seeing you in court.'

'I'll talk to you there then . . .'

He would have hung up, but Robinson spoke again. 'I hear you're going to get married, Jack. I wanted to congratulate you.'

'You heard wrong.'

'Shacked up with a lovely lady doctor, with your daughter all nice and cosy, and a new one on the way as I heard.'

Delaney breathed through his nostrils. 'You better hear this then. You're going down today, and this time you are staying down.'

'I wouldn't count your chickens.'

'You can count on this, Robinson. You get in my life or my family's life, and I will fucking destroy you.'

He clicked the phone off and put it back in his pocket. 'That sandwich ready yet?' he said to Roy.

Roy forked a few rashers of bacon onto a thick slice of white bread, added a fried egg, squirted some tomato ketchup over, slapped another slice of bread on top and handed it over to Delaney in a paper napkin.

'There you go,' he said. 'Just as you like it.'

'About bleeding time.'

115

Roy looked at him, unsmiling. 'So what was that all about?'

'A nuisance call is all.'

'Michael Robinson?'

'Yeah.'

'What? They just let him phone you up?'

'Prisoners on remand get to make phone calls, Roy. This isn't Victorian England.'

'More's the pity, you ask me. They would have that filthy, raping scum hanged and dancing the dead man's jig long before now.'

'He'll get what's coming to him.'

'Will he, though? How many fuckers like him get off?'

'He won't be getting off.'

'There's plenty as do. And what will he get anyway? Some nominal sentence and serve half of it?' Roy scraped the fat from his hot plate angrily.

'We do what we can.'

'I know.'

'And he did more than just rape the woman, Roy.'

'I'd have been in your shoes, Jack, I'd have made sure he didn't even make it to court.'

'Not the way I operate.'

Roy twitched the corner of his mouth. 'That's not what they say in the papers.'

'Not true, Roy.'

'Might influence the jury, though.'

Delaney took another bite of his sandwich. Drops of the red sauce squirting from it stained the snow beside his feet. He looked down at the bright red splatters glistening against the brilliance of the snow in the early-morning sunlight, and then back up at the roadside chef.

116

'Like I said, he'll get what's coming to him.'

He scuffed his foot over the crimson stain, crushing it under the snow.

Delaney walked along the platform towards the steps leading up to the ancient courthouse. He was aware of the barrage of questions being shouted at him, of the lights flashing as photographs were taken, of the fact that film cameras were being pointed at him. But he ignored it all. He walked through them, not even bothering to say: *No comment.*

'Knock 'em dead, Delaney.'

Delaney turned, recognising the familiar voice. Melanie Jones, the Sky News reporter, was standing close by, her cameraman training a state-of-the-art HD video camera on him. Time was when Delaney would have ignored her too. But things had changed. Maybe Delaney was getting less cynical, maybe Melanie Jones was. Either way, when Delaney looked across at the woman, she seemed to be genuinely encouraging. He gave the smallest, barely noticeable nod to her and walked into the court building.

His boss, Superintendent George Napier, was standing in full dress uniform inside, waiting for him.

He strode across and pulled Delaney to one side. 'Where the bloody hell have you been?'

'Something came up, sir.'

'What?'

'Breakfast, sir. Needed to get something to eat.'

'You better be bloody joking, Delaney.'

'The car was playing up. The cold, sir. Took longer to sort out than I thought.'

'And in the meantime you didn't think to call or return any of Diane's calls?'

'The phone was inside on charge, boss. Didn't see the calls missed until I was halfway here.'

Napier looked at Delaney closely. He was pretty certain the man was lying to him, treating him as he did everything else – like it was some kind of joke. Only Napier wasn't laughing. The man had been skating on thin ice so long, it was a miracle to him that Delaney was still in the force. If Diane hadn't protected him like a jealous tiger protects her cubs, he'd have been gone long ago. True, he had cleaned his act up in recent months – Dr Kate Walker was clearly having an influence on the man. But he didn't trust him. Not as far as he could kick him.

'Just make sure you stick to the script, Delaney.'

'Of course, sir,' said Delaney and smiled, walking onwards into the court.

The look in his eyes told a very different story, however.

24.

Patricia Hunt took the large aluminium kettle from the trivet it was sitting on beside her range-style cooker and carried it over to the sink to fill. As she did so, she watched her husband, still working in the garden. He had cleared the pathway to his wooden studio completely of snow and was now clearing the birdbath. He brushed the snow aside and, with the handle of a small trowel, tapped the surface of the frozen water, tilting it so that he could remove the top layer of ice. It came loose in one frozen circle, which he put to one side, and then filled the bath with fresh water from a can.

Patricia smiled, for she knew the water would be frozen again in no time at all, but Geoffrey hated to see the birds suffer. He hated to see anything or anybody suffer. It was one of the things she loved so much about him. It broke her heart to see him in so much pain himself. But they had done what they had to do. It was for the best, they had both agreed that.

In the background West London radio was playing. Another single from this year's X *Factor* winner. She wasn't sure if she preferred the old days when it would be Cliff Richard on the radio all the time, come Christmas. Sometimes it was good to know where you stood. She put bread in the toaster and fetched a jar of home-made marmalade from the dresser. Seville orange, a bit too bitter for her taste, she preferred lime marmalade, but Geoffrey liked it. She put it on the table and laid out some plates. As the song finished, she picked up the teapot and took it over to the work surface beside the range.

An announcer came on the radio with the local news. Patricia wasn't listening until the announcer mentioned St Luke's Church.

'. . . *St Luke's Church south of Queen's Park Rangers football ground. It is not known at this stage how the body came to be buried there, or how long it has been there. The police pathologist is onsite and we will update you with developments.*'

Patricia Hunt screamed and looked down at her hand, which she had spilled boiling water from the kettle on. She dropped the kettle back on the range and ran to the sink to run cold water, putting her hand under it. As her husband came hurrying up the garden to see what had happened, Patricia found tears in her eyes.

Stephanie Hewson was an above-average-height woman with dark, curly hair. She exuded confidence and authority, and dressed accordingly. A pin-striped two-piece suit with a dark-red silk blouse. Her hair was tied back and she wore plain-framed black glasses.

Her voice, when she spoke, however, belied the assertiveness that her dress and bearing seemed to wish to present to the world. Her voice trembled in fact.

'It was a Friday night. Ten o'clock . . .' She paused to take a drink of water.

'It's okay, Miss Hewson. Take your time,' said the judge, Helen Johns, a stern-faced woman in her late fifties. The severity of her expression softened, however, as she looked across at the woman standing in the witness dock.

'Thank you, Your Honour. I know it was ten o'clock,' she continued, 'because I had just missed a train. And there were eight minutes until the next one. I was worried about missing my connection at Marylebone and having to wait another half-hour.'

The counsel for the prosecution, Selena Carrow, inclined her head solicitously. She was a woman in her late thirties, of medium height with a soft voice that belied her single-mindedness.

'And were you alone on the platform?'

'I was initially. Like I said, I had just missed my train. But other passengers came onto the platform.'

'Could you describe them?'

'It was a long time ago.'

Selena Carrow, QC, sketched her hand in the air. 'Any stand out in particular?'

'There was a group of young women, in their twenties, I should say. They had been on a hen-night, I think, some kind of party. It was close to Christmas. Maybe a works outing.'

'What makes you say hen-party?'

'They were drunk, unsteady, holding onto each other. Giggling loudly. One of them had on a pair of bunny ears, and they all had short skirts or dresses. Light coats on. It was cold but they didn't seem to notice.'

'And anyone else?'

Stephanie Hewson looked to her left across the courtroom to the gallery, where DI Jack Delaney was sitting, watching events with an impassive expression on his face.

The defence barrister, Hector Douglas – a tall, balding man in his fifties, a leading light in the firm of Gable & Wilson, and wearing a suit that cost more than Jack Delaney's monthly salary – leapt to his feet.

'Objection! Counsel is leading the witness.'

Selena shook her head, as though annoyed by the interruption. 'Not at all, My Lord. I ask only if there were other persons present that night that she might recall.'

The judge nodded. 'Overruled. You can answer the question, Miss Hewson.'

'I saw a man further along the platform, he was looking at the women.'

'And could you describe him?'

Stephanie Hewson looked across at Jack Delaney again, and once more the defence barrister sprang to his feet.

'Your Honour!' he said, seemingly outraged. 'The witness seems to be seeking advice in this regard from members of the gallery. Are we not to have her opinion unalloyed by prejudicial direction?'

The judge sighed. 'Please spare the court your theatrics, Mr Douglas, and sit down. And, Miss Hewson, please try to focus on counsel and her questions.'

'He was a long way down the platform from me.' She shrugged. 'He was of medium height, had a dark coat on, was wearing a hat and had glasses.'

'Okay. Now please tell the court what happened next?'

'I waited for my train. More people came onto the platform. The train arrived and I made it in time to Marylebone to catch my overland train to Harrow-on-the-Hill.'

'But you had to run in order to do so?'

'Relevance, My Lord,' asked Hector Douglas, this time not bothering to rise.

The judge gestured to Selena Carrow.

'Goes to her state of mind, Your Honour. Focus as to who she may or may not have seen.'

'Continue.'

'So you were running, Miss Hewson?'

'I was. As fast as I could, I had court shoes on.'

'And did you notice the man you had seen in the hat earlier?'

Douglas stood up. 'Objection, My Lord!'

'You know better than to lead the witness, Miss Carrow.'

'Sorry, My Lord.' She turned back to the witness. 'Did you take any notice of the people around you?'

'I did not. No. Like I said, I was running as fast as I could.'

'Quite so. And you made your train?'

'I did.'

'And then what happened that evening?'

'The train came into Harrow station some twelve or so minutes later and I continued my journey home on foot.'

'Could you describe that journey for us?'

'I live on the hill, so it is a ten-minute walk. Usually I take a taxi.'

'But that night you didn't.'

Stephanie Hewson looked at the woman for a minute, her hand trembling. She took a sip of water, spilling some, then placed the glass down. 'No,' she said. 'I did not.'

'Why was that?'

'It was a nice evening.'

'You said earlier it had been cold?'

'It was cold. But it was a nice night. Clear sky. The moon was full, so there was plenty of light, there were stars in the sky . . .' She shrugged. 'I don't know, I was in a good mood. I thought I would enjoy the walk.'

'But you didn't enjoy the walk?'

Stephanie Hewson looked down at her feet for a moment, then looked back up, her eyes wet. 'No, I did not enjoy the walk.'

'Can you tell the court what happened?'

The judge looked sympathetically at the woman in the witness dock. 'It's okay. Take as long as you like.'

'Thank you,' she said and raised the glass to her lips once more, taking a few more sips of the water. She placed the glass back down and then straightened herself, as if steeling herself for what was to come. 'I was gagged and raped. And when he was done with me, he took a sharp knife and sliced it across my breasts, my stomach and my thighs.'

25

The woman looked across at the accused, who was watching her intently, but seemed neither agitated nor concerned.

Michael Robinson was in his early fifties with receding sandy-coloured hair, of medium height, but stocky with broad shoulders. He wore tortoiseshell retro-style glasses, and the skin on his balding pate was flaky. He was dressed in a two-piece suit and wore a white shirt with a green tie. He met the woman's gaze with unblinking eyes, then turned his gaze on Delaney, a hint of a smile playing on his lips.

Stephanie Hewson took another sip of her water and the prosecuting attorney waited for her to collect herself.

'Please tell the court exactly what happened, Miss Hewson.'

'I left the station at approximately ten to eleven.'

'Had you looked at your watch?'

'No, but the ten-thirty train was on time from Marylebone. It takes about twelve minutes to get to Harrow, and so a few minutes to walk up the steps, through the concourse and out the back entrance.'

'The one that leads out to the hill, and not to the shopping centre?'

'Yes. I walked down the steps and up to the alley-way that runs through to Roxborough Park.'

'Were you aware of being followed?'

The defence counsel stood smoothly to his feet. 'Objection, My Lord, it has not been established that Miss Hewson was indeed followed. Counsel is leading the witness yet again!'

'Sustained.' The judge threw Selena Carrow a look. 'You really do know better than this.'

'Sorry, Your Honour.' If she meant it, it wasn't evident in her expression. She turned to the witness stand again. 'At that time were you aware of anyone else?'

'No, I was not. I was walking home and didn't notice anybody else out. But, like I said earlier, I was lost in my thoughts a little.'

The prosecution lawyer consulted her notes. 'Yes, you said you were in a happy mood.'

'Relevance, Your Honour?' asked Hector Douglas.

The judge gestured to the prosecution counsel.

'State of mind, Your Honour. We intend to establish that the accused, Michael Robinson, targeted Miss Hewson, that he followed her home on the train, that he pursued her down the alleyway that she has just described. That Miss Hewson was not aware of anyone else that night was because her thoughts were preoccupied.'

'Your Honour,' Douglas stood up. 'My client has never denied being on that train – he lives in Harrow. That her mind was elsewhere prior to this terrible assault taking place is evident in that she has mistakenly identified my client as the man who attacked her.'

'Sit down.' The judge rapped her gavel sharply. 'You will have ample opportunity to cross-examine, Mr Douglas. Please continue, Miss Carrow.'

'I am obliged, My Lord. Miss Hewson, please tell us what happened next.'

'I came out of the alleyway into Roxborough Avenue, when a man suddenly appeared behind me and said that if I screamed, he would kill me.'

'And did you believe him?'

'Your Honour, leading the witness!'

'Sustained.'

'He had a knife in his hand, which he held to my side. I was too terrified to scream.'

'This alleyway, and the one opposite, is overlooked by housing.'

'Yes, there are apartments. But I was too scared to call for help. His voice . . .' She took another sip of water. 'His voice was ugly, terrifying!'

'So, as you say, you were in fear for your life?'

'Yes.'

'What happened next?'

'He stood beside me telling me to keep my head down, so as not to see his face, and led me into the alley that leads to the hill.'

'And did you see his face?'

'Not at that time.'

Selena Carrow consulted her notes again. 'So he led you across the road into the opposite alleyway. This is the one that runs alongside the Catholic church of Our Lady and St Thomas, past a junior school and out onto Harrow Hill itself.'

'Yes, only we didn't go so far.'

'What did happen then, Miss Hewson?'

127

'Just past the church, before the primary school, there is a Scout hut.'

The lawyer made a show of consulting her notes again. 'The Seventeenth Roxborough?'

'Yes. He opened the door and pushed me inside, telling me to be quiet.'

'How did he open the door?'

'He had a key.'

Selena Carrow turned pointedly and looked at Michael Robinson for a moment or two, letting the jury see the scorn on her face.

'Can you tell the court, please, what took place in that hut, Miss Hewson.'

'He closed the door behind him; it was dark inside.'

'Even though it was a moonlit night?'

'The windows were grimy, it was dark. He came in, like I said, and closed the door. He ordered me not to look round. He said he would hurt me if I didn't do exactly what he said. He held the point of the blade to my throat as he said it. It was a very sharp blade.'

'What did you do?'

'I . . .' She paused for a moment and took another sip of water. 'I voided my bladder,' she said.

'You wet yourself?' Selena Carrow clarified and looked at the jury.

'Yes.'

'And what did the man do?'

'He laughed and said I would be punished for it, then ordered me to take my clothes off.'

'And what did you do?'

The woman put a hand to her neck, in an involuntary gesture.

'I did as he said.'

'You stripped naked?'

Stephanie Hewson shook her head. 'I left my knickers on.'

'And what did he do?'

'He told me to get on all fours, pushing me down. Then he held my knickers and ripped them up hard. I gasped with pain as they pulled between me and then he tore them right off, stuffing them in my mouth and ordering me to keep quiet.'

Selena Carrow nodded sympathetically, letting the words hang in the air as she consulted her notes.

'And you did?'

'Yes.'

'What did he do?'

'I heard a zip being pulled. He said he was going to put on a condom, that he couldn't afford to pick up diseases in his line of work.'

'And then he raped you?'

'Yes.'

'Repeatedly?'

'Yes, first he . . .'

She trailed off and Selena Carrow held her notes up. 'It's okay, Miss Hewson. I know it is hard for you to talk about it. To relive the horror. I have your police statement here. You informed the police surgeon on duty that night at Harrow Police Station that you had been anally and vaginally raped. Is that correct?'

Stephanie Hewson nodded her head, tears springing in her eyes.

'I am sorry, but we will need to hear your answer. Is it true that you were brutally raped, anally and then vaginally?'

'Yes! And when he was done he sliced me with his knife and left.'

'And what did you do?'

'I got up and went to the window.'

'You weren't feeling any pain?'

'I didn't register the knife at the time. I was in shock. The surgeon said I was in shock. It was later . . . it didn't really hit me until later.'

'So you went to the window. Could you see anything?'

'He was outside, adjusting his hat, and then he hurried off past the school towards the hill.'

'Did you see his face?'

'Sideways on.'

'Enough to recognise him?'

'Yes.'

'Then what did you do?'

'I waited some minutes, then I put my coat on, grabbed my other clothes and ran to the apartment block to raise help.'

'And then the police and ambulance came, and they treated you and took your statement.'

'They took my statement the next day at the police station. I was sedated overnight and kept in at Northwick Park Hospital.'

'Thank you very much, Miss Hewson. I know this hasn't been easy for you.'

'I can go now?'

'Not just yet, my learned colleague will have some questions for you. But I have one final question?'

'Yes?'

'You said you could recognise the man again, from what you saw of him through that Scout-hut window?'

'Yes, I would.'

Selena Carrow nodded and paused for a moment. 'Can you look around this room then, please, and tell the court if you can see him here.'

Stephanie Hewson slowly looked around the courtroom, at the accused, at the visitors' gallery, at the jury and finally at Jack Delaney. She looked at him for about three seconds, studying him, and then turned back to the lawyer.

'No,' she said. 'I don't see the man who attacked me.'

26.

There was uproar in the courtroom. The judge had to bang her gavel several times to get order restored. Selena Carrow was about to speak, but the judge motioned her to silence.

'Sit down, please, Miss Carrow,' she said, then turned to the woman in the witness box.

'Miss Hewson, you do understand you are on oath?'

'I do.'

'Mr Robinson was arrested and charged and brought to court, largely based on the identification you made of him.'

'Yes.'

'You picked him out of a police line-up. How were you able to do that, if he was not the man that you saw through the window of the Scout hut?'

'Because I had seen a photo of him, Your Honour.'

'When did you see the photo?'

'Before the line-up took place.'

'Days before the line-up, weeks?'

'It was less than an hour.'

Murmurs ran around the court once more, and yet again the judge gave a couple of sharp raps with her gavel. 'And who showed you this photo of Michael Robinson?' she asked.

'He did,' said Stephanie Hewson and pointed at the visitors' gallery. 'Detective Inspector Jack Delaney showed me the photo.'

27

DI Jack Delaney took a sip of his pint of Guinness and looked at his watch.

He was sitting at the bar in the Viaduct Tavern on the corner of Newgate Street and Giltspur Street, right opposite the Old Bailey. He took another sip and smiled approvingly at the barmaid; it was a Fuller's pub and they kept their beer well.

'So what's new and different then, Lily?'

'How do you know my name?'

Delaney pointed to her polo shirt with her name printed on it.

'Keep forgetting about that. Only started yesterday.'

'Well, you're doing a magnificent job!' He flashed her a smile and she smiled back, a tad embarrassed, and went off to serve another customer.

Delaney put his beer glass neatly on a London Pride coaster and looked around the bar. It wasn't the first time he had been there and as sure as Shinola wouldn't be the last, he figured. Fighting for the cause of justice was thirsty work after all, and the tall lady on the dome of the building across the road was famous for turning a blind eye. The Viaduct Tavern had been built in 1869, the selfsame year that Her

Britannic Majesty Queen Victoria had opened the Holborn Viaduct opposite, after which it had been named. The world's first flyover connecting Holborn to Newgate Street over the River Fleet, which likewise gave its name to the famous street of shame nearby. A river that fittingly enough had become a sewer by the eighteenth century and was now the largest of London's subterranean rivers. Subsumed as London grew. The Viaduct Tavern was a reverse Tardis of a pub, smaller on the inside than the large, curved frontage on the outside would suggest. But it kept its Victorian origins proudly evident. A square-shaped wooden and canopied bar in the centre of the room, with silvered and gilt mirrors on the wall and original art.

Delaney liked it.

A stool was moved beside him and DS Diane Campbell sat on it. She gestured to the barmaid. 'Large vodka and slimline tonic, please.'

'Cheers, Lily,' said Delaney and smiled at her again.

'Lily?' said Diane and looked at him.

'She's got her name printed on her polo shirt.'

'Hard for a man like you not to notice a thing like that.'

'As a trained and experienced detective, you mean?'

'I was thinking more of as a committed lecher.'

Delaney held up his hands. 'I'm a reformed man, Diane. There's only one woman in my life now. Two, if you count my daughter.'

'I'm glad to hear it. Kate is a lovely woman.'

'So she is.'

'And she's been through enough.'

'Yeah, I know.' Delaney's eyes darkened, remembering how close he had been to losing her, and sipped his Guinness.

Diane picked up her change from the barmaid and took a sip of her vodka too.

She looked back up at Delaney for a moment or two and then jerked her head backwards in the direction of the Old Bailey. 'Well, that certainly didn't go according to plan.'

'No. Seems someone had rewritten the script.'

'A clusterfuck in fact, as our ex-colonial cousins across the pond would have it.'

'I take it Napier is not pleased?'

'I would go so far as to say Superintendent George Napier would quite like to have your balls removed with a rusty pair of secateurs and fed to his pet dog.'

'I didn't know he had a dog?'

'Small one.'

'Figures.'

'So what Stephanie Hewson said in court – you showed her a photograph of Michael Robinson just prior to the line-up?'

Delaney shrugged. 'I don't think so.'

Diane took a contemplative sip of her drink. 'You don't *think* so?'

'It was a while ago, Diane.'

'I know. We had to wait until the man's bones healed.'

'That was nothing to do with me.'

'You remember that then?'

'I had nothing personal against the man.'

'You had everything personal against any man who hurt women, Jack. You still do.'

'I'm not a vigilante.'

'No – what you are is a pain in the bloody arse.'

Delaney winked at her. 'Nice arse, though!'

'This one is out of my ability to control.'

'What I figured.'

'There's going to be an investigation.'

Delaney shrugged. 'I'm on holiday after Christmas anyway.'

'Yeah, I know, Jack. Not really the point here.'

'I guess not.'

'You're going to lose your job over this, if it isn't sorted. Napier will see to that. The official interview is for Monday afternoon. So you have the weekend to get your facts straight.'

'Maybe that's not such a bad thing.'

'What isn't?'

'Losing my job.'

'Really? What would Kate think? What with a baby on the way and all?'

'Kind of my point. This job is toxic, Diane. This whole city is toxic.'

'No, it's not. People are toxic, Jack. Some of them. That's why we do the job we do.'

'Sanitation engineers?'

'About that.'

'I can't remember what happened that morning, Diane. But I am pretty sure Eddie Bonner covered for me. I didn't get in until just before the line-up.'

'Jesus, Delaney!'

'I know.'

'The CPS knew that, this would never even have made it to court.'

'The man is guilty, boss.'

137

Diane Campbell shook her head, disgusted. 'Eddie-fucking-Bonner!'

Sergeant Eddie Bonner had been Jack Delaney's partner for a while. Up until the time he tried to kill him, that is. Bonner had been involved in serious and criminal corruption within the force, working with Kate Walker's uncle, a senior police figure now in jail awaiting trial for murder, attempted murder and child-rape charges, amongst others. Delaney was getting close to exposing him, and Bonner, who wasn't involved in the child crimes, changed horses mid-gallop. He was going to give Delaney information to help put Walker away. He didn't get the chance to, for Bonner was killed in a hit arranged by Walker, and Delaney was nearly taken out too.

'Bonner may well have shown her a photo – I wouldn't put it past him, but I doubt it.'

'Why?'

'She could have said Bonner showed her the photo, if in fact he ever did. But she didn't; she said I did.'

'Why?'

'I don't know. But Michael Robinson called me this morning. He seemed very upbeat.'

'Jesus, Jack! You didn't think a little detail like that was important enough to mention it to me?'

'I'm mentioning it now.'

Diane took a healthy glug of her vodka. 'What the fuck was that sick flake calling you for?'

'He mentioned Kate and Siobhan, Diane. And *the baby on the way*.'

Diane gestured to the barmaid. 'Can we get some more drinks over here, and make mine a large one,' she said and turned back to Delaney. 'You want a whiskey with that?'

'No. I'm okay with this, thanks,' he gestured at his half-finished glass of Guinness.

'You reckon he was making some kind of threat?'

'That was my understanding. Plus he seemed confident about the court case. Almost as if he knew Stephanie Hewson was going to recant on her testimony.'

'What did he actually say?'

'Just that. He knew he was getting off.'

'How?'

'Somebody got to the woman. Someone has been in contact with him. Watching me. Intimidating her.'

'He had a partner?'

'He has a partner. Maybe not that night. But yeah. There's two of them.'

'He's definitely guilty, Jack? He did rape and slice the woman?'

'Stephanie picked him out, Diane. I saw her when she did it. She wasn't faking it. And what would be the motive?'

'So what do we do?'

'We go over everything again.'

'Something you might have missed?' she asked, taking the glass from the barmaid and swallowing at least half the contents.

'There's two of them, Diane. Stephanie Hewson wasn't the first. I'd bet my mortgage on it.'

'They are going to turn over every stone in your career, Jack.'

'Of course they will. But it's bureaucracy, Diane. Red tape. We haven't got time for that.'

'Okay. You've got the weekend. I'll try and stall things as best I can.'

'Napier won't like it.'

'Napier can kiss my arse.'

'He might enjoy that.'

Diane looked at him coolly for a moment or two and then nodded. 'Just don't fuck me over on this, Jack. Nail the sick son of a bitch!'

'Boss.'

Diane tossed back the remains of her drink and headed to the door. Delaney grinned at the barmaid. 'Be an absolute darling, Lily. And give me a shot of Jameson's, will you?'

The barmaid placed the shot glass in front of him and he looked at it for a long moment. A woman came up the bar and sat next to him. She had a tumble of auburn hair framing a heart-shaped face. Her eyes were big and blue. As she turned to Delaney, she had a smile on her face that could have melted frozen tundra.

'Are you going to drink that whiskey or just look at it?' she said.

'I haven't decided yet,' Delaney replied.

'Could go either way?'

'Life's a lot like that. Sometimes the small decisions help you make some big ones.'

'And have you got a big decision to make?'

'Seems like my life is full of big decisions,' Delaney said and smiled back at her.

'My name's Kimberley Gold,' she said.

'Hello Kimberley, my name's Jack Delaney.'

'And don't you shake a lady by the hand when you meet one?'

140

'I'm married,' he said and held his hand out.

Kimberley looked at his open hand for a moment and then slapped an envelope in it. 'And you're served, Jack Delaney!' she said, got off her stool and walked out.

Jack watched her leave, then put the envelope on the bar counter and looked at his whiskey. Then he stood up, picked up the envelope and headed out himself. Leaving the whiskey untouched.

28.

Kate Walker was seated at her desk drinking a cup of coffee and reading the morning paper when there was a quick knock on her door and Laura Chilvers stuck her head round.

'Have you got a minute?'

'Sure, come in.'

'Thanks.'

Kate looked at her. 'What's up? You look terrible.'

'I feel terrible.'

'What's happened?'

'I'm not sure.'

She held her hands out – they were raw. Streaks of blood dried on her fingers, her knuckles puffy and swollen. Split.

'Dear God, Laura, what's happened? Have you been attacked?'

'Like I said, I don't know, Kate. I can't remember.'

'Let me clean that up for you.'

'No!' said Laura sharply and drew her hands back, clasping them together and holding them on her lap. 'There's more.'

'Go on?'

'I think I was raped.'

Kate looked for a moment too stunned to say

anything, remembering the trauma she had gone through when she thought she had been raped. Only she hadn't.

'Oh my God, I'm sorry.'

'The thing is, I can't remember what happened last night. I'm okay up to a point and then it goes hazy.'

'You think you might have been drugged?'

'I'm not sure.'

'What do you mean?'

'I was at a club. I had some drinks. Took some other stuff.'

'Laura!'

'Yeah, I know, I know. I should have known better! I'm a doctor. But if every doctor who took drugs was fired today, there would be queues at every health centre stretching for miles.'

'I know – sorry. I wasn't judging you.'

And Kate wasn't. She recalled again the time she thought she had been raped. She had had a big argument with Jack and had got herself completely plastered at The Holly Bush in Hampstead. Drowned her sorrows, as they say, in a small pond of vodka. She had allowed herself to be chatted up by a smooth Delaney lookalike. Dark curly hair, handsome, full of charm. Except that was where the similarities ended. His charm was as false as the smile on a double-glazing salesman's face. He was a children's doctor and she thought she could trust him, only she couldn't. She let him stay in her bed and was con-vinced he had raped her. Only he hadn't, and was playing sick mind-games with her. Delaney had busted him on the nose, and she wished he had done more than that.

'I know what it's like to lose control, Laura,' she said.

'I had things . . . I don't know, I couldn't deal with them, Kate. I wanted to be in a different place. I was stupid.'

'Whatever happened, it isn't your fault.'

'That's just it, though. It *is* my fault. All of it. I deserve this.'

'Don't say that. Don't ever say that.'

Laura wiped the sleeve of her overcoat across her eyes. 'I need your help.'

'Of course.'

'You'll need your rape-kit.'

29

Jack Delaney stood by the side of the ditch watching as 'Bowlalong' Bowman, the forensic pathologist, and his team worked on uncovering the body. A protective marquee had been erected over the site. It had stopped snowing, but judging by the heavy sky overhead, it wouldn't be long before it started again.

The skeleton had nearly been fully uncovered, and rags still clung to part of the body, bits of a suit by the looks of it. The rest had decomposed over the years that the body had lain there. The skull had been broken in several places and what looked like a book lay under the skeleton's right arm.

'You want to talk me through it?' said Delaney, putting an unlit cigarette into his mouth.

Derek 'Bowlalong' Bowman looked up at the detective. He was a large, portly, cheerful man. His hair, as ever, was a tangled mass of grey curls, his dress sense equally scruffy, although he was now encased in a white forensic examination suit. 'Hello, Jack. Didn't expect to see you here. I'd have thought Napier would have had you on a convict ship to the colonies by now. Hard labour under the Australian sun.'

'If he had his way, he probably would,' Delaney

agreed. 'Some minor details to sort out first. Things have to be investigated thoroughly after all – innocent before being found guilty, and all that kind of malarkey.'

The large man smiled. 'I know you're a stickler for due process yourself.'

'Famous for it.'

'I take it you didn't show the woman in question the photograph of Robinson?'

'I hope not.'

'Yes, I can see that might be awkward. No clear recollection?'

Delaney shook his head. 'I certainly don't remember doing that, no.'

'Lost-weekend kind of thing.'

Delaney nodded drily. 'Sometimes a little longer.'

'The man was guilty, though?'

'And now he's walked free. But not for long.'

'Best tread careful, Jack.'

'My middle name.'

'Really, I thought it was Daniel.'

Delaney gestured at the skeleton. 'Our friend here a John or a Jane?'

'Definitely male. Probably somewhere in his fifties.'

'Can you tell how long he's been in there?'

'Bowlalong' shrugged. 'Not recent – the best I can do for you. For now at least.'

'They look like old bones. Might have been moved here, you mean?'

'I don't think so.'

'Why not?'

'The clothing has decomposed, you can see it in the

soil. We'll do some tests, but the bone alignment, the clothing . . . I'd say this was the original site of burial.'

'But you can't say when.'

'Bones react differently with different soil. Acids, alkalis, chemicals.' He waggled his hands. 'All manner of things either preserve or speed up the decaying process. I'll know more when Lorraine and I get him back to the office.'

Delaney nodded at the young woman 'Bowlalong' had just gestured at. She was Kate's former assistant, when Kate still worked as a forensic pathologist, until she decided she preferred working with the living to the dead and quit. Lorraine was a shy woman, with an expressive face that blushed readily. She was blushing now as Delaney nodded to her and he found himself wondering, not for the first time, why she was in a job like this. Kate had explained to him that Lorraine couldn't cope with people dying on her, but didn't want her medical training to go to waste.

'Here you go, sir.'

Delaney turned round as DC Sally Cartwright handed him a styrofoam cup of coffee. Another attractive young woman working amongst the dead. He would probably be called a sexist pig, but it seemed wrong to him somehow. He didn't articulate the thought.

'Cheers, Sally,' he said instead.

'Any further forward?' she asked the pathologist.

'Not till we get back to the lab.'

'What about the skull injuries?'

'The doctor thinks they're post-mortem.'

Derek Bowman nodded. 'Like as not the workman with his spade.'

'Maybe,' said Delaney. 'Maybe not.'

Lorraine delicately lifted the rotting book from under the dead man's arm. She placed it to one side on a plastic sheet. The book was leather-covered, black originally by the look of it, although slimed with mud and moisture from the years it had lain with the man in the ground. She brushed away some of the mud on the cover with a stiff brush, revealing the object mounted on the book's cover.

A crucifix.

'Indeed, detective,' said Doctor Bowman as he looked back at the fractured skull of the dead man. 'Maybe not the workman's spade at all.'

30.

Patricia Hunt rubbed some cream onto her hand.

'You should see a doctor, darling,' said her husband, watching her, concerned.

'I'll be fine, I ran it under cold water straight away; don't fuss, Geoffrey.'

'When I heard you scream, I didn't know what had happened.'

'I know, dear. It was nothing.'

'But how did you spill it on your hand? That's not like you at all. I'm supposed to be the clumsy one.'

'I'm tired. And I'm not as strong as I used to be. My hand shook holding the kettle, that's all.'

She looked away, unable to meet his eyes.

Geoffrey would have responded, but he suddenly went into a paroxysm of coughing, his whole body shaking as he held a handkerchief to his mouth.

His wife looked across at him, her hand forgotten. 'I told you, you shouldn't have gone out there this morning.'

He took a moment or two to catch his breath, his breathing ragged and wet. 'There was work to be done.'

'Standing here in the kitchen in the dead of night.

With no slippers on, in the freezing cold. No wonder you've got a cough.'

'Fresh air never killed anyone, Patricia.'

His wife looked at him for a moment. 'You know that's not true!'

Jack Delaney walked through A&E reception towards the intensive-care units, talking on his mobile telephone and ignoring the hostile glances that he was getting from the hospital staff as he passed.

'I'll give you a call when I'm heading in. Thanks, Tony, appreciate the heads-up.'

He closed the phone and put it in his pocket.

'The ball rolling?' asked DC Cartwright.

'Yeah, a bloody big ball made of stone, and heading straight for me.'

'Indiana Delaney.'

'Yeah, only I might not make it out of the tunnel this time, Sally.'

'Who was on the phone?' she asked, trying to make the enquiry as casual as possible.

'Detective Inspector Tony Hamilton, Constable,' said Delaney, a small smile tugging at the corner of his mouth. 'Didn't you and he . . .?' Delaney wiggled his hand suggestively.

'No, sir, we didn't,' said Sally Cartwright, feeling a blush rise to her cheeks despite herself.

'Oh, I thought—' continued Delaney, amused.

'Well, we didn't!' Sally repeated, ending the discussion. 'Seems he's the go-to man for any investigations involving you, sir.'

'Seems that way, but you'd be wrong.'

'Oh?'

'Diane arranged it. He's part of the investigation team anyway. Much better him than that little prick Richard Stoker.'

'True. I don't like that man. And Tony Hamilton did save your life a few months back.'

Delaney smiled at her as he pushed the swing doors at the end of the corridor open. 'Sure now, I had that covered.'

Sally gave him a little jab in the arm. 'Of course you did, boss. And besides, it was your picture on the front of all those papers, not his.'

'Jeez, don't remind me.'

At the end of the summer Delaney had made headline news when he had rescued a young boy. The boy, Ashley Woods, had been kidnapped by a woman who had herself been kidnapped some fifteen years or so earlier. When she escaped she returned to Harrow to seek revenge. Whilst killing those she thought responsible, she also took the little boy, the grandson of one of the men in the group. As the killings mounted, Delaney had nearly been killed himself before rescuing the boy and making the front pages all over again.

'Just saying, sir . . .' said Sally Cartwright, amused at her boss's discomfiture.

'Well, don't.'

'Either way, it's probably a good thing he is the one investigating you.'

'It's not an investigation – it is a preliminary inquiry to ascertain whether there is a case for formal investigation, at which time it will be turned over to the appropriate people.'

'Which isn't going to happen, is it?'

'God knows, Sally. God only knows what that toerag Bonner did or didn't do.'

'Never trusted him myself. Too good-looking, with sleazy eyes.'

'Right.'

They arrived at the intensive-care unit. A doctor, a very petite woman, and a nurse stood outside the first room. Delaney glanced inside. An elderly Chinese woman was lying on a bed, with drips and heart monitors attached.

'I'm Detective Inspector Jack Delaney,' he said. 'And this is my assistant, Detective Constable Sally Cartwright.'

'Lily Crabbe, the consultant registrar,' said the doctor, a woman in her late twenties, but didn't hold her hand out. The nurse, an older man, nodded but didn't speak.

'How is she?'

Dr Crabbe flicked a glance through the window. 'She's an elderly woman. We're keeping a close eye on her.'

'Was she attacked?'

'That is more in your line of expertise, surely?'

'The inspector means were there any signs of assault?'

'There are bruises on her arms and legs, and her head has suffered some trauma.'

'So she could have been attacked?'

'She could have been, Detective Inspector. We ran an ECG scan and it looks like she has suffered from some form of stroke. That could of course have occurred if she was being assaulted. It could also have occurred and caused her to fall. Her injuries would be consistent with that.'

'Even though there was snow on the ground?'

'Hard snow, it was cold out there this morning.'

'Yes. And the pavement would have been frozen. How do you rate her chances?'

'I'm not a loss adjuster, Detective. She has a chance, but she is not in a good place right now.'

Delaney nodded, pointed to the next room along and walked towards it. 'And the homeless man?'

'Bible Steve.'

'You know him?'

'He's been in before. The ambulance crew recognised him.'

'How is he?'

'To be honest, Detective Delaney, the fact that he is alive at all is what I would class as a minor miracle.'

'How so?'

'He was attacked some time in the night, as far as I can tell. It was cold this morning, it was below freezing last night. He was knocked into a comatose state. God knows how long he spent out there. He's been living rough on the streets for years. He had a blood alcohol level that was through the roof. He should be dead, in my opinion.'

'Somebody else's opinion too, it would look like,' said Sally Cartwright as she looked through the window. Bible Steve had as many tubes and monitors attached to him as the Chinese woman next door. But his hair was matted with dried blood, where it was visible; the rest was hidden under a thick white bandage wrapped around the top of his head. 'My diagnosis . . . that looks like a clear case of attempted murder.'

'I would hold fire on the "attempted" if I were you, Detective Constable,' said the young doctor.

Delaney turned back to look at her. 'You don't think he's going to make it?'

'It's not looking good for him, given what I said earlier. He's in a coma. I'm not sure he has the health to pull himself out of it.'

'There's nothing you can do to help?'

'We'll do everything we can, of course. But short of further divine intervention, I am afraid his chances aren't good.'

'Why would someone want to kill a harmless old street person?' asked DC Cartwright.

'He's not harmless, Sally. Look at his knuckles. "Slimline" Matthews tells me Bible Steve is a bit of a fighter.'

'Let's hope he is,' said Dr Crabbe.

'I still don't get it. Why would someone want to murder him?'

'This is London, Constable,' said Jack Delaney. 'Who needs a reason!'

31

Dr Laura Chilvers came out of the police surgeon's office, her face drawn, her eyes still haunted, her pupils dancing nervously.

'I'll make sure this is given top priority, Laura,' said Kate Walker reassuringly as she followed close behind.

'I don't want anyone knowing, promise me,' Laura whispered, leaning in and gripping Kate's arm tightly.

'I already have promised.'

'I know you have, sorry. It's my head. I can't take it all in.'

'I understand, Laura. It's a perfectly natural state after what you have been through.'

'It's just the paperwork, I don't want you getting into trouble.'

'Let me worry about that. I have plenty of favours I can call in.'

'Thanks, Kate. For everything.'

'I haven't done anything. But I will. Anything that's needed.'

'I appreciate it.'

'Go home, take a shower, get some rest. I'll call you as soon as I hear anything.'

Laura shook her head, trying to compose herself. 'I don't know if I want to go home. An empty house?'

'Take a shower here, then. I know it sounds trite, but it will help.'

Laura knuckled her fist, furious with frustration, against her temple. 'I just wish I could remember.'

'I know you do.'

'Christ, though, Kate! Maybe it's best if I don't.'

Kate stroked her arm.

'Go and take that shower. You've got something to change into?'

'I brought clothes. I know what the procedure entails, don't I?'

Kate gave her arm a final rub. 'You have my number. Just give me a call. Any time.'

Laura nodded and headed off. Kate watched her for a moment and then went back into her office.

Laura was pushing through the door into the corridor leading to the staff changing rooms when the sound of someone running made her spin round, terrified for a moment.

'God, Dave!' she said. 'You nearly gave me a heart attack.'

'Sorry, Dr Chilvers, but I need to speak to you.'

'What about? This isn't a good time right now.'

'I tried phoning you at home, on your mobile.'

'I've been busy.'

'You're not rostered in for today?' said the sergeant, puzzled.

'I had things to take care of.'

'We've got things to take care of too.'

'Spit it out, Sergeant. Like I said, this really isn't a good time for me.'

'It's Bible Steve.'

'What about him?'

'He's lying in an intensive-care bed, Laura.'

Her hand flew to her mouth. 'Oh, my God, what's happened to him?'

'We don't know.'

'I knew you should have kept him in last night.'

'We have to be very clear on what happened last night.'

'I am.'

'You asked me to keep him in, but you also said he was fit to be released.'

'He was. But it was freezing out there, and you said he doesn't always stay in the shelter.'

'I know. But we're not a homeless refuge.'

'I do know that.'

Dave Matthews looked at her. 'Are you all right, Laura?'

'Of course I'm all right, what do you mean?'

'You seem very distraught.'

'I'm a doctor, Sergeant! Forgive me for being concerned if someone who was under my care is now in an intensive-care bed.'

'He was under both our care. We charged him and released him on your judgement—'

'And?' snapped Laura, interrupting.

'And,' he continued pointedly, 'another woman was found unconscious beside him, and is also in that same unit fighting for her life.'

'I don't understand?'

'We don't know if he attacked her or not. So, like I say, we have to be very clear about what happened last night. His state of mind when we released him.

His blood alcohol levels were sky-high this morning.'

Laura's eyes danced nervously again as she ran a hand through her dishevelled hair. 'He must have got hold of some more.'

'Bible Steve may have killed that woman.'

Laura blinked, taking it in. She ran a hand through her bedraggled hair. 'What happens next?'

'Detective Inspector Delaney is at the hospital now. If Bible Steve recovers, he'll take a statement and we'll take it from there, I guess.'

'And if he doesn't?'

'There'll be an inquiry. But our hands are clean, aren't they?'

Laura didn't reply for a moment or two. 'I may go to the hospital myself. See how he is.'

'Why?'

'I don't know. Maybe I feel responsible.'

'But you're not, are you?'

'What if I missed something?'

'Let's find out why he collapsed, and what happened to the woman, before we decide who's to blame.'

Laura nodded distractedly. 'I've got to go,' she said and hurried off towards the changing rooms.

Sergeant Dave Matthews watched her for a while, absent-mindedly scratching his chin and unaware that he was doing so.

32

Geoffrey Hunt stood up from adjusting the thermostat on his electric radiator mounted on the back wall, and stretched his aching back once more.

He was in the studio that he had built in the garden. It had been made from breezeblocks, with split-beamed pine logs clad on the front and stained wooden panels on the inside, so that it looked like a log cabin. His wife had called it his folly, and she didn't just mean in the architectural sense. Inside it was very comfortable, with a dark-stained wooden floor that was covered with colourful rugs. A stable door looked out to the garden, the top half open when the weather allowed. A large desk stood in front of a broad panelled window beside the door. An antique captain's chair rested in front of the desk. On the walls were a clutter of photographs and memorabilia. His wife, his family, old friends. Bookshelves lined one side-wall of the cabin; they were full of jumbled books. Geoffrey liked to read, almost as much as he liked to write.

On his desk top stood a modern laptop that his wife had bought him for his birthday a couple of months ago. The truth was, though, that he never felt comfortable using it. A stack of notebooks stood beside it. One open. He was supposed to have started transcribing what he had written so far of his latest story from the notebooks into the computer. But he hadn't. He hadn't even turned the laptop on. He sat at his desk and slowly moved the pen, which lay on the open book, in a circle with the index finger of his right hand. The other truth was that he hadn't picked up a book to read in two weeks and hadn't written a single word, either.

But he liked coming out to his studio. It gave him space to think, even if he didn't like the thoughts that came to him. He looked at the wall to his left. A large crucifix was centred above the desk, and below it another small bookshelf. These books were kept neatly. A collection of his diaries over the years and, at the end, a copy of the Bible. Given to him when he was seven years old by his favourite aunt.

He took it from the shelf and held it in his hands for a moment, his thin fingers trembling as he felt the weight of it. He placed it down on the desk and laid his right hand on it, tracing the outline of the crucifix stamped onto the cover. The fading gold leaf was as much testimony to that ritual as it was to the passing of the years.

The door opened and Patricia came in, bundled in an oversized duffel coat, her feet in blue wellingtons, a large university scarf wrapped around her neck. She held a plate in her hand with a sandwich resting on it.

'You shouldn't have come out in this weather, Patricia,' her husband said.

'And neither should you. Here, I've brought you a sandwich,' she said, placing the plate on his desk.

'And a thermos of tea. Got to feed the creative mind.'

'Thanks, darling,' he replied and then coughed into his hand.

Patricia looked at him fondly and shook her head. 'Why you can't work inside I'll never know.'

'It's as warm here as it is there. The radiator works a treat. Probably warmer, if anything.'

Patricia took a thermos flask from the bag she had slung over her shoulder and put it beside the sandwich plate. Then she rummaged in her bag and brought out a bottle of pills. 'It's time for your medicine.'

'Yes, dear.' Geoffrey sighed and took a bite of his sandwich, chewed it and then peered inside. 'You put butter on the bread. You know I don't like my bread buttered.'

'Oh, for God's sake, Geoffrey!' his wife snapped suddenly. 'I can't think of everything! Not now, not today.'

Geoffrey looked up at her, concerned. 'What's happened?'

Patricia shook her head, wiping the back of her hand across her eyes. 'Nothing – it's just my hand is sore. Sorry, I shouldn't have snapped.'

'No, it's my fault.'

'Nothing is your fault, Geoffrey. God made us, didn't he?' she said, pointing at the Bible. 'He made us and he can judge us. Everyone else can go hang.'

'Yes, dear.'

'We agreed. So eat your sandwich and try not to think of the butter. You know you're supposed to feed a cold.'

'Yes, dear,' he said again. He picked up the

sandwich once more, giving his wife a small smile as she left. Not seeing the tears coming to her eyes again. He contemplated the sandwich for a while as he had contemplated the Bible earlier – as though he might find within the answers that he sought. He sighed again and put down the sandwich. Made the sign of the cross on his forehead and chest, closed his eyes and then started praying softly.

'Our Father in heaven, hallowed be thy name. Your kingdom come, your will be done, on earth as it is in heaven. Give us this day our daily bread, and forgive us our debts as we have also forgiven our debtors.'

His eyes opened and seemed to shine as he gazed out on his snow-covered lawn.

'Lead us not into temptation, but deliver us from evil.'

33

Derek 'Bowlalong' Bowman contemplated the skeletal form laid on his forensic-examination desk.

'So what have we learned?' he asked his young assistant.

'Definitely male.'

'Yes.'

'A tall man, somewhere in the six-foot range.'

'Correct.'

'Been in the ground for some twenty-odd years.'

'Probably.'

'Cause of death?'

'Ah, now that's the thirty-two-thousand-dollar question.'

Lorraine smiled. 'I thought it was the sixty-four-thousand-dollar question, Derek?'

'Was, Lorraine. Don't you know there's a recession on?' He stepped up to the skeleton. 'Come and give me a hand.'

Lorraine slipped on a pair of latex gloves and joined him at the examination table.

'These skull fragments, if you can give me a hand holding them together.' The doctor held the section of skull that had been broken into four pieces. 'You take those two pieces and hold them together with mine.'

They each picked up two pieces of broken bone and held them together, forming the gap that was missing from the left-hand side of the skull.

Bowman smiled grimly. 'Can you see that?'

'That wasn't made by a workman's spade.'

'No, you can see here where the spade shattered the skull – the edges are different, whiter. But the edges here are as brown as the rest of the bone.'

'Which means that it was made at the same time, or thereabouts, as the body was put into the ground.'

'Exactly so, Lorraine.'

'He was shot?'

Derek Bowman looked down at the ragged hole formed in the centre of the bone pieces they were holding together. 'Looks that way: left temple, small-calibre pistol, close-range.'

'No exit wound for the bullet.'

'No.' The forensic pathologist put down the two fragments he was holding and picked up the larger section of skull, turning it over. The openings to the skull were packed with earth. As he held it up, a worm wriggled loose and Lorraine grimaced.

'Once we've cleaned this up, I should imagine we will find it still *in situ*.'

'The workman was right, then.'

'Indeed. It looks like Jack Delaney has got a murder on his hands!'

34.

DI Tony Hamilton was a tall well-built man in his thirties. He had dark hair, blue eyes and was dressed in an immaculate suit. He could have been Jack Delaney's younger brother, if it wasn't for his accent, his Protestantism and his all-round clean-cut image. Whereas Jack Delaney charmed people, unaware that he was doing so – his rough moodiness attracting women against their better sensibilities – Tony Hamilton used his charm as he used his intelligence. Like a tool. But the woman standing on the doorstep of her house and giving him a cool, level gaze was going to be impervious to any charm he could muster. He was pretty certain about that.

'Didn't take you long,' said Stephanie Hewson.

'Do you mind if I come in?' asked the detective.

'Do I have a choice?'

'I need to speak to you formally. It might be more comfortable here than down at the police station.'

'Is that a threat?'

DI Hamilton smiled at her reassuringly. 'Not at all, Ms Hewson.'

'Why is it, then, that I feel like it's going to be me on trial now?'

'You have made some very serious allegations.'

'I have simply told the truth.'

'And yet a man has spent a year in prison when, if you had told the truth earlier, he might have been released sooner.'

The woman looked at him for a moment, containing her anger. Then she seemed to calm herself, shivering almost, and her eyes dropped from his gaze to look at the detective's highly polished shoes.

'Why don't you come in for a nice cup of tea then?' she said in a flat voice, unable to hide the sarcasm inherent in her invitation.

A few minutes later, she handed Tony Hamilton a mug of tea. The mug was decorated with a scene from *Winnie-the-Pooh*. Pooh and Piglet playing Poohsticks. He wondered if there was any significance to it. He knew Stephanie Hewson didn't have children. She still lived in the same downstairs apartment that she had been in at the time of the attack. He wondered if she would move, now that the man she had said was her attacker had been released from prison; but he didn't articulate the thought.

'Thank you,' he said simply instead. 'You have a lovely home.'

'You can buy it if you want, it's going on the market.' She sat down on the sofa opposite the wing-backed chair in which the detective was sitting.

Tony Hamilton kept his face level, wondering when the decision had been made. 'Had many offers?'

'Not many. It's not on the Internet yet.'

He took a sip of his tea. 'Why did you recant your statement, Ms Hewson?'

'Straight down to business?'

'It's a very serious matter.'

'Did you see the scars on my stomach and on my breasts, Detective? I presume you have seen the photos?'

'I did.'

'Do you think I need telling how *serious a business* it is, then?'

'Why did you change your mind?' Hamilton persisted.

Stephanie Hewson took a sip of her tea. 'I was shown that man's photo. That's not right, is it?'

'And you are sure it was DI Jack Delaney who showed you that photo?'

She looked up at him defiantly. 'Yes. Who else would it have been?'

'Sergeant Bonner maybe?'

'His assistant?'

'Yes.'

Stephanie shook her head, flustered for a moment. 'No. It was Inspector Delaney.'

'Jack Delaney doesn't remember meeting with you before the line-up.'

'What do you mean, he doesn't remember?'

DI Hamilton took a sip of his own tea. 'In his recollection, he met you just before taking you through for the identity parade. Are you sure it was not Sergeant Bonner you met with?'

'Yes, I'm positive.'

'Was Eddie Bonner with him?'

'I can't remember.'

'Why is that?'

'Why do you think? I'm shown a photo of the man who raped me and cut me. What am I going to do: take an inventory of everybody in the room?'

'So you do think Michael Robinson was the man who raped you, then?'

'I was told he was,' she replied angrily. 'I was shown his picture. Why would somebody lie about something like that?'

'We don't know that anybody did. Why do you now think he wasn't the man who attacked you?'

'I never said that.'

'But your statement in court this morning meant that he walked free.'

'That wasn't my fault.'

'What do you mean?'

'I took an oath to tell the truth. It was your job to find the man who did this to me. Your job to find the evidence, not just make it up.'

'Jack Delaney says he never did show you that photo.'

'Then he's a liar!'

DI Hamilton looked her in the eye. She was angry, no doubt about that, but there was something else in her eyes. Something that looked a lot like fear.

'We will find out exactly what happened, Ms Hewson. You have my word on that.'

'I couldn't stand up in court and perjure myself, Detective. I let myself believe that Michael Robinson was the man who assaulted me. Who hurt me. Detective Delaney showed me that photo, and I believed it. I believed it because I had to. Do you understand me?'

DI Hamilton could see tears forming in her eyes. 'No, tell me,' he said.

'It meant that they had the man. That he would be put away, and that I wouldn't have to flinch at every little noise. That I could leave my house without feeling absolutely terrified that he was there again. Watching me. That he would hurt me again. If it was him, then I had some of my life back.'

'Okay. We absolutely believe Michael Robinson was the man who raped you, Stephanie. You know that.'

DI Hamilton looked at her sympathetically, but she wouldn't meet his gaze. She stood up and took his mug from him. 'I couldn't lie in court. I didn't see him clearly. It was too dark, the window was too grimy. You need to find evidence. Proper evidence.'

'It was over a year ago, Ms Hewson.'

'I know exactly when it was, thank you, Detective!' she said, the anger flaring back into her voice.

Tony Hamilton stood up. 'Of course you do, I'm sorry.'

'Will Detective Inspector Delaney be arrested?'

Hamilton shook his head. 'No. He won't be. At worst there will be a disciplinary hearing. He's been served with a notice of investigation – that's all.'

'Good.' Stephanie Hewson walked him to the front door and opened it. 'All I want is justice, Detective.'

Hamilton looked at her for a moment and then nodded.

'Welcome to the club,' he said.

35

In the intensive-care ward Delaney crumpled the plastic coffee cup he had just been drinking from and looked around for a bin to put it in. A young nurse who was passing held her hand out.

'It's all right, I'll take it for you.'

'Cheers, darling,' Delaney said, flashing her a smile.

'Any time,' she said and carried on walking, swinging her hips a little more.

Sally Cartwright shook her head, pulling a face.

'What?' Delaney asked her. 'What?'

'Just my gender, sir. Sometimes I despair for it.'

'What can I tell you? She's a nurse. The caring profession, Sally. She sees a person in need and her natural instinct is to help him out.'

'She sees a man in need, maybe. And I can imagine the kind of help she'd like to administer.'

'Sally, I am a happily . . .' He paused.

'Were you about to say "married man", sir?'

'No, I was not.'

'What were you going to say?'

'As a happily partnered man, I have no interest in other women, Constable,' he said, looking as the nurse pushed through the swing doors at the end of the corridor. 'No matter how pretty they are.'

Sally punched him lightly on the arm. 'I'll tell Kate you said that!'

Delaney gave her a stern look. 'Did you just strike a superior officer?'

Sally Cartwright grinned. 'Yeah, I did.'

Delaney would have responded, but the doors swung open again and Dr Laura Chilvers walked down the corridor towards them. She had changed her outfit, and was now dressed in black trousers with a large red jumper and flat, sensible shoes. Her face was scrubbed of make-up and her hair was tied back. She looked about ten years younger to Delaney. She still had her coat on, but it was open and the flaps sailed behind her like a cloak as she hurried down the corridor.

'How's Bible Steve?' she asked.

'Not in good shape, Dr Chilvers.'

Laura carried on past them into the room. She picked up the medical chart at the base of the man's bed. Delaney followed behind her.

'What are you doing here, Laura?'

'Sergeant Matthews told me what happened. I wanted to see for myself.'

'We don't know what happened yet.'

'That he was hurt, I meant,' she said, flustered, as the consultant registrar came into the room and took the chart from her hand.

'Can I help you? What are you doing in here?'

'I'm a doctor. Laura Chilvers. I'm with the police.'

'Dr Chilvers is a police pathologist,' Delaney confirmed.

'I treated Mr . . .' She gestured at the comatose man. 'Bible Steve last night.'

171

'Treated him? With what exactly?'

'I didn't mean treated him in that sense. He was brought into the police station. He was drunk. He had been urinating on the window of a Chinese restaurant. He passed out in front of it.'

'So you didn't give him any medication?'

'No. He was drunk, that was all.'

'But he was lucid when you released him?'

'When the desk sergeant released him, yes. Well, as lucid as he ever is apparently.'

'What do you mean?'

'He has mental-health issues, I am led to believe.'

'You haven't treated him before?'

'He's quite well known to us at the station, Dr Crabbe,' said Delaney, flashing her a quick smile.

'It's Lily, please.' She returned the smile.

Behind her, Sally Cartwright, who had followed the registrar in, rolled her eyes.

'So what is the prognosis?' Laura asked the smaller woman.

Dr Crabbe shrugged. 'He's stable. That's all I can give you for now. You have read his notes.'

'When do you think we will be able to speak to him?' Delaney asked.

'I am afraid, like I said earlier, it's an "if", not "when", Detective.'

'He's comatose, Jack,' agreed Laura. 'It's something we just can't tell.'

'He may never regain consciousness,' agreed the registrar.

'But he's stable, you said,' Delaney replied. 'That means he is not going to die on us?'

'It's not that simple, Inspector,' said Laura Chilvers.

172

'He is stabilised, yes,' said the registrar. 'But that can change. His overall health is extremely poor. Judging by his alcohol levels when he came in and his general appearance, his skin, it looks like he has serious alcoholism issues. I would suspect cirrhosis of the liver. Possibly quite advanced. He could deteriorate at any time. And I gather he has been living rough on the streets for quite some time?'

Delaney nodded. 'Years.'

'So it is unlikely he will have received any recent medical treatment?'

'Very unlikely. I get the sense that he's extremely wary of any kind of authority figures.'

'He's homeless,' Sally added. 'It kind of goes with the territory.'

'The blow to the head. Is that what knocked him unconscious?' asked Delaney.

The surgical registrar adjusted Bible Steve's intravenous drip and made some notes on his chart as she spoke. 'Probably. But not necessarily.'

Delaney gestured for her to elaborate. 'What do you mean?'

'He could have collapsed some time after receiving the blow.'

'How much later?'

'It could be many hours. If he suffered a subdural haematoma for example. Or he could have fallen or been pushed to the pavement at some stage, occasioning the trauma.'

'So it could have been an accident?' Delaney asked.

'It could be,' replied the registrar. 'But unlikely. He has fresh abrasions to his hands and knuckles. I would say he had been in a fight, wouldn't you?'

Despite cleaning, there was still blood crusting on Bible Steve's inflamed knuckles. 'Yes, I would.'

'I'm not a detective, but it looks to me like someone wanted to hurt him.'

Delaney looked over at Laura who was staring at the man on the bed. 'Did he have any bruising to his head when he was brought into custody last night?' he asked her.

Laura shook her head, her forehead creasing.

Delaney picked up on her hesitation. 'You did check?'

'Of course I did!' she snapped back. 'I treated his hands. He was drunk. I was just assessing how drunk, and whether he was fit to be released.'

The registrar looked down at the comatose man. The monitor sounded louder now that no one was speaking. 'Doesn't look like he was, does it?'

'This isn't my fault!' said Laura.

The registrar leaned back, a little surprised. 'Nobody says it was.'

Delaney would have said something, but a loud alarm sounded from the intensive-care room next door and the registrar ran out.

Five minutes later, the crash team came out of Dongmei Chang's room, wheeling their resuscitation equipment away. A short while afterwards, Dr Lily Crabbe came out of the room and shook her head at Delaney who was standing outside in the corridor.

'We did everything we could,' she said.

From inside the room, the sound of wailing could be heard. A Chinese man came out. He was in his late twenties, dark-haired, about five foot nine and thin. His hair was slicked back and he had a black jacket over a white T-shirt and black jeans. He looked like an Asian Fonz, Delaney thought.

'You are the police detective?' he asked.

'Detective Inspector Jack Delaney, yes. And you are?'

'My name is David Chang. Dongmei Chang was my aunt.'

'I'm sorry for your loss.'

'I don't need your pity.' The man practically spat the words out. 'What are you going to do about it?'

'Trust me, there will be a thorough investigation into how she came to be injured.'

'She wasn't injured, Detective. She was murdered!'

Delaney zipped up his coat, his shoes crunching in the snow as he and Sally Cartwright walked back towards his car. Pulling out his mobile phone, he saw that he had a number of missed calls.

He punched in some numbers and tossed his car keys to Sally, who pushed the button to open the doors.

'You drive,' he said as he waited for the phone call to be answered.

'That will make a nice change,' said Sally wryly.

'Hi, Bowlalong. It's Jack Delaney. What have you got for me?' He listened for a while. 'Okay, Derek, thanks for that. Let me know if Ballistics can get anything off of that shell. Will do.' He clicked his phone shut. 'Bowman sends his love,' he said to Sally, who was pulling on her seatbelt.

'What did he have for us?'

'Our body in the churchyard this morning . . .'

'Yeah?'

'He and Lorraine fitted all the pieces together like an osteopathic jigsaw.'

'And?'

'And . . . there was a piece missing.'

'Left behind in the grave?'

'No. It was a piece missing,' he put a finger to his temple, right in the middle of his temple. 'Bullet-sized.'

'He was shot.'

'Yes,' said Delaney as he hit the speed-dial on his phone.

Sally turned the key in the ignition and kicked the engine into life. 'Back to the office?'

Delaney nodded. 'Hi, Tony,' he said as his call was answered. 'It's Jack Delaney.'

Sally reversed Delaney's old Saab out of its parking spot and headed for the car-park entrance as he listened to Tony Hamilton on the phone.

'Where are you now?' He nodded again. 'Okay, we'll meet you in The Castle in about fifty minutes. Change of plan, Sally.'

'Where to now then?'

'Harrow-on-the-Hill. The Castle pub. Do you know it?'

Sally shook her head.

'Don't worry, the Saab knows the way.'

Sally changed gears, the crunching audible. 'This car should know its way to the knacker's yard, if you ask me.'

'Well, no one is asking you! So step on it. Your boyfriend's waiting for us.'

Sally grimaced. 'Bloody men!'

Delaney smiled, but not for long, as what DI Tony Hamilton had told him ticked over in his brain.

Sally looked over at him as a thought struck her. 'It's not going to take fifty minutes to get to Harrow-on-the Hill, sir,' she said.

'I know, Sally, got to make a little visit first,' he

replied, all humour having vanished now from his blue eyes.

Laura was sitting on a chair by the base of Bible Steve's bed. A uniformed constable stood outside. Next door, CID officers from Paddington Green were interviewing Dongmei Chang's relatives.

She sipped on a clear plastic cup of water, her eyes unfocused, lost in thought.

She remembered taking the girl to a play area of the club. She remembered dark lights, throbbing music. Velvet Underground. Lou Reed, the song playing in her mind continuously – she couldn't seem to stop it. An earworm. Lyrics about leather and boots. Tasting a whip. She remembered the whip in her hand. She remembered lashing down with it hard. Again and again. But the memories blurred. She couldn't see who or what she was hitting. Just the song and a red mist. Flashes of images came back. Outside, in the snow, blood on her hands. Putting her hands in the snow to ease the pain.

She held her hands to her ears, trying to stop the song. Trying to remember.

'Dr Chilvers! Are you all right?'

Her eyes flew open, startled. Dave Matthews was standing in the doorway, practically filling it with his massive shoulders and looking at her, concerned.

It took her a moment to find her voice. 'Yeah, I'm fine, thank you, Sergeant.' She finished her cup of water and held it out to him. 'Just a touch of migraine; it will pass in a minute, but could you get me some more water?'

Dave Matthews left and Laura closed her eyes

again. Steadying her breathing. Willing her heart to slow down. For Christ's sake, Laura! Get a grip on yourself, she said to herself.

And then screamed as a strong hand seized her arm.

Sally Cartwright brought Delaney's Saab to a stop in a suburban street in Harrow. Warrington Road, just a few streets away from Carlton Row, where the children had been kidnapped all those years ago and made Jack Delaney a household name for a while. His face plastered over the front covers of most of the papers. Not once, but twice.

There was a huddle of press outside a house about fifty yards up the road.

'Do you think this is wise, sir?' asked Sally as they stepped out of the car and shut the doors.

'I don't know, Sally,' said Delaney as they walked up the road towards them. 'What do you think?'

'I think, sir, in the words of Chief Inspector Diane Campbell, that George Napier will want your balls dipped in chocolate and served up at the ambassador's ball.'

'That's Superintendent Napier to you!'

'Yes, sir.'

'And George-fecking-Napier can kiss my black Irish arse.'

'Glad to hear it, sir.'

'Detective Inspector Delaney!'

Delaney didn't know who had called out to him from the gaggle of press outside Michael Robinson's front door. Because they were all shouting the same thing.

Delaney held a hand up to silence them. 'I have no comment to make at this time,' he said and pushed through them, Sally Cartwright trailing in his wake.

Delaney let the noise wash over him. Aware of the photo flashes bursting behind him, but not much caring.

A short while later and the door opened. Michael Robinson blinked at the barrage of white light that ensued, then smiled.

'Detective Inspector Delaney. What a pleasant surprise!'

'Good. May we come in?'

'I'm not sure that would be appropriate under the circumstances.'

Delaney stepped forward so that Robinson had to take a step backwards. 'Come on, Detective Constable,' he said to Sally. 'The nice man is going to put the kettle on.'

He took hold of Robinson's arm and steered him further inside. Sally followed closely behind and shut the door.

'What do you want, Delaney?' Robinson asked, all veneer of politeness stripped away as they stood in his hall.

'You sent me some mail, Robinson. I'm sending it back.' He took out the summons that he had been served in the Viaduct Tavern and tossed it against the man's chest.

Robinson let the envelope fall to the floor. 'It makes no difference. You've been served, Detective Inspector. I'll see you in court.'

'I'll see you in hell first.'

Robinson grinned. It made Sally Cartwright's skin

creep as he looked at her. 'I hope you're making notes of all this, Detective Constable? Sounds like your boss was threatening me.'

'See, that's where matters of opinion vary,' Sally replied with a sweet smile of her own. 'What I heard the detective inspector say to you is that he won't need to see you in court on a trumped-up civil case. Because the CPS will have you banged up long before that.'

'The case was thrown out of court.'

'For now. But you know that you are cowardly rapist scum. I know you are, and what is more important . . . is that Detective Inspector Delaney does too. And he really doesn't like people like you.'

Robinson kept the grin on his face. 'I couldn't really give a shit what you or DI Bogtrotter of the Yard here thinks. You have nothing on me, and you know it.'

Delaney stepped forward and grabbed the man in the groin.

'You're hurting me,' Robinson said through clenched teeth.

'Ah that's a shame.' Delaney looked over his shoulder at Sally Cartwright. 'See, that's the thing about bullies, rapists and paedophiles – they're all cowards at heart.'

'I'm no paedophile!' said Robinson, his eyes watering.

'You mentioned my partner and child, on the phone this morning. I just came here to tell you. You go near either one of them and you, my friend, are a dead man!' Delaney squeezed his hand and Robinson stood up on his toes. 'We have a congruence of understanding on this matter?'

Michael Robinson nodded his head and Delaney released him.

'You're crazy,' said Robinson, his breath ragged.

'Certifiable,' Sally Cartwright agreed.

'I'm a stone-cold killer. You'd do well to remember it.'

Robinson cowered back against the wall, unable to meet Delaney's gaze.

Delaney gestured to Sally Cartwright and they left. Robinson took a moment to collect himself. 'Motherfucker,' he said in a low whisper, then 'Motherfucker!' more loudly. Calming his breathing, he snatched up the phone stabbing in some numbers. 'We have to meet,' he said when the call was answered.

37.

Outside in Delaney's car, Sally put the key into the ignition and looked across at her boss. 'Did you mean what you said in there, sir?' she asked.

'Every fucking word.'

Sally thought about it for a moment and turned the engine over. She guessed he had his reasons.

Bible Steve was sitting up looking at his bruised knuckles. Sergeant Dave Matthews stood beside him at the head of his bed. Dr Chilvers waited by the door.

'Just tell us what you remember?' said the sergeant.

The man blinked his haunted eyes for a moment or two. 'I can't remember anything!' he said finally.

Dr Lily Crabbe came into the room, followed by a nurse. 'I am not sure this is the right time to be interrogating him, Sergeant,' she said, with the kind of voice a teacher might reserve for an unruly child throwing litter in the playground.

'I'm simply asking some questions, Doctor. A woman did die, you know.'

'Yes, thank you, Sergeant, I am well aware of that!'

'It was nothing to do with me,' said Bible Steve, shaking his head.

183

'Nobody is saying it was, Steve.'

'I want to leave,' said the homeless man, pulling at the tubes still attached to him.

Dr Crabbe rushed over. 'Try not to get excited, please. You will hurt yourself.'

'But I want to leave, I don't belong here.'

'You are still a far-from-well man. You need to stay here, so that we can take care of you.'

'Listen to the doctor, Steve. She's trying to help,' said Dave Matthews.

Bible Steve looked up at him angrily. 'Stop calling me that. Why are you calling me that?'

'It's what everybody calls you, Steve. *Bible Steve*, that's your name.'

'Isn't that your name?' asked the registrar as Steve's eyes darted wildly.

'No,' he said.

'What should we call you then?'

Steve screwed his eyes shut. When he opened them there were tears on his cheeks. 'I don't know,' he said.

The registrar held out her hand. 'It's okay. Really, it's okay. You have had a blow to the head.'

'I know he is your patient,' said Laura Chilvers to Dr Crabbe, speaking for the first time, 'but he is clearly still in shock. Maybe a mild sedative?'

Dave Matthews turned to the registrar. 'I'd like to talk to him a little first, if that is okay?'

'He's had a head injury. We need to check his consciousness levels before we can sedate him.'

Bible Steve was swivelling his head like an audience member at Wimbledon.

'Of course,' said Laura, feeling the colour rise into

her cheeks a little. 'I meant a painkiller.'

'Who are you? Who are you all?' Bible Steve cried.

'I'm Sergeant Dave Matthews,' said the policeman. 'Don't you remember me, Bible?'

'Don't call me that! And no I don't remember you.' His gaze flicked from person to person, coming to stop as he stared at Laura.

'Who are you?' he asked. Laura looked away. 'Who am I?' he said in a hoarse whisper.

Geoffrey Hunt sat in the snug that lay just off the kitchen. They called it a snug, a small affectation, but one that amused them. A smallish lounge, but cosy, with an open log fire opposite a comfortable sofa and a wide arched opening to the kitchen beyond. On the left was a pair of leaded-light windows that looked out to the front garden.

There were logs burning in the firedog and the crackle and spit of the flames seemed to add to the festive decorations that bedecked the walls and beams overhead. There were more than a hundred Christmas cards displayed. In the corner stood a small tree: a six-foot-high Norwegian Blue. Patricia always insisted on a Norwegian Blue, as it didn't shed needles into every nook and cranny, and take a month to clean up after Twelfth Night when it was carried into the garden. Geoffrey usually laughed and made a joke about the old *Monty Python* sketch featuring a Norwegian Blue parrot, but this year he hadn't laughed when he made the joke, and neither had his wife. They were saying things to each other but half the time they weren't really listening. He supposed a lot of old couples got like that. They didn't really need language to

185

communicate their thoughts, their feelings. In the background the radio was playing some classical Christmas carol. Geoffrey always had the radio on. Hated the television. Always had. Patricia occasionally insisted they watch some programme or other, but it never held his attention. He'd rather listen to his record collection or read a good book. Not that he had done that recently either.

He took out his handkerchief and coughed into it, then coughed again uncontrollably.

Patricia came through from the kitchen where she had been making a hot-drink remedy and waited for him to stop. After a moment or two Geoffrey wiped his eyes with the sleeve of his shirt and smiled gratefully to her as she handed him the steaming mug.

'Thanks, darling.'

'Your cold does seem to be getting worse, Geoffrey.'

'I'm fine.'

'I'm worried about you, that's all. What with your asthma.'

'Like I say, I'm fine. I've got my sprays and my inhalers.'

The classical music finished on the radio and the presenter announced that the news would be following the adverts.

Patricia crossed over to the small, occasional table where the radio stood and turned it off.

'I was listening to that, darling,' Geoffrey said.

'I know you were, but we need to talk.'

'I wanted to catch the news!'

'Later, Geoffrey, this is important.'

'What is it?'

Patricia sat down next to him. 'You know we were always talking about moving away. To Spain. To Barcelona.'

'A pipe-dream. We're too old now.'

'Rubbish! But we are getting older. There is no denying that, and this climate here does nothing for your lungs.'

'What's put this in your mind all of a sudden?'

'It's your chest, and this damned cold. And now there's this snow and goodness knows when it will end.'

'If Winter comes, can Spring be far behind.'

'That's all very well for Shelley, darling, but he didn't live in Queen's Park.'

'Well we can certainly think about it. Turn the radio back on.'

'But that's all we ever do, Geoffrey. *Think* about it, let's seize the horn right now, today!'

'What do you mean?'

'I've been on the computer . . .'

'Again!'

'Yes, and I've found some really cheap flights to Barcelona.'

'For when?'

'For tomorrow, Geoffrey. Why don't we go and spend Christmas in Spain and see what we think?'

Geoffrey coughed into his handkerchief again. 'I know what I think?'

'What's that?'

'I think you've finally lost your marbles,' he said. 'And we've no chance of making a quick sale, what with the housing market as it is. Let's wait till the market picks up and then we'll talk about it.'

'It might be too late by then.'

'There's nothing to connect us, Patricia. Nobody will know who he is now, even if he does turn up.'

Patricia nodded, close to tears. 'I just worry about what's to become of us.'

Geoffrey took her hand and patted it. 'I promised you I'd take care of everything, didn't I?'

She nodded, blinking back the tears. 'Yes.'

'And I will, darling,' he said, his eyes suddenly clear and focused. 'I will!'

38.

Jack Delaney parked his car at the Harrow School theatre. Built in 1994, the Ryan Theatre had cost more than four million pounds, and was worth more than many professional theatres. Then again, the school charged pupils thirty grand a year to attend. Getting on for a quarter of a million pounds for their time at school, and with approximately 850 pupils in attendance, they could pretty much afford it. Pretty much afford anything! Most of the land and the buildings on the Hill were owned by the school. They had invented the game of squash and Harrow's old-boy honours list contained eight former prime ministers, amongst many other luminaries.

Delaney was not surprised, therefore, as he slammed shut the passenger door of his battered old Saab, to see an outraged figure with curly hair strolling from the theatre towards him.

'You can't park there!' the man said.

'And you'd be?' replied Delaney.

'I'd be the technical manager. And this is school property.'

'We won't be long,' said Sally Cartwright, smiling sweetly at him. 'We've got a quick meeting at The Castle.'

189

The technical manager looked across at her and beamed. 'Good choice,' he said. 'Take as long as you like. Tell them I sent you.'

'Cheers,' she said and walked out of the car park with Delaney. 'See, sir, didn't even have to flash my warrant card.'

'Not your warrant card, no, Sally,' said Delaney.

'Sir!' Sally replied in mock-outrage.

They walked up to the main road and down towards The Castle. 'They do a nice drop of ale here apparently, Sally.'

'Bit early for me, boss.'

Delaney looked at his watch. 'Past lunchtime, isn't it?'

'Maybe a cheese and onion roll.'

They turned right out of the car park and walked downhill on West Street a few yards to the pub. Loud singing was coming from the larger of the two bars, and Delaney figured that Tony Hamilton would have gone into the smaller one. He figured right. There were a few regulars drinking pints of London Pride and scowling at the noise emanating from next door. Delaney wasn't sure if it was an office party that had started early or was finishing late. The school had closed a while back for the holidays, but there was a pantomime running in the theatre and plenty of people still living on the hill.

Delaney used to come to the pub in the old days, when he walked the beat in the area. It was usually a lively pub on a Friday back then, at any time of the year, as he recalled.

'Second Fuller's pub I've been into today,' he said to Tony Hamilton as he steered Sally to the bar.

'What's it to be, then?' said the detective inspector, taking a sip from a tall glass of what looked suspiciously like Coca-Cola to Delaney.

'I'll have a pint of Guinness.'

'And the lovely detective constable?'

'The lovely detective constable will have a soda water and lime. She's driving.'

'Yes and the lovely detective constable can speak for herself as well, sir.'

'At least we all agree she's lovely,' said Hamilton and Delaney groaned.

'Dear God, do you not have a Saturday job selling cheese in the market?' he said.

Hamilton pulled a stool out for Sally to sit on and gestured the barman over. 'Pint of Guinness please.' He looked enquiringly at Sally.

'I'll have a soda and lime, and a cheese and onion roll, if they have one?'

The barman grunted, indicating that they had, and set about pouring Delaney's pint.

'So what did you learn from the woman?' asked Delaney.

'She wasn't exactly keen to talk.'

'You think she was lying?'

'I don't know. Did you show her the photo?'

Delaney shrugged. 'I don't think I did.'

'Well there you go then. She's lying. Lying about something anyway. Not about being raped and slashed with a knife. Not about that.'

'No, she wasn't lying about that,' agreed Sally Cartwright.

'So someone got to her?' said DI Hamilton.

'Yeah.'

'She's put her house on the market. Suddenly. And she's put it on cheap.'

'Can't blame her for wanting to leave the area.'

'No.'

'Specially if she knew that Michael Robinson was moving back in.'

'Which she would know, when she decided to make that statement in court.'

'Exactly.' Delaney took a pull on his pint of Guinness and placed the glass down. 'I want you to go to Northwick Park Hospital this afternoon, Sally.'

'Why?'

'Michael Robinson is a sick fuck. But he has a friend, one assumes.'

'A partner-in-crime.'

'Yeah, someone has put the frighteners on Stephanie Hewson, is my guess. Maybe he has put the frighteners on other women. Maybe he has hurt other women. Check the records, see if there have been any women in with knife injuries over the last few years.'

'We'd have known if something similar had happened before, sir.'

'No we wouldn't. Not necessarily. How many women who are raped come forward do you reckon, Sally?'

'We can't know for sure.'

'We do know it is a great deal more who don't come forward than do,' agreed Tony Hamilton.

'With six per cent conviction rates, I'm not too surprised, are you?'

Hamilton shook his head. 'We're just the rat-catchers, that's all. Other people's job to decide what to do with them.'

Sally looked at Delaney. 'That's your expression, isn't it, sir?'

Delaney ignored her. 'The thing is a woman might not report a rape, but she would have to report a knife assault.'

'Unless she claimed it was self-harming.'

'Self-harmers don't slash themselves across the belly, Constable.'

'Some might.'

Delaney drained his Guinness and stood up. 'Can you give her a lift to Northwick Park?'

DI Hamilton considered for a moment, then smiled at Sally. 'I'd be delighted.'

'Where are you going, sir?'

'Just a little call to make and then I have to go and see the vicar.'

'Sorting out the wedding?' said Sally with an innocent expression.

'Just give me my car keys and save your wit for someone who might appreciate it.'

He nodded at Hamilton who couldn't see him, and Sally rolled her eyes.

'Don't get up to anything I wouldn't,' Delaney said as he headed out the door.

Hamilton took a sip of his drink. 'Just you and me then.'

'What's going to happen to Jack?'

'Not a lot, I should imagine.'

'Aren't you supposed to be investigating him?'

'I'm interviewing you, aren't I?'

'Is that what you're doing?'

'Yeah, I'm the good cop. It's my technique.'

'All charm?'

'Is it working?'

'Not yet.'

'Rome wasn't built in a day.'

'It was destroyed in one.'

'So you think he showed her the photo?'

'I wouldn't put it past him, but he doesn't think he did. And that's good enough for me.'

'I don't think he did either.'

'So what are we going to do about it?'

'Prove him innocent.'

'Good.'

'And then, maybe dinner? Do you like Chinese?'

Sally finished her drink, then stood up. 'Still not working.'

DI Hamilton stood up and jangled his keys. 'Northwick Park then?'

'Sounds as good a plan as any!'

Sally walked to the door and Hamilton watched her for a moment then grinned and followed her out.

39.

Stephanie Hewson hesitated for a moment before slamming the door shut. Delaney took that moment to hold his hands up in an *I surrender* gesture.

'I'm not here to give you a hard time, Stephanie.'

'What are you here for then?'

'To help.'

'You'd help me by leaving me alone.'

'Is that what they said?'

'Who?'

'Someone has threatened you, I know that much.'

'You don't know anything at all.'

'I know Michael Robinson was the man who hurt you.'

'He didn't just hurt me. He raped me and sliced me like a carcass of meat.'

'And I am going to make him pay for what he did.'

'You can do what you like, as long as it is not at my expense.'

Delaney took a card out of his pocket. 'I know nothing I say can make up to you for what has happened. The truth is there is never the kind of justice that that man deserves.'

Stephanie Hewson looked at the detective standing

on her doorstep, some of her anger evaporating. 'I have to protect myself.'

'I know,' said Delaney and then nodded sadly. 'Take my card. It has my mobile number on it. Call me any time, day or night. I promise I'll be there for you.'

'I'm not going to change my statement.'

'I'm not asking you to. I know why you did it, and that's all that's important to me.'

Stephanie looked down at the card Delaney was holding out.

'Take it, Stephanie. Please,' he said. 'I can't promise you that the Metropolitan Police force will do everything in its power to bring Michael Robinson down. But I do promise you *I* will. It was personal to me when I was assigned the case in the first place. I wasn't functioning properly then. I was borderline alcoholic.'

'Why are you telling me this?'

'Because I want you to understand. My wife was killed and it was partly my fault. I didn't pull the trigger on the shotgun, but I put her in harm's way. I blamed myself and I couldn't deal with that, so I drank. My eye was off the ball. We should have had a stronger case against Robinson. What we had was circumstantial and it mainly came down to your identification in the end.'

'I know.'

'So you have been put in a place you shouldn't have been. Twice.'

She looked at him, waiting for him to continue.

'But I am going to make that stop now.'

'Thank you,' she said and took the card.

Delaney waited until she had closed the door and listened to the bolts being slid home, and then walked back to his car.

40

Delaney looked up at the sky for the hundredth time that day and frowned. Thick flakes of snow had begun to fall, settling in his long eyelashes. He blinked and locked the door to his Saab. The snow was crusty and slippery underfoot as he walked into the churchyard.

It was starting to get dark now and there was a glow coming from the forensic 'marquee' that had been erected over the grave where the body of the unknown man had been discovered.

Diane Campbell was standing outside the tent with a lit cigarette in her hand. Beside her stood a tall thin woman, with silver-grey hair slicked back. She wore a dark woollen overcoat but a dog collar was just about visible.

'Jack,' said Diane as he approached. 'This is the Reverend Leslie Hynd. She's the vicar here.'

'Was the vicar here,' she corrected her. 'The church is deconsecrated, remember.'

'Detective Inspector Jack Delaney.' He shook the vicar's hand.

'Are we any further forward in finding out who the unfortunate man might be?'

'No. Which is why we wanted to talk to you.'

'Of course. Anything I can do to help.'

Delaney nodded and turned to his boss. 'Could I get one of those, Diane?'

'Thought you'd given up?'

'New Year's resolution. It's not the New Year yet, is it?'

'Not unless I missed Christmas.'

Diane tapped out a couple of cigarettes, lit one from the dying embers of her own and handed it to Delaney. Then lit herself a fresh one.

The vicar gestured towards the church. 'Why don't we talk inside,' she said.

'You go ahead. We'll finish these and catch up with you.'

'As you wish.' The Reverend Hynd headed off towards the church.

Diane looked at Delaney for a moment. 'Are we any the wiser, Jack?'

'A day older nearly, no wiser.'

'I hear you talked to Michael Robinson.'

'Yes. And Stephanie Hewson.'

The deputy superintendent blew out a long stream of smoke. 'At the risk of sounding like John Le Mesurier in *Dad's Army,* "Do you think that wise?"'

'The man served a civil suit on me.'

'I know.'

'So I'm entitled to prepare my side of the case.'

'That's what you were doing, was it?'

'No. I had his balls in my hand and told him that he ever went anywhere near Kate or Siobhan I'd tear them off.'

'I imagine that got his attention.'

'The cockroach is guilty, Diane.'

'Yes.'

'Stephanie Hewson is absolutely terrified. Someone has got to her.'

'Who?'

'I don't know yet. But I intend to find out.'

'She didn't say?'

'She's not saying anything.'

'But she talked to you.'

'I promised her I'd take care of things, whatever it took.'

'You make a lot of promises, cowboy.'

'Only ones that I can keep.'

'Good,' said Diane Campbell, grinding the cigarette butt under the heel of her boot. 'Make sure that you do.'

Delaney didn't reply, just flicked his cigarette away, watching the trail of tiny sparks as it wheeled through the air, the light winking out as it hit the snow-covered ground, then followed Diane into the church building.

The Reverend Leslie Hynd was closing her mobile phone as they both walked in.

The church was a shell, stripped of pews, altar, decorations. A vast, empty hall of a room now. The last of the day's light came weakly through the stained-glass windows, but electric lighting had been set up. And a kettle, mugs and the fixings for cups of tea were on a side-table near the entrance door.

'Sad to see the place like this,' said the vicar, gesturing at the dust-covered floor of the church, broken tiles scattered here and there. 'So many services, wedding, funerals, baptisms, Easters, Christmases. So

200

many years, so many people.' She sighed. 'So many stories. It seems criminal.'

'How long were you the vicar here?' Delaney asked.

'Not long. About three years.'

'And before you?'

'The Reverend Patrick Hennessy.'

'And how long was he here?' asked Diane Campbell.

'About sixteen or seventeen years, I believe.'

'And where is he now?'

'He is doing missionary work in the People's Democratic Republic of the Congo.'

'And can he be contacted?'

'Not easily. But I have put a message out for him to get in touch.'

'And who was in charge here before then?' asked Delaney.

'My assistant is looking into it, Detective. I'll let you know as soon as I do.'

'Thanks. Do you have any idea who the person might be that we found in your grounds?'

'Absolutely none, I'm afraid. I understand he has been there for quite some time.'

'About twenty years, we think.'

'And the cause of death?'

'This is a murder investigation, Reverend. He was shot in the head.'

'Oh, my goodness, that's terrible. Why would they bury him here?'

'We don't know,' said Sally Cartwright.

'If we knew that, then maybe we'll know why he was killed, Reverend,' said Delaney.

41

Michael Robinson stood on the platform at Baker Street waiting for the east-bound train that had just left Edgware Road and would take him to Piccadilly Circus.

He jiggled some coins in his jacket pocket. Not that he was scared as such, more a nervous excitement. He had a meeting first and then he was free to spend some time in Soho. It had been more than twelve months since he had enjoyed female company and he intended to savour the opportunity now. Ideally, he would have liked to pay that haughty bitch Stephanie Hewson another visit. He felt himself harden as he remembered the look she had given him in the courtroom that morning. Since he had recovered consciousness in hospital, every day, every night he had replayed in his mind what he had done to her in that Scout hut in Harrow-on-the-Hill. Grunting as he entered her, her gasps of pain making him harder still. He could remember the feel of her. His hands on her cool buttocks as he rammed himself into her. He remembered taking his knife and cutting her. Her sudden intake of breath. He remembered walking home over the back of the hill. Her scent in his nostrils, and he hardened again almost immediately.

He'd look for someone just like her. There were plenty of women to choose from in Soho, if you had the cash in your pocket. He hadn't bought a new knife, though. The old one was hidden somewhere no one would ever find it and he wasn't going to risk trying to recover it. He was many things, but one thing Michael Robinson wasn't, was any man's fool. He wasn't any man's bitch, either. And certainly not that arrogant fuck DI Jack Delaney's. Coming into his house. Threatening him. The fuck didn't have any idea who he was dealing with. But he was going to find out soon enough just what kind of man Robinson was. Delaney could wait, howevert. Wheels were in motion and the bastard would get what was coming to him.

Stephanie Hewson – she'd get what was coming to her soon too. But for now he was going to concentrate on himself. He jingled the coins in his pocket again, and a slow smile spread across his face as he imagined what lay ahead for him that evening.

He stepped forward as the train came clattering out of the tunnel from Marylebone.

And then he felt a lancing needle of pain in his right thigh. An unbearable pain searing through his neural pathways. His body convulsed and he stepped forward into thin air. He didn't even have time to scream before the east-bound train hit him.

And then he didn't think much of anything at all.

He was dead.

42.

Delaney came into the bedroom loosening his tie.

Kate was sitting up in bed reading the latest Shardlake novel. The hunchback of Olde London town solving crimes for Henry the Eighth. Not Delaney's cup of tea. It seemed to him that the serial killer Shardlake never caught was old Henry himself. Kate's glasses were perched on the end of her nose and she peered over them at Jack as he tossed his tie on the chair beside the bed.

'Where've you been, Jack?' she said.

Delaney leaned over and kissed her. 'My car broke down.'

'Again? Isn't it about time you got rid of that old thing?'

'Probably. But I like my Saab.'

'It doesn't like you.'

'Got the Tube.'

Kate wrinkled her nose suspiciously. 'After a couple of beers, by the smell of you, I'd say.'

'I might have had a couple. It's been a bit of a day.'

'Funny how your car often breaks down when you've had a bit of a day.'

Delaney lay on the bed and rested his head on the pillow. 'Just a coincidence.'

'I don't believe in coincidences.'

Delaney grinned. 'Me neither.'

'I heard about the court case.'

'Hard not to.'

'Yes. Pretty much over the news continually.'

'Small-news day.'

'What's going to happen?'

'Nothing, darling. Old cowboy here, he's pretty much bullet-proof.'

'Man from Krypton?'

'Something like that.'

Kate rested her head on his chest and he stroked her hair. 'How was your day?' he asked her.

'Not the best, if I am honest.'

'Want to talk about it?'

'Not yet.'

Delaney nodded. 'Fair play.'

'What about yours?'

'Started bad, got worse, ending up nice, though.' He stroked her hair some more. She looked up and kissed him.

'Glad to hear it.'

Delaney's mobile trilled and he fetched it out of his pocket, checked the caller ID, then answered the call. 'What's up, Sally . . . Yeah, yeah, I know. I had it switched off for a couple of hours. Okay, let me grab a piece of paper.'

Delaney fumbled in his pocket for his notebook and grabbed a pen off the bedside table. 'Shoot.'

'Reverend Geoffrey Hunt. Okay, got that. How did you get on at Northwick Park Hospital?' He listened for a while. 'All right, I'll meet you seven tomorrow morning. Usual place. And how did Inspector Hamilton behave himself?'

He grimaced and held the phone way from his ear. 'No, you hang up,' he said and closed his phone.

'So you switched your phone off for a couple of hours?' said Kate.

'Forgot to turn it back on.'

'Another coincidence.'

'Mobile phones in pubs, they shouldn't be allowed. I am very consistent on that point.'

Kate laughed. 'Nothing should come between a man and his Guinness.'

'Only you, sweetheart.'

'What was that about Reverend Hunt?'

'You know him?'

'Sort of. I know his wife. She used to teach at the university, still registered to the practice there.'

'What did she teach?'

'She's a doctor of divinity. Why?'

'I don't know. I'm a detective, Kate. I like asking questions. Ask enough, and sometimes things make sense.'

'And sometimes they don't.'

'True.'

'Is her husband in some kind of trouble?'

'Not that I know of. St Luke's is his old church.'

Kate sat up. 'I didn't know that. I was called out there this morning. Before they knew it was human remains.'

'Your friend's husband was the incumbent vicar at the time the body was put in the ground.'

'So they've got you on that case?'

'Amongst others. Till I get suspended, that is.'

'The Devil finds work for idle digits.'

Delaney slipped his hand down the duvet. 'Best keep them busy then,' he said.

Kate slapped his hand. 'You can have a shower first, busy boy.'

'Good idea.' Delaney swang his legs round and stood up. He leaned over and kissed the bump of Kate's belly.

'Henry the Eighth got one thing right,' he said.

'And what would that be?'

'It's good to have lots of children.' He smiled and headed to the bathroom.

Part Three

43

Sunday morning

'Deck the halls with boughs of holly! Fa la la la la, la la la la. 'Tis the season to be jolly . . . Fa la la la la, la la la la!'

'Do you want to button it, Roy?' said Jack Delaney as he leaned against the counter and contemplated lighting a cigarette. Roy stopped singing and grinned over his shoulder at him.

'What's up with you this morning, Jack? Or do I even need to ask? You being normally such a ray of emerald-green Fenian sunshine.'

'What does that even mean, Roy? How in the name of St Joseph on a fucking bicycle can you have green sunshine?'

'I was talking metaphorically, Jack.'

'You were talking bollocks.'

'You want an egg with this?' asked the portly short-order cook as he flipped some slices of bacon.

'I do.'

'I see the piece of shit we talked about yesterday walked free.'

'Yeah, he did.'

'Anything going to come down on your head?'

'I should think so.'

'If you'd handled things a little differently back then, Jack . . .'

'You saying this is my fault?'

'Nothing of the sort. Like I say, I wouldn't even have let the scum make it to court.'

'Yeah, well, I'm a changed man nowadays.'

'Are you?'

'You see me smoking this cigarette?' Delaney asked, holding up an unlit Marlboro.

'Not yet.'

'Exactly.'

'Don we now our gay apparel, troll the ancient Yuletide carol!' sang Roy happily, as he cracked an egg that spattered and sizzled when it landed on the hot griddle plate. 'Fa la la la la, la la la la.'

'God give me strength,' muttered Delaney as Sally Cartwright walked up to the van. She was dressed in black trousers, with higher heels than usual and a smart black parka with faux-fur trim. Her long, blonde hair was tied back in a loose ponytail. She had on more make-up than usual too, and was altogether too bright and perky-looking for seven o'clock on a Sunday morning.

'Are you on a promise, Cartwright?' he said.

'Sir?'

'Never mind. But I am guessing you are not dolled up like a tart's breakfast for Roy's and my benefit.'

'You look gorgeous as ever, Sally darling,' said Roy and started buttering some bread.

'I don't want butter on mine,' said Delaney.

'Jeez, Jack. How long have you been coming here?'

'Too bloody long. Next year I'm going vegan!'

Roy laughed as he slipped some bacon into the buttered slices and handed the sandwich over to Sally Cartwright in a paper napkin. 'Beauty before age,' he said.

'Cheers, Roy,' said Sally, and squirted some tomato ketchup into her sarnie.

Roy Smiley flipped the egg briefly, put three slices of bacon on a slice of unbuttered bread, added the egg, topped it with another slice of bread and handed it over to Delaney, who grunted approvingly.

'Reckon it's going to snow?' asked Sally.

'Sing we joyous, all together, heedless of the wind and weather,' sang Roy.

'Fa la la la la, la la la la,' added Sally.

Delaney shook his head despairingly and took another bite of his sandwich.

'So I've done a bit of looking into the Reverend Geoffrey Hunt,' said DC Cartwright.

'And?'

'He retired from the church twenty years ago.'

'About the same time our man was planted in his churchyard.'

'Give or take, I guess. As you know, Derek Bowman couldn't be very specific. Could be after Hunt's time. Could be during, as you say.'

Delaney finished his sandwich and wiped his lips clean with the paper napkin, before screwing it into a ball and handing it over to Roy.

'How old was Hunt when he retired?'

'Late forties. Health reasons apparently. And his wife was on a good wage.

'University lecturers? Wasn't aware they were well paid . . .'

Sally looked at him curiously.

'Yeah, well, I didn't just go to the pub last night, Sally. I did some research of my own.'

'Where?'

'Never mind where.'

'Anyway Dr Hunt was a publishing academic. She had one book which sold an awful lot overseas as well as here. Particularly in America.'

'So he could afford to retire.'

'Yes. Just about.'

'What else do we know?'

'Well this is where it gets interesting.'

'Get on with it then, Sally. For God's sake. We've got a murder to investigate.'

'I know, sir.'

'Well?' added Roy.

Sally smiled. 'We did a missing-persons check for the area, going back nineteen to twenty-one years.'

'And?'

'And it seems that the Reverend Geoffrey Hunt's brother, Jeremy Hunt, went missing in that period.'

'And?'

'And he was never found, sir.'

44.

Bible Steve was floating in a sea of mist and fog.

He held his hands fanned in front of him, moving his arms in a slow breaststroke, but the milky light slipped between his fingers and he seemed hardly to be moving at all. His eyes were fogged with the stuff and it filled his lungs with a cold moistness. And then the mist thickened into a cloud and started sliding down his body. And a light overhead grew brighter and brighter. And his feet came forward, and the white stuff around him sank down around his ankles. And the light dazzled, reflecting off the cold steel in his hands, and the blood poured over his hands like hot soup.

Then he opened his eyes and screamed.

Patricia Hunt took the kettle off the stove and placed it carefully on the trivet beside it. Her hand throbbed a little, but she had been quick to run it under cold water, so that it hadn't blistered and worsened overnight.

She looked across at her husband, who was dressed in pyjamas and a dressing gown and was hanging up the phone.

'It was the police,' he said.

Patricia nodded without replying.

'They'll be here a little later. I had better get dressed.'

'Better had.'

'We have to be very sure of what we say, Patricia.'

'I know.'

'Everything's going to be all right.' He nodded reassuringly and then his whole body shook again as he coughed and fought for breath. He gestured to the dresser, and his wife hurried across to fetch his inhaler for him, shaking it vigorously. He took a quick breath and, after a few moments, squeezed it again and took a deeper breath.

'I really think we should go and see the doctor, Geoffrey.'

'And what will she tell us? There's nothing different. It's a cold. You have to wait it out, that's all.'

'Well, dress up warm!'

'Yes, dear,' he said, smiling, his breathing steady now, and kissed her on the forehead.

Detective Inspector Emma Halliday had only been in the job for a few months. As a detective, that is. She had been promoted from sergeant back at the tail end of summer. She was in her mid-thirties, six foot one in her flat feet, with short hair that she had recently dyed black to give her a little more gravitas. She had clearly defined cheekbones and a set of perfect teeth. Her nickname back at Paddington Green was 'Catwalk', but very few people called her that to her face.

Emma's father had been a policeman, and his father before him. Her twin brother had gone to university and studied textile design and was now successful, in a small way, in the fashion industry, with his own business just off Oxford Street. Emma had opted for Hendon, even though she had grades good enough to go to Oxford and read English, which is what her mother would have preferred. But Emma was always sure what she wanted to do, and that was to join the Metropolitan Police force. Sometimes, though, she regretted it.

She was waiting outside the morgue in the South Hampstead Hospital. Her young assistant, Constable Andrew Hoyland, shorter than her by a good few inches, with short-cropped ginger hair and a spray of freckles across his cheeks, was taking notes as she talked with the constable from the Transport Police and the A&E registrar.

'He was brought in at eight-thirty last night?'

The registrar, a short man in his early thirties, nodded. His hair was dark too, but, whereas Emma Halliday's was glossy and healthy, his was matted and dull and the bags under his eyes suggested he could do with a good night's sleep. 'That's correct. He died shortly afterwards. His injuries were massive. Nothing we could do.'

'And you still have no idea who he is?'

'There was no identification on him. Do you wish to come through?'

The doctor gestured towards the morgue, and Emma Halliday could see the colour draining from her younger assistant's face. 'Are you all right, Constable?' she asked.

'Yes, ma'am. I'll be fine.' He sounded as though, by stating the fact, he hoped it might be so.

'Goes with the territory, Andrew.'

'I know.'

'Can't say you ever really get used to it. But we have to deal with it.'

The temperature dropped considerably as they entered the morgue, and Emma was glad of it. She hoped her constable would be okay, but equally she hoped she would be herself. She had made the mistake of eating a full English breakfast that morning, and prayed she'd be able to keep it down. He had seen a fair few dead bodies over her years on the force, but had never seen one that had gone under a train.

The registrar crossed to one of the large steel drawers and pulled it smoothly out. She looked over at DI Emma Halliday, who took a deep breath and nodded. The doctor pulled back the cloth covering the top part of the dead man's body. His head had been smashed on one side, but not so badly on the other side. He looked like a man wearing a particularly gruesome horror-mask. The Phantom of the Opera without his face-covering.

It was enough for Detective Inspector Halliday. She nodded to the registrar and he slid the drawer smoothly back into place.

'His belongings are over here.'

The small man led the detective over to a side-table where the man's shoes and clothes and belongings had been put in individual, clear bags. Emma picked up one of them.

'Eight hundred and fifty in cash. Lot of money to be carrying around.'

'Yes,' agreed her constable. 'And in just a plain brown envelope?'

'Yes,' answered the registrar.

'And just this card?' asked Emma Halliday as she put down one bag and lifted another.

'Just that, yes.'

Emma looked at the card in the bag. It was larger than a standard playing card. Rectangular, about six inches by four inches. The picture depicted the Angel Gabriel playing a trumpet from which hung the St George's Cross flag. Underneath him was a group of people – men, women and children who were standing in graves and looking up at him in awe. In the background was a towering ocean, a tidal wave.

'What is this?' the detective said, to no one in particular.

'It's a tarot card,' replied the registrar. 'Judgement.'

45.

Sergeant 'Slimline' Dave Matthews, on guard duty, stood with Laura Chilvers outside the intensive-care room where Bible Steve was being attended to. Laura had little make-up on, as usual, but this morning she didn't look radiant. Her eyes were red and there were the first signs of bags under her eyes. Matthews took a swig of water from the clear plastic cup he was carrying and looked over at her.

'Did you get much sleep last night?' he asked.

'Not much, why?'

'You look like shit, Doctor.'

'Yeah, thanks for that, Slimline.'

The sergeant smiled cheerily. 'Just saying.'

'Well, don't!'

He gestured towards the window. Bible Steve was under the covers with his arms outside. His head was back on the pillow and he was snoring loudly.

'Looks like he's getting plenty of sleep.'

Laura nodded.

'That's a good sign, I guess.'

'I suppose it is.'

'Means he's alive at least.'

Laura Chilvers nodded again.

Dr Lily Crabbe came out of the room. 'Sorry to keep you waiting.'

'How is he doing?' asked Laura.

'He's been sedated. We'd rather not do it, but his body needs to repair itself and sleep is the best mechanism for that sometimes.'

'Why was he sedated?' asked Laura.

'He woke up screaming this morning. Talking gibberish and wouldn't settle. We didn't have any choice. He looked like he might become violent. It took a couple of nurses to hold him down, or he might have injured himself or one of my staff.'

'Does he remember anything?' asked Laura.

'He remembers being here. He remembers being on the streets. The snow. Being cold.'

'Is that it?'

'Yes.'

Sergeant Matthews looked down at the sleeping man. 'How long will this amnesia last?'

'It really depends on what caused it in the first place. You tell me that he has had this condition for a number of years?'

'As far as we can tell, yes.'

'Well his situation has certainly changed. He doesn't remember the name Steve, or Bible Steve. But that is the name you say he has been giving for himself.'

'Yes,' agreed the sergeant. 'It's the one he responds to.'

'Not any more.'

'Is there anything that can be done, Doctor?'

The woman ran her hand through her hair. 'It depends what caused it and what type of amnesia he is suffering from.'

'There are different types?'

'Yes, Dave. There are,' Laura answered for the registrar. 'Short-term memory loss which means anterograde. That concerns recent memories only. Then there is retrograde amnesia, which means whole chunks of your life can disappear, even your identity. And it can be caused by all kinds of things: stress, physical or mental trauma.'

'What do you think caused the problem?'

'In the first place?'

'I guess so. A blow to the head?'

'Maybe. Like I said, there are all kind of causes. I'm not a neurologist,' said Dr Crabbe. 'But yes, a physical trauma is often the cause. Or a big emotional upset. Many people on the streets are ex-military. Mental illness brought on by post-traumatic stress disorder.'

'Do you think he is ex-military, Doctor?'

'I have no idea. Surely that would be more in your line?'

'He can take care of himself, from what I have heard.'

'Not very well, Sergeant.'

'Can you tell us what caused his head injuries, at least?'

'It was definitely a blow. And, looking at the bruises on his body, quite possibly a long, blunt instrument. Not metal, probably wood.'

'Something like a baseball bat?' asked Slimline Matthews.

'Possibly. Like I say, these areas are more in your line.'

The sergeant gazed down at Bible Steve. 'Looks

like somebody really wanted to hurt him.'

'If you ask me, Sergeant,' said the registrar, 'somebody tried to kill him.

And Bible Steve sat bolt upright in bed.

46

Snowflakes were dancing in the air again. A slight drift had accumulated at the base of Geoffrey Hunt's writing cabin, covering once more the path he had cleared so carefully.

Inside their kitchen Patricia Hunt's hand trembled as she poured some tea into a cup. DC Sally Cartwright noticed the bandage on her hand and wrist and went across to help.

'Why don't you let me do that?'

The older woman smiled gratefully. 'Thank you, dear.'

'Have you hurt your hand?'

'She scalded it yesterday,' said her husband, then blew his nose into a large white handkerchief. 'Refuses to see her doctor.'

'You should,' said Jack Delaney. 'I hear she is a very nice woman.'

'You know Dr Walker?' asked Patricia.

'I should do. She's having my child.'

'Oh. Well, congratulations!'

'Thank you.'

'The detective is a very lucky man,' said Sally Cartwright and handed him a cup of tea.

'We need to talk to you, Reverend Hunt, about

224

St Luke's,' said Delaney.

'I'm afraid I don't have much to do with the church any more, Detective. Not for some years.'

'You do know the church has been sold to a property developer?'

Geoffrey hesitated and blinked.

'Yes, we do know that. Don't we, dear?' said his wife.

'Yes, sorry. Of course we did. My memory. Not what it was.'

'That's okay, Reverend.'

'But I don't understand. What has that to do with us?'

'A body was discovered in the grounds.'

'Well there has been a cemetery in the grounds since the church was built.'

'It wasn't in the cemetery part.'

'Oh?'

'I still don't see what this has to do with us, Detective,' said Patricia Hunt.

'We don't know who the man is. Trying to get a lead on him. We're just making enquiries really.' Delaney smiled reassuringly.

'We heard about it on the radio,' said Patricia. 'We would of course have phoned if we thought we could help in any way.'

'As far as our forensic pathologist can tell, the body has been there for some twenty years. About the time the church was under your care, Reverend.'

Geoffrey Hunt took a hit on his inhaler, his breathing wet and ragged. 'I retired twenty years ago. Have you spoken to my successor?'

'Not as yet. He is in Africa on missionary work at present. We've left him a message.'

'He may . . .' The older man struggled to get the words out. 'He may be able to help. Maybe he knows something . . .' He trailed off, wheezing.

'Are you all right, dear?' Patricia crossed to his side and held him as Geoffrey's eyes rolled back and he collapsed in his chair. 'Help me,' she shouted to Delaney, who rushed over to catch her husband.

Sally pulled out her mobile and punched in the number nine three times.

'I need an ambulance quickly,' she said.

Bible Steve stood in the gents' bathroom, horrified at the sight of the man looking back at him from the mirror. His whole body was trembling, and tears had formed in the corner of his eyes. He turned both taps on and looked down at his shaking hands as he put them under the jets of water. The water turned pink for a moment, then clear as he rubbed harder as if to scour the skin from them.

He splashed water onto his face and through his hair. Making fists of his hands and rubbing the corner of his eyes. He opened his eyes again and leaned in closer to the mirror.

'Who are you?' he whispered. 'Who the fuck are you?'

He held his hands under the water again and then cried out as it burned his hand.

Dave Matthews came running into the room, closely followed by Laura Chilvers. 'What's happened?' he asked.

'It's hot,' said Bible Steve.

'Here,' said Laura, taking his hand, running the cold water and putting his hand under it. After a while, she dried off his hand with a paper towel and looked at it. 'You'll be okay, I'll get the nurse to put some cream on it.'

'What happened to me?' said Bible Steve.

'You scalded your hand, Steve,' replied Dave Matthews.

'That's not my name. I'm not called Steve. And I don't mean the water.'

'You need to get back into bed.' Laura took his arm and led him out of the room into the ward corridor.

Bible Steve walked docilely along, no fight in him. 'How did I get so old?' he asked.

Laura shrugged sympathetically. 'Can you remember anything at all about what happened last night?'

Bible shook his head, confused, and looked down at his hands again as they arrived back at his room. 'My skin is parchment, isn't it?' he said.

'I'm sorry.'

'How charged with punishments the scroll!' he continued.

'What are you on about, Bible?' asked Sergeant Matthews.

'The spirit is weak, so the flesh must be punished, and here that punishment is recorded.' He held up his hands, forming them into fists. 'The body is a canvas and pain is the paint with which God marks us.'

Dave Matthews held his hands up. 'Okay, Bible. Let's not do any decorating here.'

The confused man lowered his hands, looked at

227

Laura, then back at the sergeant. 'I do remember one thing,' he said, tears forming in his eyes again.

Laura put her hand on his arm. 'What?'

'A death.' He almost whispered the word.

'What do you mean?'

Tears streamed from the homeless man's eyes now. 'I murdered a young woman.' He looked down at his bunched fists again. 'I can still see her blood.'

Sergeant Matthews would have pressed him but the registrar came bustling up to them, a nurse in tow and a serious expression on her face.

'Okay. That's quite enough, Sergeant. You're upsetting him.'

'He's just confessed to a murder.'

'He is tired and confused. Your questions will have to wait and we need to do some blood tests.'

'Hold on just a minute,' said Dave Matthews. 'I need to speak to him.'

'Then you need to speak to him later.'

'It's important.'

'He's in no state to be questioned right now. That's a medical . . . and a legal opinion.' She looked over at Laura, who nodded.

'I'm not talking about a formal interview. We just want to talk.'

'Then you can do it a little later. Come on, sir. Let's get you back to bed.'

She led Bible Steve back into his room. Sergeant Matthews swore mildly under his breath. 'What the hell's going on here, Laura?'

Laura Chilvers shook her head, her eyes troubled. 'I don't know.'

'Are you all right?'

'Yes, of course I am!' she snapped back.

Dave Matthews looked down at the hand she was rubbing nervously, unaware that she was doing it.

'How did you hurt your hand?'

'I did something really stupid.'

'What?'

'I don't know.'

47

The briefing room was about half-full. Uniforms and CID, some sitting, some standing. Most with cups of coffee. The windows were steaming up, but through them you could see the snow falling in earnest. Delaney wiped his hand on the window, peering out to see a white layer covering his Saab. Maybe it was time to get a new car. As a detective inspector he was entitled to have replaced it years ago. And with a baby on the way, maybe he should. An estate maybe. Kate would probably approve of a Volvo, something dependable, reliable, safe. Words not usually associated with him. He smiled at the thought, and realised that Diane Campbell had just said something to him.

She half-sat on the desk behind her, a pint-sized mug of tea held in her petite hand.

'Sorry, what's that?' he asked.

'I said, is something amusing you, Detective?'

'Life, boss. Sometimes just looking out of the window, seeing the city stretching out in all directions. The millions of people. Some of them loving. Some of them just living. The hate, the poverty, the dirt. And then days like today with the snow falling, covering up all the dirt. Makes you wish it could do the same for the pain and hurt that human beings visit on each other on an hourly basis. But you know nothing can. You have to either smile or cry.'

'Yes, thank you, Brendan Behan. But back in the real world of the Metropolitan Police, what can you tell us about the John Doe we dug up in Queen's Park yesterday morning?'

'Not a lot more, ma'am. The lab will run a DNA analysis, but that will take a while. Likewise dental records. We're checking the missing-persons lists for the area, going back to the time we estimate he was buried there.'

'Any hits?'

'The vicar at the time, Geoffrey Hunt. His brother went missing about the same time. A little while later, the reverend's brother called to say he was okay, apparently.'

'You think the brother might be the John Doe?'

'It's possible. But I also think he might know what happened to the John Doe. Could be he had a reason for disappearing.'

'A reason like murder, you mean.'

'Someone put a hole in the man's head and tried to make sure the body was never discovered.'

'If those workmen hadn't been digging that trench, it probably never would have been,' said Diane Campbell.

'Exactly. I get the sense that there was something the retired vicar wasn't telling us.'

'You think he knows where his brother is?'

'Maybe.'

'Can you not lean on him?'

'He's in hospital, ma'am,' answered Sally Cartwright.

Diane looked over at Delaney. 'Jesus, Jack! Don't tell me—'

'Of course not,' Delaney said. 'He's an old man. He's sick. He just collapsed is all.'

'I've seen your bad-cop routine, Jack.'

Delaney held up his hands. 'I swear. Just asked him a couple of questions is all. I'll go and see him later when he's fit to question.'

'Where is he?'

'The South Hampstead.'

'Talking of which, what's the update on Bible Steve, Slimline?'

Dave Matthews shrugged his broad shoulders. 'He's still there. Out of intensive care now, but not in good shape.'

'What about his mental state?'

'In some senses worse. He doesn't even recognise the name Bible Steve any more and has no memory of being on the streets.'

Diane nodded. 'Paddington Green are not treating the Chinese woman's death as suspicious. The coroner said she died from a heart attack. She had a long history of heart problems, apparently. It could have been triggered by finding Bible. Or it could have happened any time, according to the coroner. The cold didn't help.'

'Looks like the poor old sod was attacked, though, guv.'

'Go on?'

Laura answered for him. 'The X-rays show he was hit with something. Something long and round-shaped.'

'A baseball bat?'

'Could be.'

'But it was definitely a deliberate attack. He's lucky to be alive,' added the sergeant.

'Random?'

'We've spoken to the homeless unit. No other reports of recent tramp bashing.'

'We prefer the term "homeless", Slimline.'

'But there's another problem.'

'Go on.'

'Bible Steve tells us he saw a murder the other night. A young woman. Early twenties. Blonde. Blood everywhere.'

'Where?'

'He doesn't remember.'

'And can he describe the attacker?'

'Perfectly.'

Dr Laura Chilvers uncrossed her arms. 'We think he is suffering from some kind of psychotic episode. The blows to the head, his earlier fall. Some kind of fugue, delusional fantasies.'

'What's the neurologist say?'

'They're running tests.'

'There's been no report of any young woman being murdered?'

'No, boss,' said Sergeant Matthews.

'Doesn't mean it hasn't happened.'

'It's a possibility.'

'Highly unlikely!' added Laura.

'So he can give us a good description of who this possible murderer is.'

'He said he did it himself, ma'am. He claims he killed the young woman.'

'You're not telling me you're taking him seriously?'

'I don't know.'

'This is Bible Steve we're talking about.'

'He says he killed someone. Maybe he didn't. Maybe he saw something, though.'

'Maybe.'

'He does seem different as well,' said the sergeant. 'Not like his old self at all. A different person somehow. Not just the amnesia. In a funny way he seemed more together.'

'He was just more sober,' said Laura. 'It won't last.'

'Best get a wriggle on then. Because he might have imagined or dreamed or hallucinated something last night. But someone beating him up with a baseball bat isn't a delusional fantasy, is it?'

'No.'

'Then we had better look into it.'

'Ma'am.'

Diane nodded at Dr Chilvers. 'And I don't need to remind you that if Bible Steve left here last night with a serious head injury, and you allowed his discharge without picking up on it, there could be serious consequences.'

'I'm pretty sure . . .'

Diane held a hand up to interrupt her and turned to Delaney. 'This is one for CID,' she said. 'The other case has been waiting for twenty years. I want you to get back on this, Jack. You're going to the hospital anyway.'

'Sure.'

'As Laura says, it sounds highly unlikely. I don't have Bible Steve down as a psychotic murderer. But we can't afford to ignore it and he might well have seen something.'

'I'll get on it,' said Delaney.

'I'll come with you,' said Laura.

'Kate, see if you can chase up the reverend's brother meanwhile as you know the family. What's the brother's name?'

Kate consulted her notebook. 'Jeremy Hunt, Diane. Reverend Jeremy Hunt, I should say. Runs in the family.'

There was a knock on the door and DI Tony Hamilton walked in followed by DI Emma Halliday.

'Hello, ma'am. Sorry to interrupt,' said DI Hamilton.

'That's okay, Tony. We're wrapped up here.' She gestured for the team to get on. 'So what can I do for you?'

'Like to have a word with Inspector Delaney.'

'Be my guest.' Diane left, followed by the rest of the team.

'What's going on, Tony?' asked Delaney.

'Not entirely sure.' Hamilton waited for the room to clear then closed the door on the three of them.

'Bit of a puzzle,' Emma Halliday agreed.

'Bit out of your bailiwick, aren't you, Catwalk?'

'Not really. They are going to combine White City here with Paddington Green next month apparently.'

'Why?'

'Cutbacks, Jack. Streamlining of management and operational infrastructure. Just the beginning, I'd say.'

'Be about right. What does Napier say?'

Emma grinned. 'Don't know, but if it means a sideways move for him, he'll not be happy.'

'That's something then,' said Delaney, finishing his coffee. 'So what's the puzzle that brings the Met's best and beautiful over to see little old me?'

Emma reached into the black leather bag she had slung over her shoulder and placed an evidence bag on the table.

'What's that?'

'It's a tarot card. Major Arcana.'

Delaney picked it up. A man dressed in medieval garb, hung by his one foot from a T-shaped tree. Red hose, blue jerkin and a yellow corona around his head.

'The Hanged Man,' said DI Hamilton.

'I'm Irish, not a gypsy. What's this got to do with me?'

'The card was found on a man who suicided a year ago. Jumped under a train at Piccadilly Circus station. Took a while to track him down. His name was Andrew Johnson. Came from a town called Lavenham in Suffolk. He was the landlord of a small pub called *The Crawfish* there.'

'Go on.'

'He was visiting London on business, he made the trip several times a year. In his suitcase we found women's clothing. We thought he was a transvestite. But there was also a pair of torn knickers, with semen stains, some blood and pubic hair. Male and female.'

'And?'

'Turned out the semen was his, as was the male pubic hair,' continued DI Halliday. 'The blood and the other pubic hair was from an as-yet-unidentified female.'

'So we have a suicide. And some stained underwear and a mystic tarot card, on the person of a pub landlord from Lavenham in Suffolk.'

'Except maybe it wasn't suicide,' said DI Hamilton.

'You have my attention,' replied Delaney.

'Last night,' continued Emma Halliday, 'another man jumped under a train. This time from the east-bound Bakerloo Line platform at Baker Street station.'

'More underwear in a briefcase?'

'No. But again no identification on him. And he was carrying an envelope with a lot of cash in it.'

'And something else,' said Tony, as the tall woman handed another evidence card to Delaney.

'Another tarot card.'

'This one is called Judgement,' said Emma.

'Does that have any special significance?'

'It might do, especially if he didn't jump.'

'He was pushed, you mean?'

'No witnesses said they saw him being pushed. But one of the people on the platform beside him thought they heard a sound before he went under the train.'

Delaney met her level gaze. 'There's something you're not telling me.'

'The sound she described sounded a lot like a static electric buzz.'

'He was tasered, you're saying?'

'You catch on fast.'

'I'm a detective inspector. It goes with my pay grade. And what's the rest of it?'

'The face was pretty smashed in,' said DI Halliday.

Delaney grimaced.

'But something about him . . .' She gestured with her hand. 'I got the pathologist to run a check for burn marks.'

'Evidence of a Taser?'

'Yep, hand held, close range. Enough volts to make him jump involuntarily.'

'Police-issue kind of Taser,' Emma Halliday added.

'So this guy who jumped in front of the Bakerloo Line train. We know who he is?'

'We do now. What I could see of his face looked kind of familiar. I ran some fingerprints. And bingo bongo!' replied Emma.

'So the question we need to ask you, Jack . . .'

'Yes?'

'Is where were you at eight-thirty last night?'

'Are you tugging on my lariat?'

'Sorry, cowboy,' said Emma with a wink. 'But I hear nowadays you're a married man, good as. So where were you?'

'Who's the John Doe.'

'Michael Robinson, Jack.'

'Ah.'

'Indeed.'

'So, anything you want to tell us?'

Delaney shrugged. 'It's four days to Christmas. I haven't done any shopping. I've got a tree to buy, a house to decorate. An unsolved murder to investigate, another possible murder. It's dark and I'm wearing sunglasses. Now tell me, who do you love?'

Emma smiled and Delaney smiled back at her. 'Got to love you, Jack.'

'Where were you, cowboy?' asked Hamilton. 'Just for the record.'

Delaney leaned in and whispered in Catwalk Halliday's ear. The female DI raised an eyebrow.

'You are fricking kidding me!' she said.

Delaney gestured apologetically with his hands and Emma smiled again.

'Everything they say about you is true, isn't it?'

'I guess it is.'

'Like I say, got to love you, Jack!'

'Anyone want to let me in on the secret?' said DI Tony Hamilton.

48.

Sally Cartwright flicked the windscreen wipers to full speed. The snow was really coming down in earnest now and the traffic was crawling through London.

'You reckon this snow is going to last until Christmas, boss?' she asked Delaney.

Delaney peered out at Edgware Road station, people bundled up and coming out of the entrance. The shopping spree still in full swing.

'You done all your Christmas shopping, Sally?' he asked, ignoring her question.

'Two weeks ago, sir. Presents wrapped, cards all sent.'

'What a surprise.'

'I take it you are not entirely finished?'

'I haven't even started. But yeah, I hope it does last for Christmas.'

'Turning into an old romantic?'

'Less of the old. And no. I meant for Siobhan's sake. Christmas, it's for kids, isn't it?'

'And big kids, sir. You're not fooling anyone.'

'I wouldn't be so sure of that.'

'What did Catwalk and Tony Hamilton want with you?'

'Some developments in the Michael Robinson case.'

'What kind of developments?'

'Someone pushed him under the eight-thirty to Elephant and Castle last night.'

'Bloody hell! Is he dead?'

'Let's just say he didn't need to buy a return ticket to Harrow-on-the-Hill.'

'Bloody hell,' she said again, quieter this time. 'So why the both of them? And why not just call you?'

'It was in the way of an official enquiry. They wanted to know where I was at the time.'

'Well, I can't say I'm unhappy that he's dead. What did you tell them?'

'That I had an alibi.'

'And do you?'

'Sally, I am shocked that you could even ask that question,' he said, shaking his head in mock-sadness.

'So have they got any leads on who did it?'

'They think we've got us a serial killer. There was a tarot card found in his pocket. A year or so ago another man was under a train with a tarot card from the same deck.'

'How do they know it's the same deck?'

'I meant the same style of deck. Apparently there are hundreds of different decks, different designs. These two were from the same series.'

'Who was the first guy?'

'Chap called Andrew Johnson. A publican from a quaint rural town called Lavenham, in the heart of Suffolk.'

'Any connection between them?'

'Not sure. But according to Tony Blue-Eyes, he used to live in Harrow before moving to Suffolk.'

'They knew each other?'

'Maybe.'

'Somebody knew them both.'

'Certainly looks that way.'

Sally Cartwright flicked her indicator down and turned left into the grounds of the hospital. It was an imposing Victorian building, much of the architecture as it originally was, with some modern wings and extensions added. She parked the car and placed the 'Police on call' sign on the dashboard.

She looked across as Laura Chilvers pulled her car into the adjoining slot. 'What do you make of Dr Chilvers?' she asked Delaney.

Delaney winked at her. 'I don't go for blondes,' he said.

'Yeah, funny, sir.'

'What's on your mind?'

'I don't know. There's something odd about her lately.'

'She's a lesbian, Sally. Maybe she fancies you.'

Delaney got out of the car before she could reply, and walked towards the entrance.

49.

Mrs Johnson looked down at the man who had his head placed between her legs. He was a twenty-four-year-old called Simon, who worked in the bar for her. He worked in the bedroom for her too.

She moaned and tangled her fingers in his hair, pressing his head down harder on her sex.

'That's it, work that tongue, boy. Do a good job of it and I might let you fuck me.'

She smiled as she saw his bare buttocks buck slightly on the mattress. If he came before she did, it wouldn't be the first time, but she'd keep him down until the job was done. She had had a variety of young lovers over the year since her husband had died, and regretted not starting a lot sooner. The truth was, she was never much interested in sex before his death. He was a boring man in life, and never more so than in the bedroom, where he would roll on top of her like a beached seal and, after a few cursory pumps with his small member, would reach a climax and flop back over again. In all the years since they had been married she hadn't orgasmed even once. Now she insisted on it every time. Two or three times a day.

She lay back and smiled as the boy beneath her

moaned with pleasure himself as he lapped at her like a large dog at his water bowl.

And then the phone rang.

Bible Steve was dressed in a hospital gown. Blood was dripping slightly from his arm where he had ripped the IV tube loose, and the young female nurse blocking his way to the hospital exit was holding her arms up trying to placate him.

'Please, sir. You can't leave.'

'I'm no sir,' he bellowed back at her. 'Look at me. Look at these hands.'

He held his weather-beaten, scarred and sore hands palm upwards.

'These are not the hands of a sir. They are the hands of a bum. Of a tramp. And there is blood on them. Macbeth blood. They will not be washed clean.'

'You need treatment.'

'I need scourging. I need fire. Most of all . . . I need whisky!' He brushed her aside and stumbled up to the door, where Delaney held out his hand and put it on his chest.

'Hold your horses, Bible.'

'Stop calling me that. You think if you keep calling me Bible or Steve, it will make me believe it's who I am.'

'And who are you?'

'I'm just a man in need of a drink!'

He moved to skirt around Delaney, but the DI held his hands wide.

'You need to stay here,' added Laura. 'They are doing some tests. They can help you.'

'No one can help me.'

'The thing is, we need to talk to you. You made some claims this morning,' said Delaney.

'I can't remember,' he said and stumbled past him to Laura, holding his hands out to her. 'Give me money, so I can get some hot tea and a sandwich.'

'They can give that to you here.'

Bible Steve shook his head angrily. 'I need a drink.'

'For God's sake, man. Do you want to kill yourself?' asked Laura.

The bearded man looked at her sadly for a moment. 'I must have wanted to, mustn't I? Whoever I was, that's what I've been doing.'

He turned away and then started coughing, his body shaking violently. Then Bible Steve dropped to his knees and vomited. Spattering the clean and shiny floor with bile and bright blood. Laura rushed over to him and Delaney handed her a handkerchief.

'Is he all right?'

'No, he's not.'

A few minutes later and Bible Steve was back in the intensive-care room. He watched passively as drips were once more attached to his arm, monitoring devices attached to his chest. There was no fight in him and his eyes were scared.

The registrar, Dr Lily Crabbe, came back out of the room.

'We've given him some more sedation.'

'Vomiting blood. That's quite serious, isn't it?' asked Delaney.

'It can be. We won't know till we get his blood-work back.'

'Coughing blood can mean an internal injury,' said

Laura Chilvers, looking worried. 'Something he got as a consequence of the beating he received?'

The registrar shrugged – not disinterested, just tired. 'It could also mean he has been vomiting heavily recently. Given his condition, it is not an unlikely situation. That can lead to tears in the oesophagus – the throat,' she added unnecessarily for Delaney's benefit.

'But it could be from the beating?' Laura pressed on, chewing nervously on the corner of her thumbnail. She realised what she was doing and thrust her hands into her pockets.

'It could be from many things.'

'Fair enough,' said Delaney. 'But we do need to talk to him urgently.'

'Might I ask why you people are taking so much interest in this particular homeless man? I don't mean to be rude, but from my experience such people are not usually high on the priority list of the Metropolitan Police,' said Dr Crabbe.

'That's not true,' said Delaney. 'But as it happens, this particular homeless man may be the victim of an attempted homicide.'

'Homeless people get beaten up all the time.'

'And this one may have seen a murder. Or may have committed one himself.'

'What do you mean?'

'He confessed earlier.'

'He was rambling, confused. I think he has been suffering from some kind of psychotic fugue, perhaps brought on by the attack. Or exacerbated by it,' said Laura.

'I guess we'll have to find out, then,' said Jack Delaney.

50

Kate Walker sat at her desk, her laptop computer open in front of her. She should have been responding to about fifty emails that had built up in the day she had been away from the police surgeon's office. She should have been . . . but wasn't.

She was looking to find something to buy Jack Delaney for Christmas. Their first Christmas together. They had gone shopping for presents for Siobhan and he had been as happy as she had ever seen him. Not that she had known him that long. Not even nine months, for goodness' sake, and here she was living with the man, bringing up his daughter as though her own. And a child they were having together being carried inside her. She didn't know yet whether it was a boy or a girl, and neither she nor Jack wanted to find out. She figured he would probably like a son. Replace the son that he thought was his when his first wife died. Died when Jack intervened in an armed robbery at a petrol station in Pinner Green. One of the masked men had blasted a shotgun towards him, only it had hit his car instead, critically injuring his wife who was in the passenger seat. She had died later in hospital and they were unable to save the unborn son she was carrying inside her.

Delaney had been devastated, had gone on a four-year binge of self-destruction. Wallowing in alcohol and violence. Functioning as a cop, but only just. When a friend of his, an Irish prostitute called Jackie Malone, had been killed in an attempt to stop the exposure of an organised paedophile ring, it had thrown Jack and Kate together. In more ways than one. Her own uncle, a high-ranking police officer, had been involved in the ring. Luring runaway children off the streets of London under cover of offering protection, whereas in fact the children were being taken to a large house near Henley-on-Thames, where they were subjected to horrific abuse, filmed and in some cases murdered. Jackie Malone's nephew had been used by Kate's uncle as bait on the streets and, as far as she was concerned, ex Chief Superintendent Walker could rot in hell. He was never going to see the outside world again, that much was for sure. She had given him a knife scar on his right cheek after he tried coming to her room late at night one last time. If she had been able, she would have taken his head off with it from the neck.

So she and Jack had both been in dark places when they met; she could never have thought they would get together in a million years – but they had, and now they weren't in those dark places any more. She guessed that's how it happens sometimes. She ran a hand over her stomach and smiled sadly. She kind of hoped it would be a boy too. The truth was that the unborn baby that Jack Delaney's wife had been carrying when she died wasn't his. She didn't have the heart to tell him, when she had accidentally discovered the fact. And she didn't have the heart to tell him now, either.

She looked at the Amazon gift page she was browsing and then closed it with a sigh. She was already carrying the best present she could give him, he always said. But she'd think of something!

Her phone went and she snatched it off her desk. 'Dr Kate Walker.'

The voice on the other end was male. He was speaking quietly. 'Hey Kate, it's Ben Fielding.'

Kate nodded and pushed some papers around, looking for a pen. 'What have you got for me, Ben?'

'The blood-work and sample analysis back on your mysterious woman.'

'And?'

'No semen. No blood. No foreign pubic hairs. Some evidence of lubricant.'

'Consistent with a condom?'

'No. Too much for that.'

'Okay.'

'Her blood had a cocktail of drugs showing in it, and her alcohol levels were very high for the morning after. I'll email you the report. But you didn't get anything from me.'

'Of course not. Goes without saying.'

'But I'm not at all surprised this lady didn't remember anything of what happened. It'd be amazing if she did.'

'Thanks again, Ben. I owe you one.'

'No, you don't, we're quits.'

Kate sat at her desk for a moment or two, pondering the implications after she had hung up her phone. And then moved her thumb on the touchpad of her laptop to bring up her mailbox, to see if the reports were there. They weren't yet, but another message had come in. She read the subject line and clicked it it to open.

Then she took out her mobile and hit a speed-dial button. The phone was answered after a couple of rings.

'Hey, gorgeous, I was just thinking about you.'

'Getting all hot and bothered, were you,' Delaney replied on the other end of the line, lowering his voice and putting on the brogue.

'Always. But I was thinking of what I should get you for Christmas.'

'Why don't I take you down to Agent Provocateur in Broadwick Street? I'll help you pick something out for me.'

'I don't think stockings and suspenders would be a good look for you.'

Delaney laughed. 'I wasn't planning on wearing them myself.'

'So, you still at the hospital?'

'Just grabbing a coffee. Both witnesses are unavailable for comment right now. Hope to speak to Bible Steve soon. He had a bit of a turn.'

'Well I just heard back from the World Peace Mission. Seems Geoffrey's brother, Jeremy Hunt, was a missionary with them. Also a reverend with the Church of England, but peripatetic as it were, overseas.'

'Go on.'

'The World Peace Mission is tracking down his medical records. Not easy from twenty years ago, if you think that he was in Africa at the time and the Internet wasn't anything like as accessible as it is today.'

'When will we get them?'

'This afternoon, they promised.'

'Good work.'

'I do my best.'

'And you do it very prettily.'

'Now that wouldn't be a sexist remark, would it, Jack?'

'It's a statement of fact, Doctor. My job, after all, is sifting the facts from the fiction.'

'And you do it very handsomely.'

'I do my best.'

'So are you just going to hang around until you're allowed in to speak to the witnesses?'

'I'm going to speak to the reverend's wife. See if she has anything to add.'

'Send her my regards.'

'Will do.'

'And be gentle with her, she's an old lady.'

'This is an old murder.'

'True. But Patricia Hunt is no murderer.'

'Everybody has secrets, Kate.'

'Part of your job is wheedling them out?'

'Yup.'

Kate ran her hand, slightly guiltily, over her stomach. 'You just take care of yourself, is all.'

'Hey, I'm always careful out there. Bye, darling, catch you later.'

'Bye, honey.'

Kate hung up and looked down at her stomach. 'Because he has to take care of us too, doesn't he? He has to take care of all of us,' she said in a soothing voice.

An incoming message beeped on her computer and

Kate pulled up the report just in from Ben Fielding.

She scanned it briefly, raising an eyebrow. If Laura Chilvers had been seeking oblivion that night, she had certainly gone about it the right way. Traces of enough drugs in her system to sedate an elephant. Unless someone had planted them in her drinks, of course.

She moved the cursor and clicked on the print icon.

51

DI Tony Hamilton looked over at the tall woman who was driving. It was an estimated two-and-a-bit-hour drive to Lavenham in Suffolk from White City, but DI Emma Halliday had her foot down hard on the accelerator. They had been going for an hour or so and were at Bishop's Stortford, about to leave the M11 and head towards Sudbury. The roads had been pretty clear out of central London, and even the North Circular had been remarkably hold-up-free. The heavier snowfalls expected in the capital had probably put most people off. Tony Hamilton didn't blame them. Traffic in London was like one of the seven circles of Hell at the best of times; add a snow blizzard to the mix, and he'd count himself out soon enough. The only trouble was he couldn't. The call comes and London's finest have to answer, even if it does mean driving through several counties to get there. There were flurries of snow and the clouds overhead seemed to be thickening, but Emma had driven fast and controlled; he was impressed.

The DI noticed that he was looking at her, with a small smile on his face.

'Spit it out, Detective. You got something to say?'

'Just having a little sexist thought.'

'You better not have been looking at my legs.'

DI Hamilton on reflex looked down at her very long trousered legs and then back up at her. 'Actually I was just admiring your driving skills and was admonishing myself for being surprised.'

'I surprise a lot of people with a lot of things.'

'I'm sure you do, Catwalk.'

'Yeah, Detective Inspector Halliday will do just fine thank you!'

'Hamilton and Halliday. Has a nice ring to it, don't you think?'

'No.'

'I could see it on the TV. After *Eastenders* . . . stay tuned for Hamilton and Halliday. They kick butt, but boy do they look good!'

Emma looked over at him, smiling despite herself. 'Got tickets on yourself, haven't you?'

'Is that what you think?'

'What I think is that you should let me concentrate on the driving.'

'Just trying to pass the time with some witty conversation.'

'Well you're failing. Stick the radio on.'

DI Hamilton leaned forward and pushed the button on the dashboard. A smooth announcer's voice was reading the news.

'. . . *Superintendent Napier of White City Police Station and the Metropolitan Police has today confirmed that the body recovered from under the carriages of an east-bound Bakerloo Line train was indeed that of Michael Robinson. Mister Robinson had earlier that morning walked free from the Old Bailey after several charges of rape and aggravated sexual assault and grievous bodily harm were dropped against him. The chief witness for the prosecution, who was the alleged victim of the vicious assault, herself sensationally claimed that she was shown a photograph of Michael Robinson before the formal identification parade.'*

Tony moved his hand to change the channel, but Emma flicked it away.

'The person who showed her the photo,' the announcer continued, *'was Detective Inspector Jack Delaney, she claimed. This claim is under internal investigation but it has also emerged that Michael Robinson had served a civil lawsuit on Inspector Delaney on the very morning he was released. DI Delaney has not been available for comment but Superintendent George Napier has confirmed that at this moment they are treating Michael Robinson's death as suspicious. In other news Cheryl Cole has reportedly . . .'*

Emma switched off the announcer in mid-speech. 'That sounds to me like wolves gathering, don't you think, Tony? Smelling blood.'

'Yeah I'd say so. Jumping Jack Flash better be watching his back.'

'To think a few months ago he was the poster-boy for the Met.'

'Tall poppy syndrome. The real English vice.'

'And Jack Delaney is Irish.'

'Black-as-bog Irish.'

'Just as well he's got us on his side, then.'

'Let's hope so. I can see heads rolling over this.'

Emma nodded and pressed down harder on the accelerator pedal.

Delaney walked into the family area of the intensive-care unit. It was as depressing a place as they always were in hospitals around the country. National Health hospitals, at least. Some gestures towards comfort but the effect was mainly utilitarian. An industrial-style maroon carpet on the floor. Modern wooden tables with a few magazines scattered on them. Blue moulded furniture with hard-wearing fabric on it, formed into benches and individual chairs. A cold water dispenser in the corner. The light overhead too bright. A mixture of hope and despair hung in the air in these sorts of rooms in hospitals throughout the country. Throughout the world.

Patricia Hunt was seated in the middle of the long blue bench opposite the door Delaney had just walked through. Her head was down, lost in the kind of thoughts that Delaney didn't have to imagine. He knew only too well what they were. He presumed she had her faith to find some comfort. The last time he himself had prayed was when his wife was fighting a losing battle for her life in a hospital theatre not so very many miles away. He wasn't sure if he was praying to a Catholic God. Over the years he had lost a sense of who he was in that regard. He was praying to the Catholic God or the Protestant or the Hebrew (even though it was supposedly the same thing), or to the Hindu God or to whatever power it was that created and shaped the universe. He prayed that that was the case and that this was not just some random chaos. So that someone might listen, might change the terrible course of events which were heading full speed to a tragic conclusion. But the words he mumbled in his head over and over again were Catholic ones. Drummed into him by rote as a schoolboy and altar boy back in Ballydehob. The words came as easily as breathing.

Pater noster, qui es in caelis, sanctificetur nomen tuum. Adveniat regnum tuum. Fiat voluntas tua, sicut in caelo et in terra. Panem nostrum quotidianum da nobis hodie, et dimitte nobis debita nostra sicut et nos dimittimus debitoribus nostris.

But the Father in Heaven who was hallowed by name, had not forgiven Jack Delaney his trespasses. His wife and her unborn child had both died that night. And Delaney had not been led astray into temptation because of this. He had simply lost all will to resist it. Neither was he delivered from Evil, but was put in its path like a sun-stroke victim walking blindly into a herd of stampeding cattle. But he was here now and he was sane and, even though he had not prayed since that terrible night, he didn't look angrily at the trappings of religion, he didn't bridle at the sight of a dog collar and crucifix. And he didn't curse God and his actions every time he swallowed a glass of whiskey and ordered another.

'Can I fetch you a coffee or a cup of tea,' he asked simply.

Patricia Hunt looked up at him for a moment or two and blinked. 'No thank you,' she said. 'It's Inspector Delaney, isn't it?'

'Yes.'

'You're married to the lovely Dr Walker.'

'Not married. Living together.'

'With a child on the way.'

Delaney shrugged apologetically. 'Yes.'

'Please,' said Patricia Hunt. 'You get to my age and attitudes change. I'm not sure the expression "living in sin" applies any more. Living in love is far more important. *Amor Vincit Omnia*. Isn't that what they used to say?'

Delaney smiled. 'Not in Ballydehob.'

'Do you come with news of Geoffrey? How is he?' she asked anxiously.

'No news, I'm afraid. They're keeping a close eye on him.'

'It's my fault.'

'I'm sorry?'

'This cold weather, Inspector. Letting him out. Shovelling snow. He's not a well man, said the fresh air would do him good.'

'You mustn't blame yourself, Mrs Hunt.'

'You're a Catholic, or once were?'

Delaney nodded.

'Well then, you should be familiar with the concept?'

'I am. And it's not a helpful one. I know that from experience.'

'So how can I help you?'

'I need to ask you some questions about your husband's brother.'

'Is that really necessary right now?'

'As you know, a body was found in the church your husband used to be the vicar of. The victim was murdered and buried there, about the same time as your husband's brother went missing.'

'I really don't see the relevance. This has waited twenty years for your attention. Do you not think it could wait a little longer?'

258

'I know this is a difficult time for you, Mrs Hunt, but if you could tell me anything about the last time you saw or spoke to him.'

'Do you think it is him then, Inspector?'

'We're not ruling it out.'

'It can't be Jeremy.'

'You're sure?'

'I am not sure of anything any more, Inspector. As a young girl, and later as a lecturer in theology, I was pretty sure. Pretty sure about most things. Now that I am just a silly old woman, it is quite the opposite.'

'You have lost your faith?'

'Not in God. Never in him.'

'The Reverend Jeremy Hunt had been in Africa . . .?'

'Yes.'

'For how long?'

'Oh I am sure if you check his records, you'll see he had been over there for many, many years. He would pop back to England every so often. But rarely. More as a holiday. Taking care of affairs, that kind of thing.'

'What kind of affairs?'

'The usual. Banking, investments. Like I say, it was more of a holiday and he didn't ever stop long. We didn't see much of him.'

'Your husband had had a falling-out with him?'

'Not at all. Why do you ask that?'

'The way you say you didn't see much of him.'

'They are both busy men. And some families . . . well they are not all the same, are they, Inspector.'

'Certainly not.'

'Do you have any siblings?'

'I have a sister.'

'And do you see much of her?'

'Sadly not. She lives in America. In Pennsylvania.'

'Once a very religious part of the world.'

'Not these days. My sister's married to a cop. Seems he is kept pretty busy.'

'I can imagine.'

'So the last time you spoke to Jeremy . . .'

'He had come back from Africa. Twenty years ago. He had phoned us.'

'Did he speak to you or your husband?'

'He spoke to me, Inspector.'

'And what did he say?'

'Very little. He said he'd come to attend to some matters of pressing urgency and arranged to come to the vicarage for dinner a couple of nights later.'

'Did he say what the matters were?'

'No. But he did say that he had left the missionary society that he was working for.'

'Was that a surprise?'

'I really couldn't say, Detective. He didn't really say much.'

'Not even at dinner?'

'He never turned up, Inspector Delaney. And we never saw him again.'

'And you have no idea what happened to him?'

'One phone call, a message left on our answerphone to say he was fine and would be in touch. But that was the last we heard.'

'He just vanished?'

'We prayed every night for him. But, no. That was it. We never did find out what happened.'

Delaney made a note in his small, black notebook. 'Do you know if your husband's brother had any enemies, Mrs Hunt?'

'Enemies? What do you mean?'

'Anyone who may have wanted to do him harm?'

'No. Why would they?' She took a sip of water and blinked back some tears. 'Please, if there is nothing else. I am not up to this at the moment.'

'Of course.' Delaney closed his notebook and stood up. 'I'm sorry to have troubled you.'

'Inspector,' she said, as he walked over to the door. 'Don't give up on your prayers.'

52

Kate Walker approached Dave Matthews, who was back in his usual spot behind the desk.

'Doctor,' he said with a smile and a nod.

'Hello, Slimline,' Kate responded. 'Just to let you know I'm expecting a package couriered over to me sometime soon, I hope. Let me know when it gets here, will you?'

'Of course I will.'

Kate smiled, but made no attempt to move away.

'Was there anything else?'

Kate leaned on the desk, keeping her voice neutral, but low. 'Dr Laura Chilvers,' she said.

'Yes.'

'Friday night – how did she seem to you?'

The desk sergeant shrugged. 'Much as she ever is, I suppose.'

'I don't know,' said Kate. 'She seemed a bit . . . I'm not so sure. Can't put my finger on it.'

'She was in a hurry to get out. Some kind of date, I think. A club opening. She didn't say where. Why do you ask?'

'Because if she dropped the ball on Bible Steve, that could come back to bite the station. Particularly her.'

'He seemed all right to me.'

'And have you studied for seven years, and then worked in the field for years more, to make that kind of qualified judgement?' Kate asked, but not unkindly.

'Maybe not.' The sergeant smiled ruefully. 'But I've done over twenty years dealing with drunks.'

'The point is that Bible Steve, or whatever his name is, had a fall before he came in, didn't he?'

'He collapsed outside the restaurant. Not sure how.'

'As I understand it, he was found in a cruciform position?'

'Come again.'

Kate demonstrated. 'His feet together, his hands outstretched like this.'

'Yes, like that.'

'Which suggests to me that he toppled over backwards, his arms outstretched for balance. Rather than crumpling in on himself, to land in a kind of foetal position.'

'I guess so.'

'Which means that he could have slapped his head hard on the pavement when he fell. He could have suffered some kind of subdural haematoma.'

'Which means?'

'That we shouldn't have released him unless we were very sure he hadn't.'

'Laura Chilvers did ask if we could keep him in overnight.'

'Why?'

'Because of the cold, she said.'

'If she was worried that Bible Steve had suffered a

serious head injury then she should have called an ambulance.'

'Which she didn't.'

'No.'

'But yet she wanted you to keep him in, even though in your opinion he was fit to be released?'

'Yes, but you know what it is like on a Friday night here, Kate, at the best of times. Friday night a week before Christmas, it was like the biblical Bethlehem.'

'No room at the inn?'

'Exactly. And she knows that. I'm surprised she even asked. She knows we would have taken Bible to the homeless shelter anyway.'

'Not that he stayed there.'

'No.'

'What if we released him when we shouldn't, and he really did go out and murder someone?'

'If he has, then we're missing a corpse.'

'Maybe we should have kept him in?'

'If *if and ans*, as my granny used to say,' said the desk sergeant, '*were pots and pans*, we could set up a bloody department store.'

Kate chewed at her thumbnail. 'I don't know. Laura did seem distracted. She got that call, do you remember? Seemed very snappy after it. Not herself.'

'Like I say, Kate. It was a very busy night.'

'Too busy, it seems.'

'It's not going to get any quieter this side of the silly season,' said Matthews.

'Never does,' said Kate.

'Never does,' agreed the sergeant.

'I wonder who it was that called Laura,' said Kate,

not really intending to voice the thought to the large man behind the desk, but he answered it for her anyway.

'I guess only Dr Chilvers can tell you that.'

53

Delaney sat in his car with the engine running, an unlit cigarette between his lips as he looked out of the window.

The heavy precipitation promised by forecasters and amateur pundits all day was yet to materialise. Delaney watched the glistening snowflakes crystallising like pieces of coral fusing together on the ground. An ice carpet built up of millions and millions of flakes, no one of them alike, each unique and yet coming together.

Delaney wished he could manage that with the various elements of the cases he was working on. Fit the disparate particles together and make some sense.

Patricia Hunt had lied to him. He knew that much. Or if she had not lied exactly, had not told him the entire truth. A sin of omission rather than commission, as the brothers and sisters back at Ballydehob would have told him. The kind of brothers and sisters who don't tease you on your birthday or give you home-made Christmas presents. The kind of brothers and sisters who would put the fear of God in you and made sure it stayed there.

Delaney didn't read the Holy Book much any more. But what he did read, and could read very well, was people. Not just the old body-language trick of people looking up and to the left if they remembered something when asked a question, or up and to the right if they were making up the answer. No, Delaney knew intuitively. Maybe the story he had told his daughter Siobhan the other night was true, he thought to himself as he dragged his thumb across the wheel of his lighter, scratching against the flint and flaring it into flame. He lit his cigarette and took a drag. Not long to go to New Year's Eve and he was making a conscious effort to cut down. It wasn't so much Kate's wafting of her fingers when he came in from having one, or the fact he didn't want to smoke around his newborn baby when he or she was born. Well, perhaps it was. But it was mainly Siobhan's critical eyes that spurred him on. Family, he thought to himself, what a powerful thing it is. How it makes people and breaks people. Nearly broke him, and he wasn't going to let that happen again.

But what was happening in the Hunt family? Patricia Hunt was not being honest with him. And, in his experience, people who were not honest with the police usually had a very good reason not to be so.

Kate Walker fished the herbal teabag from the mug it had been sitting in, white china with the words 'I'd rather be in Ballydehob' written on the front. She had ordered it for Jack online, but somehow appropriated it for herself. Crystal Mountain organic Himalayan green tea. Blended with four botanical herbs, she discovered from the packet: peppermint, angelica, lemon verbena and ginseng. It was supposed to create a deliciously refreshing infusion that would awaken the mind and revitalise the body. Kate blew on the surface, took a cautious sip then added a squirt of honey from a squeezy bottle she kept on her desk. She liked the drink and found it worked for her. Maybe it was a combination of a sense of well-being from being pregnant and giving up the alcohol. Maybe it wasn't. One thing she did know for sure, though, was that it wasn't a few glasses of ice-chilled Marlborough Sauvignon Blanc after a hard day's work that she missed. It was the jolt in the morning that the espresso machine in her kitchen gave her. Coffee was her secret vice. In that respect, she empathised with Jack's senior boss Superintendent George Napier, if with little else. She took a sip of her tea and permitted herself a small smile. Actually she empathised with the man in one other major way. He had to deal with Detective Inspector Jack Delaney and that could drive any man, or woman, to stronger stimulants than freshly ground Jamaican Blue.

She pulled out the folder she had recently liberated from the courier's padded envelope and started reading the medical files on the missing man. The Reverend Jeremy Hunt. Last seen in the parish some twenty years previously. She pulled her notepad towards her and started to make notes, correcting herself as she did so. According to the conversation she had just had with Jack, he hadn't actually been seen twenty years ago. Just made a phone call and never turned up. Jack had put a call though to immigration to chase up entry and exit visas, but, as she well knew, the wheels of that particular bureaucratic engine could turn very slowly, and neither of them had access to the kind of grease required to speed up their progress. Kate made a few jottings as she turned the pages of the various reports and papers, not just Jeremy Hunt's medical record but his history of service through Africa in the Seventies onwards. Her cup of tea grew cool.

After a while, she picked up her phone and punched a speed-dial button.

'Hey, Jack,' she said as the call was answered. 'Whoever we dug up yesterday from St Luke's church . . .'

'Go on,' said the familiar voice.

'Are you smoking?'

'Never mind that.' Delaney adopted a professional tone that didn't fool Kate for one second. 'What do you want to tell me, Doctor Walker?'

'Well, *Detective Inspector Delaney*, I can tell you for a fact that whoever it was we dug up . . . it wasn't Jeremy Hunt!'

54

PC Danny Vine and PC Bob Wilkinson were out on foot and none too happy about it.

'Jeez, Bob,' said Danny. 'Why couldn't they give us a car? My plates are freezing here.'

'Feet are a part of the job. You know that, Danny.'

'I think I'm going to go into CID,' he continued as the two of them walked to the top end of Oxford Street. 'Yeah, lookit . . .'

Bob Wilkinson stopped and stared at him. 'Did you just say "lookit" to me?'

The younger constable shrugged. 'What about it?'

'I'll tell you what about it, Danny Vine. You ever use the expression, "lookit", "innit" or "knowwhatimean", and I will stamp on your size-ten plates of meat, and then you will really know what chilblains are.'

'You going racist on me, Bob?'

'I'll go racist with my asp up your arse in a minute.'

'Seriously though, why not?' Danny persisted as they passed the only pub genuinely to be found on Oxford Street, The Tottenham.

'Did you know, Danny, that in 1852 there were thirty-eight pubs in Oxford Street and now there is only one?' Bob jerked his thumb sideways as they passed it. 'Now, if that ain't a sign of the times, I don't know what is.'

'Seriously though, Bob, what do you reckon? Should I go for CID?'

'Get to work a bit closer with the lovely Sally Cartwright. Is that the idea?'

Danny Vine shook his head, a little flustered. 'No. Not at all.'

'You don't have to be coy with me, son. I've worn out enough shoe leather in this game to know a thing or two or the mating dance of the lesser spotted constable.'

They turned left at the intersection and walked up Tottenham Court Road. The snow underfoot had turned to mush although the temperature was definitely dropping again.

'Don't get me wrong, Bob. She's an attractive woman.'

'She's gorgeous. Clever. Personable,' Bob Wilkinson agreed. 'If I was sixty-eight years younger, I might be giving you a run for your money.'

'But she's made it quite clear she's not interested in me. Can't say I blame her after what happened.'

'The guy got what was coming to him, that's for sure.'

'Jack Delaney sure don't take no prisoners, does he?' said Danny.

'What's that supposed to mean?'

'First Michael Hill and now Michael Robinson. Both taken out. You've heard the gossip.'

'What, he don't like people with the name Michael?'

'Couldn't blame him if he did. I was just saying . . .'

271

'Well, don't.'

'Fair enough.'

'Seriously, Danny, DI Jack Delaney may have a lot of enemies on the force, but he's got a lot of friends too.'

'Yeah I know. Jeez, Bob! I didn't mean anything by anything.'

'Good. That's that then.'

'But CID, you know. People like Jack, they get to make a difference.'

'Sometimes.'

'That's what I want.'

'We make a difference too, lad.'

'What , out tramping in the cold and snow, homeless shelter after homeless shelter?'

'You think CID just sit around in warm pubs drinking mulled wine this time of year, and waiting for inspiration to strike?'

'Guinness maybe,' Danny laughed and held up his hand before Bob Wilkinson could reply. 'Joke, Bob. Joke.'

The constable shook his head. 'Well, you might just be right on that one.'

Five minutes later and they were in the offices of one of the many homeless shelters dotted around the capital. Not the one Bible Steve was usually taken to. That had been their first port of call. Then lots more.

The woman in charge of the centre was in her fifties, with a plump figure, thick dark hair and a sense of energy and enthusiasm that was a dramatic contrast to the hangdog attitude of Bob Wilkinson.

'So how can I help you, officers? My name is Marian Clark.'

'We're just constables, ma'am,' replied Wilkinson, although PC Danny Vine here has plans to become the next Commissioner.'

Marian Clark smiled at the young constable. 'Well, as the great man once said . . . you have to have a dream in the first place, for that dream to come true.'

'William Shakespeare?' asked Danny Vine.

'Oscar Hammerstein.'

'Oh,' said Danny. 'I've not read any of his books.'

'Anyway,' said Bob. 'We're trying to ascertain if a young woman has gone missing.'

'A runaway, you mean?'

'We're not sure. We have a confession to a murder that we are checking out.'

'It's probably a waste of time,' interrupted the younger constable. 'One of our regulars, Bible Steve. He's delusional, drinks a bit, lives rough, you know . . .'

Marian Clark's expression was replaced with something a lot less kind. 'Yes, this is a homeless centre, Constable. I think you will find we know exactly how it is.'

'Have any of your regulars not turned up for a day or two?' asked Bob Wilkinson.

'Sometimes we don't see them for days, particularly in the summer when it is hot outside, even through the night.'

Bob Wilkinson looked out of the small office's window. It was getting darker now as the clouds thickened even more ominously overhead and the snowflakes were falling more intensely.

'A young woman, you say?' The shelter manager picked up on the constable's unspoken point.

'Yes, early twenties maybe.'

'Child-like. Blonde-haired, blue-eyed. Delicate skin?'

Bob Wilkinson looked down at his notebook. 'Face like an angel.' He read out the quote.

'Oh my God,' said Marian Clark.

'You think you might know her,' asked Danny Vine.

'This man who says he murdered her . . .'

'Bible Steve,' answered PC Wilkinson.

'Is he much older than her? Grey matted hair, tall. Always quoting from the Bible or some such?'

'Hence the nickname.'

'She came in with him a few times. We don't have men here. I had to ask him to leave, and he became quite . . .'

'Violent?'

'Not violent as such. Abusive. He left with her.'

'When was this?'

'Friday afternoon.'

'And you haven't seen her since?'

The woman didn't reply, but PC Bob Wilkinson didn't have to be CID at any level to read the answer in her eyes. He pulled out his radio phone and thumbed the Call button.

'Foxtrot Alpha from Thirty-Two.'

55

Jack Delaney was sitting in the right-hand room of The Holly Bush pub in Hampstead.

Danny Vine would not have been at all surprised to learn that Jack was there with a drink in his hand. He might have been surprised at what he was drinking, though.

'What's that, sir?' asked DC Sally Cartwright as she perched herself on the stool alongside him. 'Bloody Mary?'

'Bloody half-a-chance would be a fine thing,' replied her boss with a grimace. 'Virgin Mary. All the goodness, apparently. None of the vice.'

'I'm sure the sisters would approve.'

'Not if they were drinking it.'

'So, no movement, then?'

'No, been stuck out here twiddling me thumbs watching the snow fall. Came in here for a bit of a warm.'

'Couldn't you have waited inside the hospital?'

'I hate hospitals, Sally. And I figured it wise to give White City a wide berth for a while.'

'Don't blame you, sir. The super is strutting up and down like a cock who's had his henhouse raided.'

'You got half that right. Anyway, I just took a call

from Diane. Seems like Bible Steve might not be quite so delusional after all.'

'Go on.'

'A young woman's gone missing off the streets. Pretty much matches Bible's description of the woman he claims to have murdered. Another homeless person been seen in his company a lot lately.'

'He might be telling the truth?'

'It's unusual, I grant you, but it wouldn't be the first time.'

'Jesus! I would never have had him down for that.'

'It happens. Who knows? Maybe God told him to do it.'

'Paranoid schizophrenics who kill sometimes do say they had God talking to them.'

'Or the Devil.'

'True. But Bible Steve isn't a paranoid schizophrenic, is he?'

Delaney shrugged. 'Seems to me that people sometimes get labelled properly after the event. After is usually much too late.'

'I still don't have him down as a murderer.'

'Maybe he saw someone else. Maybe there was a fight. Maybe he got in the way. A lot of maybes, I know. Time will tell, I guess. Meanwhile, what have you got for me?'

'I've been going through the records we got from Northwick Park Hospital the other night.'

'Going through it with Tony?'

'No, sir. On my own. DI Hamilton's headed up to Suffolk with DI Halliday.'

'Catwalk, eh?' Delaney raised his eyebrow, knowing it would annoy his young assistant.

'DI Emma Halliday, yes sir. I don't know why people have to belittle the woman's intelligence just because she is six feet tall.'

'She's over six feet tall and gorgeous, Sally.'

'Can you just get me one of those drinks please, sir,' she replied, not rising to the bait.

Delaney gestured to the barman and Sally opened the folder and flicked through a few pages.

A few possible women to talk to, nothing really obvious. They are all a bit vague as to how they got their injuries. Pointing more towards domestic abuse maybe, but not the sort of assault Michael Robinson made on Stephanie Hewson. But this one looks more promising, sir,' she said, removing a sheet or two of paper and closing the folder.

'Go on?'

'Her name is Lorraine Eddison. She's a thirty-three-year-old dental nurse. She lives and works in Harrow. She was assaulted four months after Michael Robinson was arrested and put on remand.'

She placed a photograph in front of her boss, taking the drink that had been put to one side for her.

'They look alike, don't they?'

'Not only do they look alike, sir. She claims she was mugged, resisted and the attacker cut her with a knife.'

'Where?'

'Down by where we parked the other day when we met DI Hamilton at The Castle pub.'

'I didn't mean where was she attacked, I mean where was she cut?'

'Sliced across the belly, sir, from behind. He had

hold of her round the neck and she struggled. So he cut her.'

'But no rape?'

'She says not, sir.'

'But she may not be telling the whole story.'

'Like you said.'

'I did. Where does she live?'

'The other side of the hill. Past the school and heading down to the main road that goes to Northwick Park. Maybe fifteen minutes' walk from where she was attacked.'

'What was she doing on the hill?'

'Had been meeting friends for a few drinks at The Castle. Someone's birthday celebration. It was a warm night. Thought she might as well walk.'

'Just like Stephanie Hewson. Maybe we should go and have a chat with her.'

'Now?'

'Not just yet. We'd better go and have another chat with Bible Steve first, don't you think?'

'Sir.'

DI Tony Hamilton held the door open leading into the lounge bar of The Crawfish pub open for his female colleague, who didn't seem impressed by the gesture.

'Save it for the uniform girls, Hamilton,' she said.

She walked past him and into the bar. The Crawfish was an old-fashioned country pub, L-shaped. Wooden beams, a wooden floor with rugs. A medium-sized bar at the top of the small part of the L, with a dining area to the left and snug bar in front. The snug had a large open fireplace with a firedog in the middle filled with flaming logs. The flames crackled and snapped as they walked past. There weren't many diners left but a few locals were dotted here and there, a couple playing dominoes, an elderly man sitting by the fireside, with a pile of scribbled receipts and notes that he was going through and entering into a notebook. The bar was L-shaped too and Tony and Emma walked up a small step and perched in the corner on a couple of bar stools.

There was one barman behind the bar. A man in his late twenties, called Lee, according to the name embroidered on his staff polo shirt. He was serving a couple of middle-aged Hooray Henrys. The Henry was in maroon-coloured corduroy trousers with a striped yellow shirt and tweed jacket, Henrietta in a pair of riding trousers a size too small for her and a white silk shirt. Apparently, the wine the barman offered to them wasn't to their liking. They were obliged to wait for a few minutes until, with a sniffy nod, they seemed pleased, if not delighted, with the best that was on offer.

Lee rang up their purchase on the till, then crossed to Tony and Emma. 'Sorry to keep you waiting. Will you be staying with us tonight?'

'No, that won't be necessary,' Emma Halliday said.

'Sorry. We're expecting a couple who booked in. Probably delayed by the snow.'

Emma nodded. She wasn't too surprised. The last leg of their journey had taken a lot longer than the first.

'It's getting a bit Winter Wonderland out there,' Tony agreed.

'Nightmare, more like,' said Emma.

'So what can I get you?' asked the barman. 'I'm afraid the kitchen is closed until six o'clock if you were looking to have something to eat.'

'We weren't,' said DI Halliday, flashing her warrant card. 'We're looking for the boss. Is she working?'

The barman pulled a face. 'You'll not find her this side of the bar. She'll be upstairs. Shall I go and tell her you're here?'

'Why don't you just take us up to see her?' said Emma with a smile.

'I don't think she'd like that, without being told.'

'Does that bother you unduly?'

The barman pretended to consider for a moment, then smiled himself. 'Not unduly,' he replied.

'Bingo bongo!' said DI Tony Hamilton, holding his hands wide as he and Emma got off their stools.

The barman led them through a pair of swing doors into a narrow hallway and up some stairs.

The landing above had a window at the far end and leaded lights, but it was dark outside now. Emma Halliday glanced at her watch and realised it wouldn't be getting any brighter.

The barman knocked on the door and opened it. A younger man rushed out, reddening a little as he mumbled an apology at DI Halliday, as she had to step swiftly aside, and hurried down the staircase.

'What is it?' Marjorie Johnson sounded less than happy with the disruption. She had a southern-counties accent.

'It's the police,' said the barman, showing the visitors into the room.

It was a large lounge with mullioned windows.

Expensively decorated. A polished wooden floor with hand-woven rugs on it. The mullioned windows looked over the street below. Overhead were ancient beams and there was another large, open fireplace. Logs were burning in the grate. A substantial antique red leather sofa stood next to a couple of matching club chairs. There was an eighteenth-century writing desk under the windows with a reading lamp on it and a tantalus, with the decanters full. A drinks cabinet was to the left of where DIs Hamilton and Halliday were standing.

Marjorie Johnson sat on the sofa. She was a large woman, with long blonde hair, expensively styled, held back in a black Alice band. She wore a low-cut, cream-coloured silk blouse and was clearly not afraid to show her cleavage and a hint of white lace beneath it. She had a black skirt, too short for Emma Halliday's taste, with a hint of lace on her stocking top. She wore high-heeled black shoes and had a cut-glass tumbler in her hand. She twirled the ice. It made a tinkling sound as she looked at Tony Hamilton appraisingly and then smiled, showing white, perfectly aligned, if slightly predatory-looking teeth.

'To what do I owe the pleasure, Detective Inspector?' She completely ignored Hamilton's female associate.

'We're here to talk about your husband, Mrs Johnson, said Emma.

She shot the DI a surly look. 'Can I offer you a drink, Detective?' Turning to DI Hamilton, she put the smile back in place.

'No thanks, we're on duty,' Emma answered for them both.

'Is that gin and tonic you're drinking?' asked Tony Hamilton.

'It certainly is. Tanqueray No. 10.'

'Excellent. I'll have one of those please.'

Marjorie Johnson stood up in one languid movement. She was nearly as tall as DI Halliday in her high-heeled shoes, but not quite.

Tony shrugged at his colleague. 'You wanted to drive,' he said with a grin.

'Sure I can't tempt you, Constable?' asked Marjorie Johnson over her shoulder.

'I'll just take a plain soda with ice, if you have such a thing. And it's Detective Inspector Emma Halliday.'

'DI Tony Hamilton,' said Tony, as he took the glass she offered him.

'Women are making great strides in business nowadays,' said Marjorie, as she squirted some soda from a Thirties-style soda siphon into a tall glass and added some ice.

'Yes. And we don't even have to burn our bras any more,' replied Emma, smiling sweetly.

'Just as well, in my case,' said the older woman, expanding her chest so that Tony Hamilton didn't miss her point.

'Need the support?' said Emma, keeping the smile hovering on her lips.

Marjorie Johnson laughed. 'No, dear, I was thinking more of the fire-hazard risks.'

She walked back to the sofa, swaying her broad hips like Mae West on steroids, and sat down. 'Please make yourself comfortable,' she said, gesturing to the two armchairs opposite.

Emma and Tony sat down. Emma put her glass,

untouched, on the sherry table beside her chair. Tony took a small sip of his. 'Very nice.'

'Not too weak?'

'No, it's certainly not that.'

'Do you think we could discuss your husband now, Mrs Johnson? We have driven a long way.'

'Yes, and in such awful conditions. I can't think what was so important. My husband has been dead for a year or so, you know.'

'I am sorry if this is painful for you,' replied DI Halliday without any hint of sarcasm in her voice. 'But there are some matters that have arisen.'

'What kind of matters?'

DI Hamilton reached into his coat pocket and handed a card over to Mrs Johnson. 'Does this mean anything to you?' he asked.

'It's a tarot card.'

'Yes.'

'Major Arcana.'

'You know about the tarot?' asked DI Hamilton, surprised.

'Oh yes, Inspector,' Marjorie said, giving the words a seductive lilt. 'I am very much in touch with my spiritual side. The Hanged Man, a significant symbol.'

'What sort of significance?' asked Emma Halliday.

'It is all down to interpretation, of course. The cards are like notes or chords in a piece of music. You need to put them together for a proper reading.'

'So what does this one mean?' prompted Hamilton.

'A good question.' She gave him a look a school-teacher might give a particularly bright pupil. 'A very good question.'

'Which is why I asked you what the significance is.' Emma could do little to hide her growing irritation with the woman.

'I am afraid I don't know, my dear. I have a lady come in and give readings once a month in the pub. It's quite an attraction. I like to have different special nights each week.'

'And what has any of this to do with your husband?' interrupted DI Halliday. 'Did he organise the tarot nights?'

'Goodness me no. Andrew never came up with any good ideas. I'm sorry, but I don't understand.' She held the card up. 'What has this got to do with Andrew?'

'We were hoping you might be able to tell us.'

'You have completely lost me.'

'The card was found on your dead husband's body when it was recovered, Mrs Johnson. It was in his pocket.'

'This one?'

'One like it. I bought another deck of cards,' explained Tony Hamilton.

'Did you not recover your husband's things?'

'They told me there was nothing of value on him. The clothes were obviously ruined. I just told them to dispose of them. His body was transported up here and it was cremated. I didn't look at him. I'm a bit squeamish about that kind of thing.'

'Did you love your husband, Mrs Johnson?' asked Emma.

'What on earth has that got to do with anything?'

'It's just you do seem, shall we say, a little dispassionate about all this.'

'It was over a year ago. My husband decided to jump in front of a train for whatever reason. Am I to wear sackcloth and ashes for the rest of my life?'

'Do you know of anyone who may have wanted to harm your husband?' DI Hamilton interjected, trying to calm the waters.

Marjorie Johnson looked at him, her smile gone and any hint of flirtation a distant memory. 'Okay, why don't you tell me what exactly is going on here?'

'We think your husband was murdered,' said Emma Halliday bluntly.

56.

Jack Delaney and Sally Cartwright were standing in the registrar's office, talking with her as she typed up some notes into her computer.

'He's okay to be interviewed now?'

The consultant stopped typing and swivelled her chair to face them. 'Yes. But try not to agitate him too much.'

'He still can't remember who assaulted him?' asked Sally Cartwright.

The petite woman shook her head. 'It's entirely possible he never will.'

'But he does have a clear idea of the woman he claims to have murdered?' asked Delaney.

'Do you know who she is?'

'Maybe.' Delaney read from his notebook. 'Early twenties, blonde hair, blue eyes, waif-like.'

Dr Lily Crabbe rose to her feet, picked her stethoscope up from her desk and swung it around her neck.

'A bit like her,' said DC Cartwright, holding out a photograph.

The registrar took it. 'Who is this?'

'A young homeless girl. She hasn't been seen at the shelter she normally uses. And the last time she was there, she was with Bible Steve. They don't take men at the hostel and so they left. She hasn't been seen since.'

'You don't think he really has killed her then?' said the registrar.

'Nothing much surprises me any more,' said Delaney. 'Not in this city.'

Bible Steve was sitting up in bed. His breathing was laboured but he seemed calmer. His eyes were still bloodshot. Tired and haunted.

Delaney sat on the chair next to him as DC Sally Cartwright and the registrar stood at the base of his bed.

'You were have been on the streets for a large number of years. When you first turned up in London, you were disorientated, confused. You didn't know who you were, or where you were. You had complete amnesia.'

Bible Steve nodded.

'You were brought into one of the shelters by the homeless unit. You couldn't remember your name, but they gave you one. Steven Collins. It's what you have been known by since. But on the street they call you Bible Steve.'

The man nodded again.

'Is it okay if I call you Steve?'

The older man shrugged wearily.

Delaney held up a picture of the young woman. 'This is Kathy Simmons. She is a homeless person like you. She is registered at the Saint Catherine's shelter in the West End. She has been in prison and on and off the streets since she was fifteen years old.'

Bible Steve looked at the picture but didn't say anything.

'You said earlier that you had killed someone. That you remembered it.'

Bible Steve blinked and gazed at Delaney. 'I can still see it. There are lights and she is lying there. Blonde hair, young. Too young to die and there is blood everywhere. My hands awash with it. And I am holding something in my hands.' His eyes started flicking nervously from side to side. 'She's dead. It's too late! You can't do anything. So much blood. I can hear her pleading, begging for help.' He squeezed his eyes shut. 'I should have died. What use am I? I'm an old, useless man. Coughing blood. I know what that means, I've seen it on the streets.'

'Is this the girl?' Delaney showed him the photo.

'It should have been me. It should have been me!'

Delaney held the photo closer. 'Is this the girl, Steve?'

The homeless man shook his head and whimpered.

'Open your eyes, please. Look at the photo.'

Bible Steve did so, but stared at the ceiling.

'Is this the woman, Steve?' Delaney asked again.

The homeless man finally looked at the photograph.

'No,' he said. 'No, it's not!' Then he leant across and vomited bright, red blood over Delaney's shoes.

57.

Detective Inspector Tony Hamilton sat happily on a stool tucked into the corner of the bar. He had a pint of Abbot in front of him, which the barmaid, who had just come on duty, cheerfully informed him was a very popular, Suffolk ale. He took an appreciative sip.

'Maybe I'll become a convert,' he said to the barmaid, a red-headed twenty-something-year-old with a blaze of curly hair and a spray of freckles across her nose. Her green eyes sparkled and she winked at the DI.

'Did I not tell you so?'

'With that accent and that colouring I am guessing you're not Welsh?' he replied.

The barmaid laughed. 'Not unless the Red Dragon invaded Cork in 1990 and someone forgot to tell me ma.'

'You a Cork lass, are you?'

'The city itself top of the bottle, as we call it.'

'I know a guy from there. He's a right miserable git sometimes.'

'Good-looking though, I'll bet.'

Tony flashed her a grin. 'Depends who else is in the room.'

'All the best-looking people come from Munster, you know.'

'That a fact?'

'Oh yeah. Born in the shadow of the Shandon Bell, me.'

'I guess that makes you an official corker?'

The red-haired woman laughed loudly. Emma Halliday came in, shaking the thick snow from her hair.

'Don't you ever give it a rest, Hamilton?'

'Use it or lose it, isn't that what they say? How did you get on?'

'Signal cut in and out, but they've closed the A134 and a lorry has jack-knifed on the M11 south-bound.'

DI Hamilton got serious quickly. 'Which means?'

'Which means you'd better order me a large glass of that mulled wine they've got sitting in the pot over there.'

Hamilton gestured to the barmaid. 'Can we get a large glass of mulled wine for Nanook here, please?'

'So this has been a wasted journey.' Emma Halliday sat on a stool next to him.

'I wouldn't go that far.'

'All we've learned is that Andrew Johnson didn't have any enemies, as far as his wife was concerned. He was a pillar of the local community. And she obviously hated his guts.'

'Enough to do something about it?'

'Her alibi checks out. I phoned the hospital where she was hosting a charity dinner. She was nowhere near London when Andrew Johnson did the hop, skip and a jump to Oblivion Central.'

'She could have contracted it out.'

'What's the motive? Not money. We already know that, the money in the relationship all came from her.'

'Maybe she was tired of bankrolling him.'

'There's something she's not telling us.'

DI Halliday picked up the glass of mulled wine that the barmaid had poured for her. 'What do I owe you?' she asked.

'I've started a tab,' said Tony Hamilton.

Jack Delaney sat staring at his laptop in the CID room back at White City Police Station. He sipped at his mug of tea. It was stone cold, but he drank some of it anyway.

DC Sally Cartwright came over, holding some pieces of paper.

'What have you got for me, Sally?'

'Someone who liked pretty young girls. School-girls. Fifteen years old. Susan Nixon and Caroline Lewis.'

'We've got names?'

'We have.'

'And who was it taking such a keen interest in them?'

'The Reverend Geoffrey Hunt.'

'The plot thickens.'

'The girls were part of a drama group attached to the church. They were in a play to be performed at Christmas in the Church Hall. Apparently the vicar didn't just get his own knickers in a twist.'

'He assaulted them?'

'Apparently.'

'And we know this, how?'

'The person who succeeded him in the vicarage. We finally tracked him down.'

'The other missionary?'

'That's him. Out in the People's Democratic Republic of the Congo.'

'So what did our missionary friend have to say?'

'At the time he was asked to take over, he remembered there was a bit of a scandal. The parents of the two girls had contacted the parish bishop making formal complaints about Reverend Hunt.'

'Were the complaints investigated? If the police were involved then we should have had records, and there weren't any. We checked.'

'I know we did. The complaints from the girls were dropped. No approaches to the police were made.'

'So what happened? Why the volte face?'

'It seems the complaints were dropped when Geoffrey Hunt agreed to retire. There could have been a lot more, of course. Girls, I mean. Some who didn't come forward.'

'And we still don't have a missing person, apart from the reverend's brother, and Forensics have confirmed that our John Doe in the shallow grave isn't him.'

'So where is he?'

'That might just be the question, Sally.' Jack Delaney stood up and put on his black leather jacket.

'You going to be warm enough in that, sir?' asked the young detective constable.

'What, are you my mother now?'

'Someone has to keep an eye on you.'

'Says who?'

'Says Kate Walker, sir.'

Delaney grunted and tossed her his car keys. 'You can drive.'

58

Danny Vine was off duty and heading down Edgware Road on his pushbike. The snow was driving into his face and he had to blink continually to see where he was going. There was still a solid gridlock of traffic running all the way from the Harrow Road onwards.

The recession might be continuing. But not on Oxford Street this Christmas. Danny was on his way to Selfridges. He wanted to buy something nice for Sally Cartwright. He didn't expect to get anything in return. He figured that boat had pretty much sailed. And he wasn't aboard. He didn't blame her for not wanting to strike up a work-based relationship after what had happened to her. If he'd had his way, he would have done exactly what Jack Delaney did to the creep who attacked Sally and wipe him off the face of the earth. But Delaney beat him to it. And you could see the gratitude in her eyes whenever Sally looked at him.

Danny darted in and out of the stationary cars, wishing he had half of the Irishman's luck. But the past was the past and, like his mother always said, sometimes you have to put the cork back in the bottle and forget about it. He had always assumed that the funny expressions she came up with were phrases lost in translation from her original Jamaican roots. Nowadays he was convinced that she just made them up. 'When the polar bear he shiver, then the whole world be cold,' was another one of hers. As Danny felt the snowflakes sticking to his cheeks, he reckoned she might be right. So he was going to Selfridges to buy a bottle of Sally's favourite perfume. It was going to cost him an arm and a leg but he figured she deserved it. A smile was good enough for him. He was picturing her face opening the present, when a woman ran straight out into the road and he crashed into her.

The woman collapsed to the floor and Danny Vine went sprawling across the bonnet of a stationary Volvo estate and smashed onto the pavement. Luckily he wasn't cycling anywhere near full pelt. He stood up painfully and the woman was already on her feet, and shouting in his face. She was tall, and was dressed in what looked like a real fur coat.

'I'm sorry, are you hurt?' he asked.

'Never mind me – that man's stolen my bag. Get him.' She spoke with a slight Scandinavian accent and was clearly used to getting her own way. She pointed to a man who was trying to make his escape down the street, his progress impeded by the multitude of Christmas shoppers.

'Okay, I am a policeman,' Danny said.

'Go and arrest him then!' said the woman, encouraging Vine on his way with a small shove as he mounted his bicycle.

Danny gradually picked up speed as he rode down the middle of the road, the traffic crawling in both directions on either side of him.

'Stop, police!' he called out.

The man, in his twenties dressed in a grey hoodie, filthy denim jeans and distinctive yellow running shoes, looked back over his shoulder and crashed into a group of middle-aged women, knocking one of them to the pavement.

PC Vine stood up on his pedals and pumped his legs.

The man ahead of him threw another backward glance at his pursuer and darted through the traffic across the road, turning right into Kendal Street. Danny jumped off his bike and followed him, threading his way through the cars which were picking up a bit of speed now that the bottle-jam at the Marble Arch end of the road had cleared.

As he turned the corner, Danny jumped back on his bike as the man turned left into Portsea Place, then left into a cul-de-sac.

As Danny swept into the cul-de-sac himself, the man was some thirty yards ahead, looking at the wall at the end of the street and wondering if he could make the climb. Suddenly he turned, and came charging back at Danny. Danny pedalled straight at him but, at that moment, a cat ran out and he swerved to avoid it, clipping the man as he went and knocking himself off balance to land in a pile of black bin bags. Danny took a moment or two to disentangle himself and cursed as he saw the man dashing out of the street. But he grinned when he noticed that the thief had dropped the bag he had stolen from the Scandinavian woman.

His grin disappeared, however, when Danny attempted to stand up and spotted the pale white arm he had uncovered. He moved the rubbish bags aside to reveal the young woman's body that the arm belonged to. Her skin was white with cold, the veins showing through its pearly translucence, the colour drained from her perfectly formed lips. Her eyes frosted, cold and immobile. The lashes brittle and her long blonde hair fanned out around the black bag beneath her, as though she were floating on some dark lake.

Danny Vine took a deep breath or two, checked for a pulse, even though he knew it was futile, then pulled out his mobile phone.

59.

Dr Kate Walker was back in her police surgeon's office at White City.

She tapped a pencil nervously on the desk as she sorted through the reports. Tap. Tap. Tap. Realising what she was doing, she put the pencil down, then snatched it up again and twirled it in her fingers. After a moment or two, she sighed and threw it to the back of her desk. Then she picked up a DVD and slid it into the player on the side of her laptop.

After a moment or two, the disc started playing. It was CCTV footage of the night when Bible Steve was brought into police reception, locked in a holding cell, to be later charged and released.

She fast-forwarded the footage to when he was first brought in, paused it and zoomed in on the man's face. His long hair obscured his forehead. She made a note on a pad by the laptop, confirming the time and noting there was no visible bruising to the man's head.

She zipped forward to footage of the custody cell and let the tape play, pushing the volume slider to maximum.

Bob Wilkinson opened the door and held it wide for Laura Chilvers to enter. 'All right, calm it down, Bible,' he said. 'You're not in Kansas now.'

Bible Steve stood up from the bench bed and, casting his eyes heavenwards and spreading his arms wide, shouted, 'It is God who arms me with strength and makes my way perfect. He makes my feet like the feet of a deer; he enables me to stand on the heights. He trains my hands for battle; my arms can bend a bow of bronze. You give me your shield of victory, and your right hand sustains me; you stoop down to make me great. You broaden the path beneath me, so that my ankles do not turn.'

Lowering his arms he looked at the doctor, then squinted his eyes and pointed at her. 'I know this harlot!'

'No you don't, Bible. She just moved down here.'

'She is a Jezebel! Satan's spawn.' He continued to point, saliva running into his beard.

'She's a police surgeon from Reading,' said PC Bob Wilkinson.

'I think you must be mistaking me for someone else,' said Laura Chilvers and smiled at him.

The drunken man clasped his hands over his ears. 'That voice,' he said, almost reverentially. 'Are you my angel?'

'No, like the constable said. 'I'm just a police surgeon.'

He opened his raw eyes and looked at her, tears welling up now. 'Are you my guardian angel?'

'I'm nobody's angel!' she said. 'He's still drunk, Sergeant. Get him some tea and I'll check back later.'

'What about . . .' the sergeant started to ask her, but Laura was already . . .

Kate paused the tape at that point and picked up the pencil again, tapping it on the desk top. She took a sip of her tea. Kate had a gut feeling that the supposed remedy the ancient herbs claimed to supply would do nothing to help. She moved the tape on to later that same evening when Bible Steve was brought from his cell.

'I'm out of here, Sergeant.'
  'Just take a minute. The cells are full back there.'
  'Are you going to charge him?'
  'You bet! I want him charged and out of here as soon as.'
  Laura's nostrils quivered. 'I can see why.'
  Bible Steve looked up at her. 'I am here, you know!'
  'No doubting of that, Mr Bible.'
  'What are you going to charge me with?'
  'Putting people off their sweet-and-sour pork balls,' said Dave Matthews and Laura laughed.

Kate forwarded the tape again.

Laura gestured for the constable to bring him to her office. As they walked towards it, Bible Steve turned and looked at her.
  'I know you,' he said.
  'No, you don't.'
  Bible Steve looked across at the constable. 'She interfered with me, the last time I was here.'

'*She wasn't even here the last time you were brought in, Steve.*'

'*Interfered, I tell you!*'

Kate stopped the tape once more and fast-forwarded to the CCTV footage from Laura's office. Glad that all areas had to be covered now.

Laura shook her head and took her hands out of his. 'No. Like I said. I met you earlier, on the street, and when you were in the cell. You were drunk. You still are.'

'*No. I know you! You are my angel. My guardian Angela!*'

He reached out for her and Laura stepped back, her eyes wide with horror.

Kate rewound the tape and played it again, focusing on Laura's expression. She paused it again and then wrote on her pad: *She knows him. What's their relationship?*

There was a knock on the door and Diane Campbell stuck her head round.

'How's it going, Kate?'

'Just doing the report on Bible Steve.'

'Are we in the clear?'

Kate hesitated before answering, then gave her a quick smile. 'I think so. There doesn't seem to be any bruising to his head while he was in custody. It looks like all the damage was done after he was released.'

'We've just had a call in. The body of a woman matching the description Bible Steve gave us has been found.'

'She's dead?'

'A couple of days, according to Derek Bowman.'

'Who is she?'

'We don't know yet.'

'Cause of death?'

'She was beaten. We know that much. Will learn more when he has done the post, I guess.'

'What kind of beating?'

'A long thin object.'

'Like Bible Steve?'

'Could be. Bowlalong wasn't specific. I'm heading to the morgue now. Want to tag along?'

Kate looked at the frozen image of Laura Chilvers and closed the laptop. 'Yeah,' she said, standing up and putting on her coat. 'Maybe whoever beat Bible Steve also battered this woman to death. Maybe Bible saw it. That's what he remembers.'

'He said he did it himself, though. Blood on his hands.'

'Maybe it was the woman who hit him. Defending herself against him, maybe?'

'Maybe.' Diane Campbell opened the door and they walked through reception towards the front doors, waving at Dave Matthews who was behind the desk talking to a couple of uniforms. 'What's the update on Bible?' she asked.

'They're operating on him shortly. He has bleeding varices, torn blood vessels in his stomach. It's why he was throwing up so much blood earlier.'

'These torn varices. Were they the result of the beating he was given?' asked Diane as they walked into the car park.

'More likely a result of his alcoholism.'

'Is he going to be all right?'

'I don't know, the poor guy is in a pretty terrible state.'

'This *poor guy* might just have beaten a twenty-three-year-old girl to death, let's not forget that.'

'I think he's mixing things up in his head. I'm pretty sure there is something going on we don't know about.'

'That's for damn sure,' Diane agreed. 'We'll take my car.'

60.

Patricia Hunt stood by the window overlooking the car park of the South Hampstead Hospital. It was full. Some of the cars had a couple of inches of snow on their roofs and some didn't. Still hot from the journey in, she guessed. She looked up at the dark sky. Soon the whole city would be covered in a white shroud.

She sat down next to her husband. His breathing was laboured and he had an oxygen mask attached to his mouth. His eyelids were closed but the eyes beneath them moved from side to side, and his body twitched every now and then, like a cat might when dreaming.

In the corridor a team of nurses and a porter wheeled a hospital bed down towards the operating theatre. Drips attached to the patient, and monitoring devices. He had long unruly hair and a bearded face.

Patricia Hunt made the sign of the cross on her forehead and chest and mumbled a prayer.

'God save us,' she said. 'God save us all.'

She picked up the leatherbound notebook she had brought from her husband's office in the garden, and started reading.

Zambia, borders of Namibia. 1989.

The missionary knelt on the floor of his hut. He ran a finger under his dog collar to loosen it slightly. It was just past dawn, but the light was brightening and the heat was building. It was a simple room. Wooden floor and walls with a pitch roof. The wood had been stained and varnished. He knelt on a simple rug. A single bed lay beside the side window. Netting covered the windows casting a mottled pattern on the floorboards. He had a plain desk and chair opposite the door that led into his hut, and a washstand with a bowl and jug on it. There was a large ceiling fan overhead that, had it worked, might have brought some relief from the growing heat. A heat that would bake the ground even harder by midday. Even at that early hour, it was enough to force beads of sweat on the missionary's brow, which he mopped with a large, cotton handkercief. Moisture from the night still hung in the air and it reminded him of the time he visited the Butterfly House in Kew Gardens. He mopped his brow once more and tried to shake the memory away.

He looked up at the simple crucifix hanging on the wall and made a sign of the cross.

'Oh Lord,' he said. 'I know I am a sinner, and I know I am not worthy. But make me strong in your service. Make me strong in my faith. Make of my weak body a weapon to fight evil on your behalf. Make of my weak mind a chalice for the purity of your love. Make my heart strong so that I might bring that strength to the weak who falter on the path of righteousness; succour them, Lord, and guide them to your glory.'

And then the screaming began.

The sound of running feet. Shots firing from automatic rifles. The whop-whop-whop of rotor blades as a helicopter came in to land. Shattering the peace of that humid dawn in the way that only man and natural catastrophes can.

The missionary threw his handkerchief to the floor and staggered outside into the village.

White men in black combat gear with no insignia, and black scarves wrapped round their lower faces, were shouting at the terrified villagers who were scattering before the automatic fire of the invaders which mowed them down.

A scream came from the church to the reverend's left. It was built of plain varnished wood, just like the reverend's hut, only some twenty times bigger with a tall cross mounted on the apex of the roof above the entrance doors. Entrance doors that stood open.

The missionary ran towards the steps leading up into the church, glad he wasn't hampered by his service vestments. He was wearing Chinos with a pale blue shirt and a dog collar. The back of his shirt was dark with sweat as he rushed into the building.

At the far end of the aisle his assistant, a young Zambian woman, stood with three young girls whose eyes were wide with horror, as they looked at the man with the automatic rifle pointed straight at them. Another man, thick-set with iron-grey hair, shifted the upturned altar to reveal a plate cover set into the ground. He opened it and brought out a small, white canvas sack.

'Stay back, Padre,' said the man holding the assault weapon.

'What are you people doing here? This is a simple mission. What harm can we do you?'

'A simple mission,' said the one holding the sack, hefting it in his hands. 'Then perhaps you could explain this.'

'I've no idea what it is.'

'It's diamonds, Meneer,' said the thick-set man. 'Diamonds to fund your so-called bloody People's Liberation Army. Diamonds stolen from the mines of South Africa by nigger-loving liberals to send bombs and death to the rightful owners of this land.'

'I know nothing of this.'

'White men!' He took off his bandana and spat on the ground. 'White men fornicating with kaffirs. Lying down like beasts of the field with the black animals.'

The man had an iron-grey beard and moustache to match his hair. There was fury in his eyes. 'Well, white men bleed,' he continued. 'Just as much as the black monkey. White men feel pain and white men talk when hot coals are held to their skin, and their genitals, and their eyes.' He smiled like a wolf baring its yellow teeth and weighed the sack of stones in his hand. 'And white men confess,' he said.

The missionary stepped in front of the children, making an extra human shield of himself.

'You have got what you have come for. Leave now. I will see no harm come to these children.'

'You have prayed to a higher power, Reverend,' said the grey-haired soldier and raised his pistol. 'And he has failed to listen to your supplication.'

Then he pulled the trigger, the bullet punching a hole into the reverend's chest, sending him flying backwards.

*

Bible Steve was staring upwards at the ceiling.

The surgical registrar, Dr Lily Crabbe, was gowned and ready as her anaesthetist brought the gas trolley over to the gurney. 'We're going to try and help you now,' she said.

'I don't want help. I want to die,' he replied.

The registrar didn't respond. She was all too aware that the homeless man might very well have his wish granted.

The anaesthetist lowered the mask over the bearded man's mouth. 'Count backwards from ten,' he said.

Bible Steve didn't respond, keeping his blood-shot eyes open. After a few seconds, though, they fluttered and closed. When the anaesthetist took the mask away he was already unconscious.

It was as dark as midnight outside now. The snow showed no sign of stopping. The traffic crept along the Harrow Road and the windscreen wipers of Delaney's old Saab had fallen into a slow, steady rhythm. An almost hypnotic sound, and, given the fact that Delaney had cranked the heating to as high as it would go, Sally was feeling sleepy.

Delaney's phone trilled in his pocket, waking Sally out of her trance, and she leaned forward concentrating on the road ahead.

'Hi darling,' said Delaney. 'What's new in Glockemorra?' He listened for a while. 'Okay, honey, keep me posted.'

DC Cartwright looked over at him. 'Bob Wilkinson?' she asked.

'Sure if you make me laugh much more today I swear my funny bone will fall out of my body, Sally.'

'Kate, I take it.'

'She's on her way to the morgue'

'What's the squeal?'

'You've been reading too many American detective novels, Constable.'

'No time to read, sir. Catching up on Sky Atlantic.'

'Well, the squeal is that someone matching the description of the woman Bible Steve says he killed has turned up. Died on Friday night according to Dr Bowlalong Bowman's best guess.'

'And Bible Steve?'

'Being operated on.'

'So we have two dead bodies. One male from twenty years ago. And one young female, recent. And the two people who might be able to tell us something about them are both in hospital and unable to speak. They don't make it easy for us, do they, boss?'

'Didn't they teach you that in Hendon?'

'Everything I learnt as a detective I learnt from you, boss.'

'God help us all then,' said Delaney.

'Exactly.'

Sally swung the wheel and parked outside a medium-sized detached house in Pinner. The driveway and pavement had been cleared. A man in his late forties was making a snowman in the middle of the left-hand lawn.

He raised a hand in greeting as Delaney and Sally Cartwright walked up to his house.

'Caroline is inside, Detectives,' he said. 'But I don't

know why you couldn't have a meeting at the school.'

'I'm sorry?' asked Sally.

The front door opened and a woman in her mid-thirties appeared. She was of medium height with a curvy figure and shiny, coppery hair. She had bright-red lipstick and long eyelashes. She reminded Delaney of somebody but he couldn't place her.

'Because the school is closed, darling, you know that.'

'Well, next term then, you bring enough work home with you as it is.'

The woman smiled at Delaney. 'Ignore him, Inspector, he's just a grouch.'

'I'm only saying . . .' said her husband.

'Well, don't, just keep at it. I want that snowman built before Natasha comes home!'

'Yes, darling,' said her husband, with a dispirited grin and picked up another handful of snow.

Inside the house Delaney and Sally sat in the lounge on a large, white leather sofa. It was a comfortably cluttered room. A boudoir grand piano had a bunch of family photos on top of it. Mainly of a young girl whom Delaney presumed was Caroline Lewis' daughter. She certainly had the same lustrous hair and easy smile.

Except Caroline Lewis wasn't smiling now. 'Are you sure I can't get you anything – tea, coffee?' she asked.

'We're fine, thanks. And sorry to disturb you on a Sunday evening. But it is urgent. A body has been discovered in the grounds of your old church.'

'What's that got to do with me?'

'We don't know. Maybe nothing.'

'It was all so long ago.'

'Twenty years ago.'

'Yes.'

'About the same time, a man was shot in the head and buried in the grounds of the church.'

'Like I say, that has nothing to do with us. With what happened.'

'What did happen?' asked Sally.

'Does it matter now? No charges were brought. We made a mistake.'

'Reverend Hunt is an old man now,' said Sally. 'He is very ill and in hospital. He can't hurt you now.'

'He never did.'

'Are you saying you made it up? He never touched you or Susan Nixon?'

Caroline Lewis reddened. 'I never said he actually touched us.'

'What did happen then, Caroline?' pressed Sally Cartwright.

'We were both in a play the church was putting on that Christmas. Part of the celebrations for the week.'

'Go on.'

'It was a play he had written. Kind of a religious pantomime, I suppose. The girls were dressed as Herod's serving women. I played Salome.'

'And he made you take off your seven veils?'

'No. Not in the play at least.'

'But when you were alone.'

'Not really. It wasn't like that.'

'What was it like?'

'He had put a clothes rail up and hung blankets to make a changing area for us girls. There was a gap and he would peek through when we were changing.'

'And you reported him.'

'The other girls didn't know. But Susan caught him one day. It was just the two of us. He was touching himself.'

'And your parents put a stop to it?'

'No. It was all Susan's idea. She said he could continue but he had to do it in front of us. And pay us. We were fifteen. We thought it was funny. He gave us fifty quid each.'

'How many times?'

'Six or seven. Susan's parents found her money and all hell broke loose. But you can't tell anyone about this. I'm a school teacher.'

'He was still to blame, Caroline. You were fifteen years old.'

'I know. We weren't exactly virgins, though. But I can't have my husband knowing. The man was sick. A Peeping Tom. But we shouldn't have done what we did.'

'Like I say, he's guilty under the law. I can't make you bring charges,' said Delaney.

'It's too late. What good would it do anyway? Susan and I will never say anything in court. You can understand why.'

'How many others were there, though?' asked Sally. 'How many other children did he peep on, abuse, maybe assault?'

'We were nearly sixteen, Detective Constable. We weren't children.'

'Yes, you were,' said Delaney.

'You said he was very ill?'

'He is.'

'Then maybe he is being punished. Maybe it's enough.'

'Maybe somebody didn't agree with you, Caroline. Maybe somebody at the time wanted to punish him more. Someone whose body we may just have found in his back yard.'

'I can't tell you that, Detective. All I can say is that I have forgiven him, and that I have forgiven myself too. 'Sometimes that's all you can do.'

Delaney looked at her for a moment. 'Sometimes,' he said. Sometimes we can do a little more.'

The woman would have responded, but at that moment her husband came into the room.

'Darling, you haven't even offered the officers a cup of tea.'

'I did do, darling, but they are just leaving.'

'That was quick. Did you get everything sorted?'

Caroline looked over at him and smiled. 'Yes, I think we know where we all stand now.'

'So you'll be giving a talk to the school next term, Inspector?' her husband asked.

Caroline looked at Delaney, her eyes pleading with him. Delaney smiled. 'Something along those lines. Thank you. I think we have all we needed here.'

'Excellent, excellent. Well why don't you come along and have a look at Sammy?'

'Sammy?' asked DC Cartwright.

'Sammy the snowman. I just need a carrot to finish him off.'

He hurried out of the room as Sally and Delaney stood up.

'Let's just hope it's for his nose,' Delaney muttered to Sally.

313

61

Detective Inspector Emma 'Catwalk' Halliday wasn't exactly drunk, but she wasn't exactly sober either.

She was on her third medium-sized glass of wine. Sauvignon Blanc, after declaring her mulled wine undrinkable. Tony Hamilton was on his second pint of Abbot, but had barely touched it.

'I don't know how you can drink that stuff,' said Emma.

'It's natural. Nutritional, no chemicals added, just barley, hops and water.'

'Still tastes like pond water.'

Hamilton laughed. 'Maybe it's an acquired taste. Some things are.'

'Are you hitting on me, Tony?'

'No. Sorry – don't do the work/personal thing. Gets too messy.'

Emma Halliday raised her eyebrows. Not sure if she was relieved or offended. 'I wasn't saying I wanted you to, Tony.'

'That's okay then.'

'Yes.'

'What about you?'

'What about me?'

'You ever had a relationship with a fellow officer?'

'Once.'

'Didn't work out?'

'In some ways I thought it would be easier. At least he'd understand the job. The hours. The stress.'

'There is that, I suppose.'

'But we never got to see each other. Different shifts. Different shouts.'

'Shame.'

'Well, I'm a big girl I guess.'

'You certainly are that!'

Emma gave him a flat gaze and finished her glass of wine as the barmaid came past.

'Can I have a word with you' the barmaid asked Tony.

'Sure,' he replied, smiling. 'What can I do for you?'

'Outside. I could do with a breath of fresh air.'

'Okay.' Tony took a slug of his ale and followed the barmaid to the entrance.

'Can I get a glass of wine here?' Emma Halliday called after them, but her words fell on deaf ears.

The snow had finally stopped and the moon was riding high in the sky. The barmaid fished a pack of cigarettes out of her pocket and offered Tony one. He shook his head and looked along the High Street as she flicked at her nearly empty Zippo lighter. It was a picture-postcard kind of town. With the snow covering the ancient buildings, he half expected a coach and horses to come clattering up the High Street. He could see why someone would want to move from Harrow-on-the-Hill to here. Was pretty sure, though, that it would drive him mad after a month or so. He'd miss the adrenaline rush London provided on a daily basis, but right now he could have stayed there for a week or two. Recharge his batteries. He thought about Emma Halliday sitting at the bar. A long streak of attitude and smiled. He wouldn't mind if she stayed with him, come to think of it.

'So, what's the mystery?' he asked the barmaid who had finally got her cigarette alight.

'No mystery as such, just wanted a fag and I didn't want the old dragon to hear.'

'She doesn't like you smoking?'

'She doesn't care as long as it's outside. I meant her not hearing what I was going to tell you.'

'Go on.'

'Lee told me you had been asking about her husband? You think he might have been murdered.'

'How did he know that?'

'He was listening at the door. He's got no time for the old dragon either. He used to be her toy boy before she traded him in for a younger model.'

'She does seem to be a woman of appetite.'

'You can say that again. Sure if sex were potatoes she'd supply the town with chips.'

'That a Cork expression, is it?'

'It is now,' she replied with a wink, drawing on her cigarette again and blowing out a long stream of smoke.

'Well, he heard right. Andrew Johnson was officially logged as a suicide.'

'I'm not surprised people believed it, especially if they've met his wife.'

'Now we think he was murdered.'

'You were asking if he had any enemies.'

'And did he? Do you know something?'

'There was an incident in his old pub back in Middlesex, at a staff party. Everybody got very drunk apparently. One of the barmaids, Michelle Riley, claimed Andrew Johnson assaulted her.'

'But she never brought charges?'

'She was flirting with him in the cellar, they had a bit of a snog. He wanted to take it further, she didn't.'

'But he still did.'

'Raped her. Didn't take long – I suppose that's something.'

'Why didn't she go to the police?'

The barmaid laughed. 'You're joking me, aren't ya? A staff party, alone in the cellar, she leading him on. His word against hers. What are the chances of that getting to court? And even if it did, what are the chances of a successful prosecution?'

'I don't know.'

'Yeah, you do. And besides she was paid off. Big time.'

'How much?'

'Fifty large, apparently.'

'And you know all this how?'

'The old dragon told Lee. One night off her head on the Tanqueray while he diddled her.'

DI Hamilton smiled. 'Diddled?'

The barmaid grinned. 'The old diddley do. Makes the world go round so they say.'

'So they do.'

The barmaid flicked her cigarette on the floor and ground it under her heel, then jerked her thumb back towards the bar. 'So the Queen of Narnia in there . . .'

317

'Detective Inspector Halliday.'

'If you say so.'

'What about her?'

'Are you diddling her?'

'Ours is a strictly professional relationship.'

'Good. I come off shift at eleven o'clock if you're snowbound and still around.'

'I'll bear it in mind.'

'Do that.' She handed the detective a piece of paper. 'Name and address. If she's still there, that is.'

'How did you get hold of this?'

'The old dragon's phone book. All their old numbers.'

'You consider a career change, come and look me up.'

'And if you fancy making the world go round, come and do the same.'

She winked at him and walked back into the bar.

A couple of minutes later, DI Halliday came out of the Ladies and up to the bar. Tony had his coat on and his beer remained untouched. She looked at the piece of paper in his hand.

'Give you her number, did she? And where's my wine, by the way?'

'She gave me a number, yes. And you won't be needing the wine.'

'I bloody will, if I have to sit here and look at your "cat that's got the cream" smile much longer.'

'They've cleared the jack-knifed lorry on the M11 and the B-roads are clear enough now. We're good to go.'

'Thank Christ for that!' She stood up and fished

the car keys out of her pocket.

Tony took them from her. 'You've had three glasses of wine, I've had a pint and I only took a sip of that gin.'

Emma Halliday was going to snap back but realised he had a point. 'Fair enough. Come on then,' she said, putting on her coat and heading for the door. Tony Hamilton shrugged apologetically at the barmaid and followed her.

'So what's the number you've got?' asked DI Halliday as the night air hit them.

'It's what you might call a bit of a clue.'

'Go on.'

'Michelle Riley. Used to work for Andrew Johnson when they ran a pub in Harrow-on-the-Hill.'

'And?'

'And,' replied Tony as he beeped the car door open, 'seems she claims that Andrew Johnson raped her one night in the pub cellar.'

'Ah!' Emma moved the seat back a little to accommodate her long legs.

'Ah, indeed. And it seems likely he did, because they paid her fifty large to keep her mouth shut about it.' Tony Hamilton pulled his seatbelt around him and clicked it into place.

'Michael Robinson. Andrew Johnson. Both from Harrow. Both rapists. Some kind of club, you're thinking.'

Tony fired up the ignition. 'Rape club? I don't know. Maybe.'

'Somebody used a police-style Taser to make them jump in front of a train. Maybe we have a vigilante?'

'I'd say we definitely have!' said Tony Hamilton as

he flicked on the windscreen wipers to clear away the fallen snow and pulled out into the High Street heading back to London.

62

Derek 'Bowlalong' Bowman was whistling rather tunelessly as he laid out his instruments on the trolley by the mortuary table. He looked at his watch and smiled as Kate Walker came into the room, followed by Diane Campbell.

'I was just about to start without you,' he said.

'That's okay, Derek. You can start when we've gone,' said Deputy Superintendent Campbell.

'Fair enough,' replied the pathologist, laying down the circular Stryker saw.

Diane and Kate walked across and looked at the naked body of the young woman lying on the table. Her hair had been straightened, her arms laid flat alongside her. Her eyes were closed, the blue veins in her eyelids even more prominent now.

Diane Campbell pulled out a photograph and compared it with the dead woman. She handed it to Kate. 'Looks like we found her,' she said.

'Who is she?' asked Derek Bowman.

'She's a statistic, Derek,' said Diane Campbell. 'More proof that we're not doing our job.'

'The police aren't responsible for homelessness, Diane,' said Kate.

'I meant as human beings.'

'She was living rough?'

'Had been on and off since she was fifteen years old. She ran away from abuse at home, into prostitution, drugs, prison. Seemed she'd been let down by society her whole life. According to the homeless shelter where she was registered, she had the mental age of a child.'

'What's her name?'

'Margaret O'Brien,' said Diane. 'Everyone called her Meg.'

'What did she die of?' asked Kate.

'Neglect.' Dr Bowman shook his her head. 'Just as the Chief says. Left on the street, sub-zero temperatures. Didn't stand a chance.'

'She wasn't murdered?'

'Depends how you define that. The cold killed her as far as I can tell pre the post. But it certainly looks like hypothermia to me.'

'It does,' agreed Kate.

'But someone beat her first. At least we know who she is, now. Maybe give you people something to go on,' he said to Diane Campbell.

Kate Walker looked at the girl's right arm. The bruises on her arms were purplish and mottled.

'Defence wounds, I'd say,' continued the pathologist.

'Similar to those on Bible Steve,' said Diane Campbell. 'What kind of instrument would have caused these injuries?'

'A baseball bat,' offered Kate.

'Possibly,' Bowman said. 'Or a policeman's truncheon.'

'We call those "asps" nowadays, Derek.'

'So you do.'

'And policewomen carry them too,' added Kate.

The pathologist crossed to an X-ray display and switched on the light. It was an X-ray of the young woman's arm. 'Whoever it was that hit her, and whatever it was he . . .' he paused and looked at Kate, 'or she hit her with, they did it hard enough to cause a hairline fracture here.' He tapped on the image.

'She had very little padding, mind,' added Kate Walker. 'Doesn't look like she had had a meal for months.'

'So we do know who she is now, as Derek said,' said Diane. 'But that does leave us with another problem.'

'Which is?'

'If this isn't the girl Bible Steve said he killed . . . then who was he talking about?'

'Assuming he saw anything at all,' said Kate.

'Maybe someone else was taken. Maybe Steve and this girl tried to stop it, got in the way and were beaten off.'

'Meg ran away to hide from whoever it was, and died in the cold.'

'Bible Steve was certainly left to die.'

'Sounds like there might be another body out there,' said Bowman.

'This is London, Doctor,' replied Diane Campbell. 'You can count on it.'

Kate's phone trilled in her pocket. She took it out and read the text message. 'Rip Van Winkle has started to get flashes of memory back apparently.'

'He's out of the operation?'

'Yup.'

'Is Jack on it?'

'No. He's in Harrow.'

'Come on then, Kate, it looks like the A-team are on the case.'

63.

Jack Delaney pushed the buzzer and stepped back from the door. He was standing outside an end-of-terrace house at the bottom end of the hill in Harrow. Sally Cartwright stood beside him, flapping her arms around herself in a vain attempt to get warm.

'Aren't you cold, sir?' she asked, looking at Delaney who was wearing his customary, battered leather jacket.

'Not particularly, Sally, I have the love of a good woman to keep me warm.'

'Bushmills in your veins, more likely.'

After a short while the door opened, as far as the chain allowed, and a woman looked nervously out. 'Are you the police?'

'Yes,' replied Delaney, immediately spotting the resemblance to Stephanie Hewson. Same height, more or less, same build, same hair-colouring. Same haunted look in her eyes and worry lines creasing a handsome face.

'Can I see some ID?'

'Of course, Miss Eddison,' said Sally.

Delaney and Sally held up their warrant cards which the woman inspected before shutting the door and opening it again with the chain clear. They followed her down a small hallway and down into a sitting room off to the right.

It was a furnished simply, with a three-piece suite in floral fabric, a television, a brown coffee table. The curtains were closed and a small gas fire was burning. Delaney opened his jacket as he sat down on the sofa. Sally didn't.

On the coffee table was a hardback copy of *When God Was a Rabbit*, with a bookmarker halfway through it and a coffee mug beside it, steam still rising from the surface.

'Good book?' Sally asked.

The woman nodded without replying. Delaney hadn't read it, but Kate had. It spoke of childhood, of happier times, but was also very sad in parts too. But then life was like that. You got dealt a mixed set of cards.

'We need to speak to you about what happened to you earlier this year, Lorraine,' he said.

The woman burst into tears.

Kate Walker ignored the stern glances the surgical registrar was giving her. She hadn't met the woman before but she looked like she only weighed six stones wet, and Kate had never been one to be intimidated by authority.

Bible Steve was sitting up in bed now. He seemed different, his eyes more focused. Not as scared.

'You say you have been having flashes of memory?'

'Just fragments really. You know, like a dream. When you wake up and try to hold onto it and sometimes you can't. Sometimes just bits of it.'

'You seem a lot more lucid.' Kate turned to

Dr Crabbe. 'Do you think his memory is returning?'

'Possibly. As I explained to Steve, amnesia can be caused by a number of things. Shock can often be a part of that. And another traumatic episode can have the reverse effect. He has been through a lot these last few days.'

'These fragments,' continued Diane Campbell. 'Can you tell us about them?'

The old man rubbed his eyes. 'Just people, faces,' he said.

'Do you know who they are?'

'No. At least, I think I did know them once. And I can see buildings. Tall, granite buildings. And I can see a house. I think it's possible I might have lived there.'

'Do you remember the road? The town?'

Bible Steve closed his eyes tight shut, then opened them and shook his head. 'I can't, I'm sorry. If I try it just fades away.'

'Don't try and force it. Sometimes these things take time,' said Kate.

'Can you remember anything of Friday night?' asked Diane, in a manner that suggested time was something they didn't have.

'No.'

'You were with a young woman. You were both attacked. Did you hurt anyone, Steve?'

'I can't remember. Why would I hurt anyone?'

Diane Campbell's phone beeped in her pocket. 'I'm sorry, I have to take this,' she said and went out into the corridor.

'Make sure that woman doesn't upset him further.' The registrar went to check on a patient next door.

The intensive care unit was always a bit of a revolving door, Kate knew only too well from her own days on rotation in the department. She didn't miss them one bit. Beds becoming vacant were not always a good sign.

She sat down on the chair beside the homeless man's bed.

'I watched the police footage of you being booked in on Friday, Steve,' she said. 'I know that Steve isn't your real name, but do you mind me calling you that?'

Steve shook his head.

'In the footage you seemed to recognise the police surgeon who attended to you.'

'I'm sorry?'

'Doctor Laura Chilvers. She has been in to see you.'

'The blonde lady. The angel.'

'Yes, you called her that in the station. Why is that?'

'I don't know. It just came into my head. I know her, I think.'

'Where from, Steve?'

'I don't know. But I can see her. And there is blood on my hands.'

His forehead furrowed as he tried to remember. 'Did I try to kill her?'

'You recognised her before you were attacked, Steve. At the police station.'

'Did I want to hurt her?'

'I don't know.'

64.

Kate Walker flipped the X-ray transparency onto the light box and clicked the switch.

She looked at the skeletal chest that was exposed and traced her finger across it.

She flicked off the light and stood there looking for a moment, contemplating.

'Did you find what you were looking for?' asked Dr Crabbe.

'Yes. I think I did.'

'Good.'

'Maybe. I'm not so sure that it is good. Do you think he'll make it?'

Dr Crabbe considered for a while, then shook her head. 'No,' she said. 'I don't think he will.'

Lorraine Eddison held a paper tissue and blew her nose. 'I'm sorry,' she said.

'You have nothing to be sorry for, Lorraine,' answered Jack Delaney.

'Yes I do.'

'It wasn't your fault you were attacked.'

'I shouldn't have been walking alone at night. I should have got a taxi. I had had too much to drink.'

'None of that makes it your fault,' said Sally

329

Cartwright. 'The man who attacked you is a sick predator.'

'Did he rape you, Lorraine?'

'No. But he tried to.'

'You managed to get away?'

'He held a knife to my side and said if I shouted out or screamed he would kill me.'

'Just like Michael Robinson,' said DC Cartwright.

'I saw on the news that he had been killed.'

'That's right, Lorraine.'

'But this wasn't him. I was attacked after he was arrested.'

'We know. We think there might be two of them. Which is why it is important you tell us exactly what happened.'

'I told the police before.'

'You didn't say he tried to rape you, just that he mugged you and cut you.'

'I didn't see the point.'

'What actually happened, Lorraine?'

'He dragged me down Church Hill to the back of the theatre there.'

'I know it.'

'It was dark. He had me up against the wall, making out we were just kissing, he ripped my knickers off. He unzipped himself but . . .'

'But what?'

'He couldn't get it up.' She held a hand to her stomach. 'Then he cut me with the knife, pushed me over and ran off.'

'And you didn't get a good look at him?'

'He had a hoodie on. It was dark.'

'But you did say he had curly hair, though.'

'Yes.'
'And his voice when he spoke?'
'It wasn't rough. Middle class more like.'
'Educated?'
'Yes.'
Delaney and Sally Cartwright exchanged a look.
'What is it?' asked Lorraine Eddison.

65.

Laura Chilvers sat at the corner of the bar in The Pig and Whistle, the local pub the police mainly favoured, a short stroll from the White City Police Station. She lifted a glass with a large measure of Pastis in it, tilted her head back and downed it in one. She held the glass out to the tall woman behind the bar. 'Same again please. A little water this time.'

The barmaid handed her a refill and put a small jug of water on the counter. Laura poured a splash in her glass and took a sip. Most offices in London were closed for the weekend, but there were still a large number of civilians in the bar, which was unusual for that time of day. Especially on a Sunday. But Laura figured there were enough workers and shoppers in town to keep all the pubs busy. She had suggested The Pig and Whistle as she thought it would be quiet. Most police workers coming off shift would be heading home for Sunday dinner. At least there was no loud music playing and mobile phone use was actively discouraged. She tuned out the chat that was buzzing around her and stared at the cloudy liquid in her glass. Fifteen minutes later the glass had been refilled, although she couldn't remember ordering another, and a hand fell on her shoulder. She was startled, then surprised.

'Oh. It's you,' she said.

Emma Halliday leaned back in the car seat and yawned. 'So what made you transfer out of special ops back into CID?' she asked Tony Hamilton.

The DI shrugged. 'Special ops is a good word. Felt more like army than the police. Not really why I joined up. I found it was taking up more and more time, especially with the cutbacks, so I was doing more of that than the detective work that I enjoyed.'

'So why apply for it in the first place?'

Tony flashed her a quick grin. 'I like a challenge. What about you?'

'What about me?'

'Why'd you sign up?'

'I had a thing for men in uniforms.'

'Really?'

'What do you think, genius?'

'I think you're pretty smart and wanted a challenge too.'

'I came from a long line of policemen. Pretty much all I wanted to do.'

She leaned back and closed her eyes. Tony looked over at her for a moment or two, a half smile playing on his lips.

Kate Walker took the change from the lady behind the bar and sat on the stool next to Laura Chilvers.

She took a sip of her soda and lime and stared at her colleague for a moment without speaking.

'What?' snapped Laura finally.

'Bible Steve.'

'What about him? Has something happened?'

'You knew him, didn't you? He said you did, and he was right.'

'I don't know what you're talking about.'

'I looked at the CCTV footage from that night, Laura. You knew him and you were covering for something. You then went out and got so blind drunk on drugs and booze that you thought you'd been raped.'

'Well I wasn't.'

'You sure of that? You've got your memory back? Seems Bible Steve's amnesia is catching.'

'You're not very funny, Kate.'

'I'm not trying to be. Something's going on, Laura. I want to know what it is.'

'You've been living with the Irishman too long, Doctor Walker. You're not a detective.'

'Bible Steve recognised you.'

'He was paralytic. He could barely stand up, let alone know who he was talking to.'

'And yet you said he was fit to be charged and released?'

'Can you cut me some slack here? All right, I was keen to get off. You know that. I had a hot date. Somebody special, maybe the one. Might be I dropped the ball a little with Bible Steve.'

'And your date can back this up, can she?'

'What are you talking about?'

Kate stared at her colleague's still-bruised knuckles. 'What happened to your hand?'

'You think I went out and attacked him myself? Are you out of your mind?'

'Something happened that night, I don't know what. But a girl is dead and a man was put in intensive care.'

'You know what, Kate. I don't have to listen to this shit!'

Laura drained her glass, stood up and snatched her jacket off the hook.

'Why are you lying, Laura?' Kate asked as the younger woman walked away. But she didn't get a reply. Laura Chilvers was too busy walking out of the door and pulling out a mobile phone.

Sally Cartwright had her laptop open on the back seat of the car, a mobile printer attached to it. Delaney was driving, cursing under his breath as the car slid on the icy road.

'Here we go, sir,' said DC Cartwright as the printer chugged out a five-by-seven-inch colour photo of the technical manager of the Ryan Theatre at Harrow School. She had googled the place and found photos of the theatre staff on their webpage.

His name was Christian Peterson.

Delaney pulled the car to a stop outside the address that DIs Tony Hamilton and Emma Halliday had phoned through to Diane Campbell. Delaney got out of the car and lit a cigarette. A few seconds later Sally joined him and gave him a sharp look.

'Yeah all right, don't you start. I'm giving up in New Year.'

'About time.'

Delaney took a couple of quick drags, then dropped the cigarette into the snow. They walked a few yards down the road and up to a mid-terraced house.

On the other side of the road a man slumped down in the seat of his van, ran his hand through a tangle of curly, dirty blond hair and watched. His eyes were blue, and intent. Filled with hate.

Delaney rang the bell and a woman in her late thirties answered the door. Michelle Riley had dark hair, cut in a bob to her shoulders. She was above average height and wore little make-up.

'Why don't you come in, detectives?' she said.

'Don't you want to see some ID?' asked DC Cartwright.

'I know who you are. I have seen the inspector in the papers and on television.'

Delaney and Sally followed her down a narrow hallway and into a medium-sized front room. It had a desk, shelves full of books and files, a small sofa and a number of plastic chairs stacked atop one another against the side-wall. On the wall beside the desk there was a poster with the words RAPE SURVIVORS ONLINE with a web address underneath it.

Michelle Riley moved a stack of files from the sofa. 'I'm sorry for the mess. This doubles as my office.' She dumped the files on the desk and perched on the chair beside it as Delaney and Sally sat on the sofa, rather squashed.

'That's fine, Miss Riley, we're not the tidiness police,' said Delaney.

'Just as well.'

'We're here to talk about Andrew Johnson.'

'I know. Your deputy superintendent told me. It was all a long time ago. I can't see why you'd need to revisit the incident. And what I did wasn't a crime.'

'No one was suggesting it was, Miss Riley.'

'Michelle, please.'

'That money he paid wasn't fair compensation, but it was some compensation. It helped me set up the support group, for one thing. We used to meet here, I'd fund a counsellor. But it's all online now, money is tight and . . . anyway I can help more people this way. Victims talking to each other can be the best kind of help, I have found.'

'Yes, I imagine so,' said Sally Cartwright.

'I can't say I shed a tear, though, when I heard that he'd jumped in front of a train.'

'How long had you worked for Andrew Johnson before he assaulted you?'

'Just over a couple of years.'

'In that time did he have any particular friends or associates?'

'Not that I recall. Can I ask what this is all about? I have to visit my mother in Watford this evening. I'll be delayed as it is, what with the weather. And you know how the elderly are – they like everything to a routine.'

'Andrew Johnson didn't commit suicide, Michelle,' Delaney said. 'We believe he was murdered. We believe the same person also killed Michael Robinson the other day.'

'I saw that on the news.'

'We believe the two knew each other, part of a ring. Rapists. So I need you to think was there anybody you saw him with, someone you might recognise or know.'

'His wife kept him on quite a short lead all the time. She was a fairly domineering character. There were the masons, of course, but that was about it.'

'He was a mason?'

'Yes. Is that relevant?'

'I don't know, Miss Riley. We're just trying to put the pieces together, and the two people who could enlighten us are both dead.'

She shrugged apologetically. 'That's all I can think of.'

'Did he have meetings at the pub?'

'We had a back room, a function room. Every fortnight or so he would get cheese and wine in. Goodness knows what went on in there.'

'You would recognise a photo of one of the men?'

'I'm pretty sure I would. I have a good memory for faces. Names are another matter. Don't get me started on names. But faces, I'm like an elephant.'

'Would you have a look at a photo for us then, please,' asked DC Cartwright.

Michelle Riley picked up a pair of black-framed glasses as Sally handed her the photo of Christian Peterson.

'No,' she said, without hesitation. 'Never seen him before in my life.'

66

Kate Walker was at her desk in her office at the station. She typed in some codes on her laptop, entered the name Dr Laura Chilvers and her police personnel file came up, starting with her full name.

Kate took a pen and wrote the name Angela Laura Chilvers. Underlining the first six letters of her name, twice.

Kate had suspected that Laura had been lying to her. Now she knew it. She flicked through her file and started checking her CV, the pen tapping on the desk once more as she read it.

She closed that page, then accessed the NHS database system, entering her security code and opening the files for Reading General Hospital. She put the pen aside and read the files from eight years ago. Twenty minutes later, she pushed the print icon and a photo printed from the wireless machine on top of her filing cabinet.

She slipped the print into an A5 envelope, then looked at her watch and cursed. She was running late. She was supposed to pick Siobhan up from dance school. The other matters would have to wait.

Stephanie Hewson drew the bolts on her door and

opened it. Delaney and Sally Cartwright were standing on her doorstep and, as they walked into the house and the door closed behind them, the man with cold blue eyes in a van on the opposite side of the road made a fist of his gloved hands as he held them on the key in his ignition, then fired up the engine and sped away heedless of the frozen snow that was turning the road into a skating rink.

'I thought now that he was dead it would all be over,' said Stephanie Hewson.

'I'm sorry, Stephanie,' said Delaney, in no hurry to take off his coat. 'But we are on it. I've spoken to Harrow nick and they are going to send some uniforms to stand guard here.'

'But I don't understand. Why would I need it?'

'Because we think there is more than just Michael Robinson.'

'A group of them,' added Sally.

'What, like some sick sort of club?' said Stephanie Hewson.

'It looks that way.'

'Do you ever drink in The Castle pub?' asked Delaney.

'No. I've never even been there.'

'You changed your testimony because someone threatened you, and I know I said I wouldn't press you,' said Delaney. 'But I need to know what these people said.'

'They didn't say anything. They left things on the doorstep.'

'Like what?'

'White lilies at first. Then a postcard with the three monkeys on it.'

'Hear no evil. See no evil. Speak no evil.'

'Yes that's the one. Finally there was a wreath, I think their message was pretty clear.'

'Yes.'

'All the time I felt like I was being followed. Watched. I know I am bound to be nervous, but it was more than that.'

Delaney nodded to Sally, who held out the photo to the distraught woman.

'Do you recognise this man?'

'No, should I?'

'He matches the description of a potential rapist. Someone else was attacked on the hill.'

'Poor woman.'

'Do you have any connection with someone called Michelle Riley?'

'She runs a rape victims support group, not far from here.'

'And were you a member of that group?'

'I went once, on the advice of a friend. But it wasn't for me. Talking about it made it all come back. Can I see that picture again, please.'

Sally handed her the photo.

'He does remind me a little of someone though,' said Stephanie Hewson.

'Of whom?' asked Jack Delaney.

'The guy who took me to the group.'

'He was a friend?'

'No. Well, sort of. I had had a blind date with him on the night I was attacked. But he came too . . . I don't know. He was always turning up with gifts asking if I was okay. He knew I didn't want a relationship. I told him that but he said he was happy just being a friend. In the end I told him to stop calling.'

'And he did?'

'Yes.'

'What's his name, Stephanie.'

'John Smith.'

'Jesus!' muttered Jack Delaney.

'Do you know him, sir?'

Delaney gave Sally a withering look. 'I should think there's a good few million people know a John Smith, Constable.'

'Sir.'

'Do you have his address?' he asked Stephanie.

'He did give me a mobile phone number but I threw it away. Sorry. Do you think he was part of this group then?'

'Possibly.'

'My God. I had him in the house. All that time.'

'I told you I'd take care of you, Stephanie, and I will. No one's going to hurt you again. Not on my watch.'

Sally Cartwright thought about commenting on the expression, then decided against it.

'Come on, Sally,' Delaney said to her. 'We need to go back a step.'

Kate Walker looked anxiously at her watch. The traffic had been horrendous. She was already twenty minutes late and had had to park quite a way from the hall where Siobhan's dancing classes were being held. She'd be looked after in the hall, but, even so, Kate felt guilty for keeping her waiting.

She tightened her coat and was walking briskly

along the pavement when a voice called out to her.

'Excuse me.'

Kate swivelled round to see a figure in a hat, a scarf wrapped around his face and a knife in his hand.

'Be very careful what you do. I know you are pregnant.'

'What do you want?'

'I want you to follow me back to my vehicle and keep very, very still.'

'Just don't hurt me, or the baby. I'll do anything you want.'

'That's a very good attitude to have.'

The man took her arm and marched her along to a black van parked behind her car. The sliding side-panel was open. 'Get in,' he said, then followed Kate inside, and shut the door.

67

Delaney rang the doorbell for a second time, long and insistent.

'She said she was going to her mother's, sir,' said Sally.

'I guess we'll just have to let ourselves in then.' Delaney kicked at the door. There was a cracking sound, but it remained closed. Another kick shattered the lock and the door flew wide open. It was dark inside. Delaney flicked on the light switch and hurried down to Michelle Riley's office. He went straight to the filing cabinet while Sally checked the desk.

'Stephanie said she had to register to join the group and John Smith likewise. Find his details, quickly.'

'I still say we should wait to get a warrant, sir,' she said.

'And I say you look good in uniform, Cartwright. So shut it or I'll bounce you back to the beat before you can say due legal process.'

'Sir.'

'Also we're not going to be arresting Michelle Riley, are we?'

Sally opened the left-hand drawer and took out a

wooden box wrapped in a red silk handkerchief. She unwrapped it and looked inside. 'Are you sure about that, sir?'

'What is that?'

Sally held up a pack of tarot cards. 'Maybe somebody crossed her palm with silver?'

'Count them. There's supposed to be twenty-six Major Arcana cards. See if there are two missing.'

Sally took out the cards, separating them into two piles, Major and Minor, while Delaney tackled the filing cabinet. It had three drawers. The bottom was filled with rape-counselling literature and pamphlets. The second had a number of textbooks, sociological studies, videos and DVDs. The top drawer had an alphabetical filing system. Delaney pulled out the index card filed under S. There was no John Smith. He tipped the cards on top of the cabinet and went through them all. Stephanie Hewson's contact details were there, but there was no sign of any John Smith. Delaney knew it probably wasn't even the man's real name. His luck wasn't that good. He looked over at Sally Cartwright. 'Full deck?' he asked.

'No. There's five missing.'

'Five?'

'Sir.'

'Shit! You know what I'm thinking now, Sally?'

'This isn't about a group of men raping. It's about a group of people taking revenge.'

'Why John Smith, if that's his name?'

'Michael Robinson queered his pitch big time, didn't he, sir? And from what Stephanie tells us, he's not actually playing with a full deck himself.'

'And then he went on to try it himself. So fixated with the woman that he acted out his fantasies on Lorraine Eddison at the back of the Ryan Theatre.'

'Or tried to.'

'What was the date Lorraine Eddison was attacked?'

Sally dug out her little black notebook and flipped back through some pages.

'Twentieth of April, sir.

Delaney snapped his fingers.

'Is that significant, sir?'

'Very significant. Come on, we're out of here.'

Kate Walker leaned against the side of the van. Her hands had been tied behind her back with the kind of plastic slip-knot cuffs the police use.

The van was moving slowly but it skidded every now and then, and Kate was thrown forward. She couldn't use her hands to protect her belly and every movement made her almost cry with despair. She knew how fragile was the life she was carrying inside her. Particularly at this relatively early stage of the pregnancy. She silently prayed to God to save them both, but mostly she prayed for Jack.

Delaney and Sally Cartwright waited impatiently in the plushly carpeted entrance foyer of the Ryan Theatre. A couple of ridiculously tall schoolboys in their mourning outfit of a school uniform watched them curiously.

A short while later, and the theatre's technical manager came hurrying through the entrance door, slightly red-faced and out of breath. He was about five foot eleven with curly, mousy hair, in his forties, but with a pampered, youthful look about him.

'What kept you?' said Delaney.

'I was in The Castle.'

'Haven't you got a show on? Shouldn't you be working?'

'Nah.' The man grinned at Sally. 'I was working on a pint of Foster's. I just open the theatre for them, lock up when they've gone.'

'It's a rep company?' asked Delaney.

'Yes.'

'And you hire the place out in school holidays, I saw your poster for this show that's on tonight when we were here the other day.'

'Yes, we hire it out. Why? Thinking of holding another Secret Policeman's Ball?'

Sally smiled but didn't let Delaney see it.

'So it was hired out last Easter?'

'Yes.'

'Who to?'

'I'd have to check the records. It was a musical, though. *Starlight Express*.'

'Not exactly opera, then?'

'Not exactly musical either, if you ask me.'

Delaney grunted. 'Sally, show him the photo.'

'It's his own photo, sir.'

'I know that. Just show him the bloody picture.'

Sally handed over the photograph to Christian Peterson.

'Any members of that visiting company look a bit like you?'

The technical director scratched his head. 'Come to think of it, I did get mistaken for one once. A woman from the audience asked for my autograph.'

'What did you do?' asked Sally.

'I gave her one.'

Sally laughed and Delaney glared at her. 'And you,' he said, turning back to the curly-haired man. 'Get his bloody details, now.'

'Can I ask what this is about?'

'No, you bloody can't!'

Twenty minutes later, DI Jack Delaney had his foot raised for the second time in an hour and was kicking in the front door of a downstairs flat. A woman opened the window to complain, but Sally held her warrant card, and she disappeared back inside, slamming the sash window down noisily.

It took a few more kicks, but eventually Delaney had the door open.

They walked into a room with a three-piece suite in beige fabric, a television and a coffee table. Nothing expensive. Seemed that John Garland – Delaney had discovered from Christian Peterson what Smith's real name was – had saved all his money for the state-of-the-art sound system and huge collection of CDs that dominated the left-hand side of the room.

They continued through the lounge into a small passageway. There was a bedroom to the right, a kitchen ahead and a bathroom with the door open leading off from the kitchen.

Delaney pushed the bedroom door open and flicked on the light.

'Jesus Christ, sir,' said Sally as she followed him.

There was a double bed in the right-hand corner. One wall was covered with newspaper cuttings and photos. Mainly of Stephanie Hewson.

The phone in his pocket trilled and he took it out. 'Delaney.' He listened for a while. 'How long has she been missing?' He glanced at his watch. 'Siobhan's safe?' His right hand was balling into a fist. 'I'm at John Garland's place now, Diane. Send back-up.'

He closed the phone and put it back in his pocket. Gazing at the photos on the wall, his mind whirred. There he was with Stephanie Hewson on her doorstep, Stephanie hugging him as if he was a long-awaited lover. And there was a picture of Kate Walker. Her curly hair every bit as dark as Stephanie Hewson's.

'He's got her, Sally,' said Delaney. 'That sick son-of-a-bitch has taken Kate.'

68.

Bible Steve smiled at the pretty young nurse as she walked alongside his bed which was being wheeled, by a porter, along the corridor to the general ward at the top of the intensive-care area.

'Sorry to have to move you, Steve, but there has been a pile-up on Western Avenue. Too many people thinking they can drive as fast as they like even in these treacherous conditions.'

Bible watched as paramedics and nurses hurried past with people on trolleys, blood-splattered, some moaning in pain. The surgical registrar ran alongside, her junior assistants with her as she talked to the paramedics, assessing the seriousness of the crash victims' injuries.

'So much blood,' said Bible Steve.

'I'm sorry?' said the nurse who was distracted by the commotion.

'More people will die.'

The nurse helped the porter wheel his bed into position in the empty space at the top of the ward.

'What do you mean, Steve?'

Bible Steve turned to look at her. 'That's not my name,' he said.

*

350

Jack Delaney took a candle from the box by the small side-chapel. He carried it to the wrought-iron candelabra. It already contained a number of candles, none of them alight. He took a lighter from his pocket and scratched the flint. The wheel turned but no flame came. Again and again he tried, but to no avail. He closed his eyes and shook the small, steel box furiously. Once more he span the wheel. A flame flared and Delaney quickly lit the candle before it winked out, and carried it over to the candelabra.

He knelt on the cold stone floor, closed his eyes once more and made a sign of the cross.

'*Pater noster qui es in caelis* . . .' But he stumbled over the words. '*Pater noster* . . .' he began again, but couldn't find the words that once upon a time had come so readily to his lips. He opened his eyes and looked upward at the statue to the woman after whom the church had been named.

'Hail Mary, full of grace,' he said. 'Our Lord is with thee. Blessed art thou amongst women, and blessed is the fruit of thy womb, Jesus. Holy Mary mother of God, pray for us sinners, now and at the hour of our death. Amen.'

Kate stumbled slightly but John Garland held her arm tightly and marched her along the alleyway. He had cut the ties from her wrists, but they still throbbed with the pain of it. She held her left arm over her stomach. Trying to feel her baby's heartbeat through the thick, woollen fabric of her coat.

She grunted with pain as the man dug his fingers into her arm.

'Shut it or you'll regret it,' hissed Garland angrily.

'Who are you? Why are you doing this?'

'Because I can.'

'What do you want?'

'You'll find out soon enough. You and that sad fuck of a boyfriend of yours.'

'What's Jack got to do with this?'

'He's been a bad boy, Kate.'

'What are you talking about?'

'Jack's been putting himself about. What's up – now you're pregnant, you don't let him fuck you?'

There was an old street lamp at the end of the alleyway. It cast a warm yellow glow of light, but she could see heavy snowflakes falling in front of it. Could feel them in her long hair, chilling the cheeks on her face. She had no idea what the man was talking about. He was clearly insane, but if she could keep him talking maybe she could figure out a way to get help.

'Has Jack done something to upset you?'

'He's been fucking the woman I'm going to marry.' John Garland's smile sent a shiver down Kate's spine.

'You must have made a mistake.'

'No mistake. Last night he was at Stephanie's house. She had her arms wrapped around him as he left. He's been fucking her and now he's going to pay.'

'Jack was with me last night.'

'I was there, watching.'

'You've got the wrong end of the stick. She was scared. He was helping her.'

The man grunted. 'Yeah. Just the kind of help I'm going to give you.' He pulled her tight to him as they reached the end of the alleyway.

A church stood almost directly opposite, with a

broader alleyway beside it. The snowflakes danced in the light of the old lamp post. Kate reckoned she was as far from Narnia as she could be, as she felt the blade jabbing in her right side.

'Across the road now. Make the slightest noise and I'll cut you right here.'

Kate walked across the road with him, her mind in turmoil. Light spilled through the cracks of the curtained windows on the apartments on the right-hand side of the alleyway. She blinked, not sure how much the moisture in her eyes was melted snow or how much was tears. As they passed the church, John Garland switched hands with the knife and pulled out a key.

'Be prepared, that's what the Scouts say, isn't it? Well you can consider me a good Scout in that regard,' he said as he led her up to the Seventeenth Roxborough's Scout hut and turned the key in the lock.

Thoughts flashed through Kate's mind. The dream she had of Siobhan being married. The daughters she was supposed to have with Jack. The baby that she was carrying. She thought about the thickness of the coat, how hard he would have to stab to penetrate it. She thought about the risks if she tried to escape. But the thought uppermost in her mind was that she was not going to be a victim. If she went into that Scout hut with that man, even if she survived if her baby was hurt, she would never forgive herself. She whispered a silent *I love you* to Jack Delaney and said, 'I consider you a sick son-of-a-bitch and you can rot in fucking hell!'

John Garland stabbed at her with his knife as Kate

reeled backwards, slamming against the wall of the hut and slid to the ground.

John Garland raised the blade above his head, then screamed as the door to the hut opened and Jack Delaney stabbed a screwdriver straight into his right eye.

69.

DI Tony Hamilton yawned and pulled the car to the side of the road. He had seen enough snow and traffic to last a lifetime.

Emma Halliday opened her eyes and stretched. 'This is my house,' she said, having wiped her side-window.

'I know.'

'How are you going to get home?'

'I figured I'd phone for a taxi.'

'You'll be lucky in this weather.'

'I didn't think you should drive.'

'I'll be fine now.'

'Well . . . like you said it's pretty foul out there.'

'Why don't you come in for a cup of coffee?' she said.

'I don't drink coffee.'

Emma smiled. 'That's okay. I haven't got any.'

'In which case I'd love a cup.'

Laura Chilvers looked at her bedside clock. It was dark and the glow of the illuminated numbers helped her locate the button for Classic FM. She pushed it and the lush sounds of Mahler's Third Symphony filled the room.

She closed her eyes and moaned as a hand cupped

her right breast, her nipples hardening, her heart beating faster in her chest.

'Do you want me to hurt you again?'

Laura opened her eyes and ran her hand down the woman's long blonde hair. 'No, Nicola,' she said. 'I just want you to hold me.'

'The other night you scared me, Laura.'

'I don't remember it. I'm sorry.'

'You made me beat you, hurt you. Use toys. You took so many drugs, drink. Punching the wall. I didn't know what to do.'

'But you brought me home, didn't you?'

'Yes. Maybe I should have stayed, but you told me to leave.'

'Probably best that you did.'

'But I don't understand. What happened? Why were you like that?'

Laura kissed Nicola on the mouth and put her arms around her. 'Just hold me,' she said.

'I only want to help.'

'You can't help.'

'What is it?'

'I did a very bad thing.'

Bible Steve walked along the corridor. He felt calm for the first time in a long while. He knew that it was due to the Valium they had given him, to help with the severe alcohol withdrawal symptoms he would be experiencing. But he felt calm. Cogs were clicking into place, wheels were in motion. He looked down at his battered, old hands and didn't recoil with horror as he had previously. He was beginning to understand, and he knew that understanding was the first step to being healed, although he very much suspected it was too late for that.

He stopped outside the room next to the one where he had been treated and looked inside. An elderly lady had fallen asleep by the side of a hospital bed. A man lay there with an oxygen mask over his face. Wires and tubes were connected to his body. The man's breath was a low, ragged gurgle. Bible walked into the room and looked at the various monitors. Staring down at the man for a moment or two, he returned to the monitoring equipment and turned a dial.

Jack Delaney held Kate's hand as she lay on the hospital bed. The technician moved the scanning device and Kate smiled as she saw the images appear on the monitor.

'Absolutely nothing to worry about,' said the ultra-sonographer.

'Not even a scratch,' added Delaney. 'Who did you think you were, Superwoman?'

'I don't know about that,' said Kate. 'I'm going to need a new coat.'

'I'm going to need a new screwdriver,' said Delaney.

Kate grimaced and gestured towards Siobhan who was busy checking the scan image.

'Yeah, sorry.'

'You've got nothing to be sorry about, Jack. You saved my life. You saved both our lives.'

'Nah, you're a tough cookie, Kate. You'd have had his measure. You sure you've not got a drop of the Irish in you?'

Kate laughed. 'Shall we go home?'

'Yeah, let's do that,' said Delaney. 'We've got a tree to decorate.'

'Yay!' said Siobhan and clapped her hands. Delaney looked from her and back to Kate and, as he ran his hand over her stomach, he had to blink his eyes, which were suddenly moist.

Part Four

70.

Monday morning . . .

Kate Walker walked into the intensive-care room. Patricia Hunt was in her usual place by her husband's side, keeping vigil. Dr Lily Crabbe was writing up some notes on Geoffrey Hunt's chart, then hung it back on the rail at the base of the bed. She smiled briefly at Kate and stifled a yawn with her hand.

'Busy night?' asked Kate.

'Always is.'

'Good morning, Kate,' said Reverend Hunt with a warm smile.

'You seem much better today, Geoffrey.'

'He's on the mend,' agreed Lily Crabbe. It was only yesterday, Kate remembered, that the registrar was telling her that she didn't think he would make it.

'Bit of a scare last night. But looks like we have the infection beaten.'

'It's a miracle,' said Patricia.

The registrar headed off and Patricia stood up. 'I am just going to get him a cup of tea. Would you like one, Dr Walker?'

'Why don't I walk with you, Patricia? Good to see

361

you looking so well, Geoffrey. You take good care of yourself.'

'I will, thank you, Doctor.'

Kate walked out with Patricia to the vending machine at the end of the corridor.

'Pneumonia can be a dangerous thing for a man of his age. He's been very lucky.'

'I know.'

'I looked at his X-rays, his chest X-rays.'

'Yes?' Patricia fished out a fifty-pence piece from her purse.

'His name's not really Geoffrey Hunt, is it?'

The older woman dropped the coin, but didn't seem to notice it as it clattered to the ground.

'What do you mean?'

'I got his brother's medical records. The man in the ground had a perfectly uninjured rib cage. The X-rays I looked at here last night showed an old bullet wound. A wound to the chest. Geoffrey's brother had such a wound. He got it in Zambia trying to defend some children, according to the report I read.'

'He did defend those children! They lived because of him.'

'And so did he! Didn't he? I'm guessing that it was Geoffrey we found in that unmarked grave. I'm right, aren't I? The man back there is his brother Jeremy.'

Patricia looked at her grim-faced. What are you going to do?'

'I don't know yet,' said Kate gently. 'Why don't you tell me what happened?'

'There were accusations that Geoffrey had been molesting young girls.'

362

'I know.'

'It wasn't the first time. He had a problem, I begged him to get help and he said that he had. That he had never actually touched any of the girls. Just looked at them.'

'Go on.'

'It was too much. I told him that I was going to divorce him. I told him I was going to report him to the police. He became very angry. He had been violent to me in the past, had been abusive. But I held my ground. He couldn't be allowed to continue hurting those poor children. He hit me.'

'And so you shot him?'

'No, Doctor,' the older woman sighed. 'He shot himself. I guess I drove him to it.'

'You didn't drive him to do anything, Patricia.'

'Jeremy was visiting, like I said. He found me in a state of absolute shock and said he would take care of everything. He always loved me, Kate. I knew that. I chose the wrong brother.'

'So what did Jeremy do?'

'In covering up for the vicar, the Church had demanded his early retirement. If his suicide was discovered, the whole sorry story would be exposed. Jeremy didn't want to put me though that. He said he would take on his brother's identity. Nobody need ever know. So we buried him that night in sanctified ground.'

'And the gun he used?'

'It was their father's service revolver, from the war. God knows why they'd kept it. Jeremy buried the gun in our garden. We laid a slab over it and put a birdbath there. He said nobody would ever find out.'

'And if they hadn't decided to demolish the church, probably nobody would have done.'

The older woman looked at Kate, her eyes moist with tears. 'No real harm was done, was there? If this all comes out now, it could kill him.'

'Were you in love with Jeremy?'

Patricia nodded her head. 'I know it was wrong. But yes, I loved him, Kate. Almost from the first day I married his brother.'

Kate patted her hand. 'Don't worry, Patricia, I'm sure everything will be okay.'

'But how can it be? We've drawn Geoffrey's pension all these years, it wasn't much but . . .' She trailed off, distraught. 'And they have found the body now. Sooner or later it will all come out. You can't take care of that.'

'No, I can't,' said Kate. 'But I know a man who can.'

Diane Campbell stood at the open window watching the uniforms clear the snow from the car park once more. The sky overhead was a brilliant blue, however, and the sun was shining brightly.

She smiled at Delaney as he came into her office.

'Full statement from Michelle Riley. Pretty much as you guessed. Five of them from the support group. Became something of a drinking club. Sharing their sorrows, their anger. Then one night at The Castle, after reading about another suspected rapist walking free from court, they decided to not just get angry but to get even. Vigilante style. John Garland's idea. They'd each pick a card, and whoever was selected they had to kill. Not the person who had raped them, however, so no trails would lead back to them.'

'First rule of the Murder Club.'

'Only when it came to Michelle's turn she got cold feet. Wouldn't do it.'

'So Garland did it for her, I guess. Pushed Michael Robinson under the train.'

'That's why he wanted Stephanie Hewson to lie in court, let him off. So that he could get to Robinson. It was his cousin who beat him up in jail originally. Only he got transferred.'

'John equals Jack.'

'Yep.'

'What's the verdict on Garland?'

'They think he'll live.'

'Shame.'

'Oh, yeah. But they also think he's going to be severely brain damaged.'

Delaney didn't look particularly displeased at the news.

'How did you know he'd take her to the Scout hut, Jack?'

'I didn't.'

'Lucky guess?'

'He'd been fixating on Stephanie Hewson. The rape. Newspaper accounts pinned to the wall. Pictures of her. Pictures of Kate. Same hair, same colouring.'

'He was acting out his fantasies?'

'Tried it before and it didn't work. But he had seen me with the woman he was obsessed with and this fixation was escalating out of control. If he couldn't have Stephanie Hewson, then Kate would do. Kill two birds with one stone. If he was re-enacting what happened to Stephanie last Christmas, then he'd take Kate to the hut.'

Diane put another cigarette between her lips. 'That was a good call.'

'Maybe I had some help.'

Diane looked at him curiously, but his face was impassive.

'Are you going to give me one of those cigarettes?' he said.

Kate walked up to Bible Steve's bed, a bunch of grapes in her hand. Laura was sitting beside him. She looked a lot better. Fresher, less haunted. Kate dangled the grapes in front of Steve. 'Bit of a cliché, I know. But . . .' She placed the grapes on his bed. 'I hear you saved a man's life last night, Steve, by adjusting his oxygen levels.'

'My name isn't Steve.'

'I know. It's Stuart. Stuart Gregor.'

'Yes.'

'You remember now?'

'His memory is coming back, parts of it anyway,' said Laura.

'Eight years ago there was a massive pile-up and an overturned coach on the motorway outside Reading,' said the homeless man. 'Seven people were killed. Thirteen people seriously injured. It was chaos at Reading General that night and a surgeon who had been drinking heavily was operating. It was me, operating without assistance, without theatre nurses, and a twenty-three-year-old blonde woman with the face of an angel and fractured ribs died because of it.'

'Except you did have assistance, didn't you, Mr Gregor? You had a young, newly qualified doctor on surgical rotation called Angela Laura Chilvers with you. After the woman died, there was a full enquiry. Only you had vanished. Nobody knew who you were. You didn't even know who you were.'

'It wasn't his fault,' said Laura. 'None of this was his fault.'

'Because you didn't stop him from operating?'

'The young woman who died that night had severe rib injuries, a haemothorax. The blood was draining into her chest area and literally suffocating her. She was in incredible pain and would have died. Stuart had to perform a chest drain. Only his hands were shaking so much he couldn't place the tube correctly in her throat. So I did it.'

'You performed the procedure?'

'Yes, and let Stuart take the blame.'

'I left her alone,' said Stuart Gregor.

'You went to find another surgeon. Only I didn't think there was time. So I went ahead anyway. I positioned the tube incorrectly. I hit her heart. By the time Stuart came back to say help was on its way, she was already dead. He thought she had died from the crash injuries, and I didn't tell him otherwise. He left there and then. I never got the chance to tell him the truth. Look what I did to him. I ruined his life.'

'It's okay. I was your supervisor, Laura.'

'I used you. And ruined you, Stuart.'

'I loved you, Laura.'

'I know. And I slept with you and used you to further my career. A woman is dead, and you very nearly died because of it.'

'Isaiah said, "Remember not the former things. Nor consider the things of old. Behold I am doing a new thing; now it springs forth, do you not perceive it? I will make a way in the wilderness and rivers in the desert."'

'Are you sure you didn't lead a double life as a vicar?' asked Kate with a wry smile.

'I was educated for thirteen years at a Catholic school, Doctor. They used to beat these things into you.'

'I've heard that.'

'I might have forgotten nearly everything else out there on the streets, but the Bible has been hardwired in here.' He tapped the side of his head.

'I wish I could go back in time, Stuart. I would do things so differently,' said Laura, tears pricking her eyes.

The elderly man took her hands and shook his head. 'You are a healer now. You have made your own way in the wilderness. Just think of the lives you have saved. Regret nothing, lass. I made my own bed. I knew you were gay, but I didn't care. I used you, I was your supervisor and I abused my trust. You should have just told them the truth. Nobody would have blamed you. Everything was just a terrible accident.'

'When I saw what I had done to you the other night, I couldn't forgive myself, Stuart. I tried to save her life, but I destroyed yours instead.'

'There is nothing to forgive. Nobody had to show me the way to drink, my angel. Believe me, the demons were in my head long before we ever met. Falling in love with you didn't make me what I am, but what you are is why I fell in love with you.'

'I'm sorry.'

Stuart Gregor looked over at Dr Walker. 'What are you going to do?'

She smiled. 'It's really nothing to do with me, is it?'

'Don't worry, Kate,' Laura said, her cheeks wet with tears, her hands still held in the surgeon's clasp. 'I'll make things right. I promise.'

Jack Delaney walked along Edgware Road with Sally Cartwright beside him. 'This sunshine keeps up, the snow will all be melted by Christmas, sir,' she said.

'I wouldn't bank on it, Sally. Besides, I promised Siobhan a White Christmas.'

'Was that wise, sir?'

Delaney laughed. 'I'm not sure if many of my decisions fall into that category.'

They turned into the side street and walked up to a female, uniformed police sergeant with a younger constable who were drinking mugs of tea with a homeless couple.

'Morning, sir. Good work last night.'

'Thanks. These the two?'

'Yes sir, Mr and Mrs Stubbs.'

'Is there a reward?' asked the man.

'There might be,' said Delaney. 'Depends what you can tell us.'

The man gestured at the uniforms. 'The bobbies have been out and about asking if anybody saw anything last Friday night.' He rubbed his thumb and fingers together. 'Thought there might be some coin in it.'

'Just tell us what you saw.'

'Well me and the missus, we was here. With Bible Steve and the young lass. I don't know her name.'

'Meg,' said Delaney. 'Her name was Meg O'Brien.'

'The four of us were just here, for the warmth, you know. And Bible had got lucky. Made a big score. He had whisky and was passing it around. Later on the police came and took him away. Blonde woman and a miserable, old geezer.'

'Go on.'

'Well we stayed there for a bit. Then the old lady closed up the Chinese restaurant about ten-thirty. Half an hour after that, a bunch of the Chinese came back.'

'What Chinese?'

'I don't know, the waiters, cooks.' One of them had a leather jacket on. Thought he was Elvis fucking Presley.'

'What were they doing there?'

'They come back to play cards and that funny game with the little bricks.'

'So what happened?'

'They told us to clear off. I think Bible really pissed them off when he pissed all over their front window.'

His wife chuckled.

'And did you move?'

'Not at first. We was still a bit bladdered, to be honest. But Elvis, he gets out these couple of sticks with a chain in the middle and we figured we'd best get out of there.'

'Nunchuckas,' said Sally Cartwright.

'I beg yours, darling?'

'It's what the sticks are called,' said Delaney, walking over to the restaurant. As they went in, Dongmei Chang's nephew shouted over his shoulder.

'Go away, we're closed!'

'You're going to be closed for a very long time, sunshine!' said Delaney.

The Chinese man looked round and the snarl on his face disappeared. Then he turned tail and raced off to the kitchen.

'Get him, Constable!' shouted Delaney. The young uniform charged after him followed by the sergeant, both of them flicking their asps out as they ran.

'Aren't you going with them?' Sally asked.

'Stuff that for a game of coconuts,' said Delaney. 'I'm getting too old for this malarkey.' He put a cigarette in his mouth and patted his pockets. 'Have you got a light, Sally?'

'No, sir!'

'Never mind,' said Delaney and picked up one of the restaurant's paper matchbooks from one of the tables and lit his cigarette.

71

Hampstead, north-west London. Christmas Eve.

The sky was mostly clear, a few clouds drifting past the waning moon. The moon had a crisp white colour that night, twinkling stars in the background. All it needed was Santa on his sleigh riding in front of it, and it could have been the poster shot for a Disney film. Santa comes to Hampstead.

Delaney took one last puff of his cigarette, flicked the lighted end into the snow, then put the stub in the bin outside Kate's kitchen door.

Through the glass in the door Delaney could see that Kate was making mulled cider. An old recipe she claimed came from some distant Norfolk relative. Delaney had never been a fan of mulled wine, but Kate had promised to convert him. His daughter Siobhan was helping her make it. Her laughter was as musical as ever. Delaney stood for a moment just watching them. Not aware that a smile had crept across his face. He thought back to last Christmas, what he could remember of it, and couldn't believe where he was now. He hadn't believed he could fall in love again, but he had.

He cursed himself for being all kinds of fool and took out his mobile phone.

When the familiar female voice answered he smiled and slipped another cigarette in his mouth. He moved away from the window and leant against the wall.

'Hi, sweetheart,' he said. 'It's Jack. I've got an early Christmas present for you.'

Kate held out the spoon of the cooled liquid and let Siobhan take a tiny sip. Siobhan considered for a moment, her brow furrowed. 'I don't mind it,' she said finally. 'But I think I prefer cream soda.'

Kate laughed as the back door opened and Delaney walked into the kitchen.

'I'm going to look at the presents again!' said Siobhan and ran excitedly out of the room.

'How many times does that make it now?' asked Delaney.

'Ooh, I don't know. About a thousand.'

Delaney laughed, but Kate noticed the expression on his face. 'What is it, Jack?'

'What do you mean?'

'There's something in your eye. I know you by now. You're up to something.'

'Maybe you know me too well.'

'None better.'

Delaney held up his mobile phone.

'Go on,' said Kate.

'I just called Diane Campbell. Told her I was resigning from the Metropolitan Police.'

'Why?'

'Because I have brought the people I love into harm's way and I can't do that any more.'

'Why don't you just phone her back then, and tell her you were only joking?'

'Fuck that!' said Jack Delaney.
And kissed her.

ACKNOWLEDGEMENTS

Many thanks, as ever, to the stalwart team at Random House for their continuing faith in the recovering Irishman, Jack Delaney. Paul Sidey, Paulette Hearn, Caroline Gascoigne, the brilliant design and sales teams, and especially Susan Sandon, who let me have extra time to deliver the book so I could work on another little project!

Muchos Gracios to the Marchioness of Camden, Lucy Dundas, who read the book first and was kind about it, and to the Uber-agent Robert Caskie, for continuing to be a thoroughly good egg and friend, and everyone at PFD!

Special mention to Irish John for his continuing advice in Cork based matters, and . . . also of Ireland.

It's been a busy year, and Lynn has been brilliant, as usual, in keeping my feet on the ground, my nose to the grindstone, my powder dry and my chin up. She has been less than successful, however, in stopping me from mixing my metaphors.

Parts of London in the book are real and some are imaginary. As I write this, some areas of the capital city are in flames and turmoil as rioting spreads. DI Delaney bangs on about London continually, but deep down he loves the place, as do I. In *Private*

London, Dan Carter says London is the best city in the world, and I can't help but feel Jack Delaney would agree with him – not that they will ever meet – and would wish that by publication of this story some peace has returned to the streets.

And thanks, finally, to the most important person of all – you the reader, without whom JD would just be a very nice thing to drink with ice and crushed mint!

Slainte!
MP
August 2011